MW01132915

DINOSAUR TALES

THOMAS P. HOPP

Fourth book of the Dinosaur Wars series

I dedicate this book to park rangers and wildlife biologists. Their task of bringing humanity and nature together gets more complicated every day—and more rewarding.

"The great poets, philosophers, prophets, able men whose thoughts and deeds have moved the world, have come down from the mountains."

—*John Muir*

Praise for Dinosaur Wars

"Solid science and pacing that never quits." —Kay Kenyon, Philip K. Dick Award nominated author of *Maximum Ice*

"Fills the void since *Jurassic Park*. And Hopp's book may be better."   —Steve Brusatte, *DinoLand Review*

"The moon will never look the same."   —Bob Gue

PART ONE

HATCHING ALAMOSAURUS

"The eggs are in no danger of being crushed."

THOMAS P. HOPP

CHAPTER 1

The army helicopter followed the alamosaurus herd from a safe distance—a safe distance above. Several of the long-necked behemoths were nearly a hundred feet long from their heads, atop giraffe-like necks, through their elephantine bodies, to the tips of their striped, bullwhip-like tails.

The herd, maybe two dozen animals of various sizes, moved among tall evergreen trees in hilly land on the Quinault Indian Reservation, headed due south. The pilot, Chief Warrant Officer Marsha Demerest, in flight helmet and combat fatigues, trailed the creatures with the thumping rotors of her OH-58D Kiowa Warrior helicopter nearly clipping the tree-tops. The animals had reacted to the noise from above at first, but now seemed content to ignore it and continue their southbound trek.

"Don't get within a tail flick of those things," Demerest's front-seat passenger, General Victor Suarez, said. "I have it on good authority they can smack down a full-grown T rex with a crack of that whip. They would make hash out of this Kiowa."

The passenger in one of the two back observer seats, Major Joseph Abercromby, held a portable computer on his knees. "Map says they're already halfway to the coastal towns of Hoquiam and Aberdeen. I wonder how fast they're moving?"

"Instruments say we're tailing them at about 20 miles an hour, ground speed," Demerest replied. "They move pretty fast for such big beasties. And they're only walking!"

"At that rate," Crom said, "they'll be in Aberdeen this afternoon."

"Unless they stop for lunch," Demerest said.

"Not likely," Suarez said. "Look at that one!"

A medium sized alamosaur, about sixty feet long, passed a tall hemlock tree. Without pausing, it raked its muzzle of peg-like teeth along one of the tree's highest branches, stripping it of needles and small twigs and leaving the naked branch and the treetop wagging after it as it moved on. It swallowed the mouthful of bristling food without chewing, tipping its bulbous-crowned head back, and gulping several times. Meanwhile, it didn't miss a stride.

"What I want to know," Suarez wondered, "is how do we head them off before they mix it up with people?"

"Sir," Demerest said. "I've got a Hellfire missile on my right pylon and a 7-shot Hydra rocket pod on the left. If you want, I can give 'em a reason to turn back."

"You mean, shoot one?" Crom asked.

"Or put a rocket in front of 'em to scare 'em."

"Negative, Demerest," Suarez said. "This mission is logged as 'observation-only.' No fireworks allowed unless we're attacked. I don't think something that heavy can get more than a couple feet off the ground. And, last time I checked, only the Kra have laser weapons. These are just big dumb beasts."

"Pretty dumb, alright," Demerest agreed, "if they're heading where people live."

"Another thing I'd really like to know," Suarez went on, "is where the heck do they think they're going?"

Crom looked at the map again. "Beats me. Another twenty miles in this direction takes them straight into Hoquiam and Aberdeen. There are more than twenty thousand people living in the combined towns, according to Google."

"All I know for sure," Suarez said, "is I woke up this morning at the forward base in Forks, thinking everything was okay. The Kra army had stood down, our lines were quiet, and everything was just fine. And then came a call from General Davis down at NORAD, telling me dinosaurs were south of the truce line at the Hoh River. No mention of what kind of dinosaur. I assumed it was a force of Kra in their fighting machines, not a bunch of big thunder lizards. Davis said we were now on a war footing and Congress was meeting in a hurry-up session to decide what to do. He told me to get south and have a look ASAP. So here we are."

Crom glanced at his computer again. "They came out of the Olympic National Park along the Snahapish River Valley. Spotted early this morning by guards at the Olympic Corrections Center. Spotted again moving down the Clearwater River and crossing Highway 101 south of the Queets River, onto the Quinault Indian Reservation. The sheriff that was following them couldn't follow them into the forests here. It's all rough country with evergreen forests, where they came from as well as where they're going right now."

"And now that we've found 'em again," Demerest said. "What are we supposed to do?"

As they watched, the alamosaurs, six adult pairs and a dozen younger animals, forded the Quinault River at a boulder-bottomed oxbow bend, scarcely slowing to dip drinks, which they took in at a single gulp by lying ten feet of their necks along the water's surface and sucking in a huge throat-full, which they swallowed by raising their heads high, like drinking geese. Then they continued south, stepping across hundred-foot long, eight-foot thick logs on the bank, and plunging into the tall forest again.

The biggest beasts strode ponderously but swiftly, like migrating elephants. The smaller animals trotted agilely to keep pace.

"Man," Crom said. "They move fast."

"Too fast," Suarez said. "We don't have much time to figure out what to do."

***

"The world's biggest science project is coming along nicely!" Professor David Ogilvey exclaimed.

In front of him and Chase Armstrong and Kit Daniels stretched the skeleton of a tyrannosaurus rex, nearly fifty feet from its toothy premaxilla bone to its last tail vertebra. It lay in a clearing in the paper-birch woods near the ranch house, and it was no fossil. Lying entirely aboveground, its bones were fresh and pink. It had been stripped almost completely by scavenging creatures large and small, leaving the long, nicely articulated framework of the animal free of flesh and accessible to Dr. Ogilvey's observations—and lectures.

As he had done on several previous visits, Dr. O moved around the skeleton, exclaiming in delight about the fine condition of the specimen and Kit's college project to collect the first-ever complete T-rex skeleton and then reassemble it for display at the National Museum in Washington DC.

At one point, standing near the skeleton's chest, he turned to Chase, grinning a long-toothed smile that dimpled his gray-bearded cheeks. His eyes twinkled behind his thick glasses.

"I hope what you see relieves your conscience, my boy," he said.

The tall, dark-haired wildlife biologist shook his head in the negative. "Nothing is going to ease my guilt about killing this magnificent beast," he said. "Why would you think looking at its skeleton is going to help? Because it gave its life for science?"

"No, Chase. Because the evidence I see here proves you didn't kill it."

"How do you figure?"

"Look here." He pointed at the animal's shoulder blade, now cleaned of flesh. "When you shot his flank, you hit the wing of his scapula. Just winged him, you might say." The professor paused and looked at Chase as if wondering whether his quip might get a chuckle. It did not.

Ogilvey went on cheerily. "The bullet sank into bone and did no more harm. Look carefully at the wound. See how new bone had begun to fill the hole? The wound was healing, Chase! This rex didn't die from this gunshot wound at all!"

"I fired two more shots," Chase said, unconvinced.

"Yes, yes," Ogilvey agreed. "But all three of your bullets struck bone—one in the left iliac crest at the hip, this one on the left scapula, and one in the right coracoid, on the breast.

None penetrated the chest or abdominal cavity. So none harmed internal organs."

"Come to think of it," Chase said, "I did try to hit those bones."

Kit made a little astonished gasp. "You mean to say you were picking and choosing your shots while this thing was trying to eat me?" She frowned her disapproval.

"Well, just for a moment," he said, apologetically. "My wildlife biologist instincts got the best of me."

"And a job well done," the professor said. "You chased him away from Kit, who was fending him off with nothing more than a pitchfork, but you didn't kill him. And notably, all three of those bones had begun to heal. I think it is safe to say your record of never having killed a T rex remains intact."

"So what killed him? Kit's pitchfork to the mouth?"

"Not at all, by my reckoning."

"What then?"

"Look here, on the flank. Three ribs broken severely, with splinters that could have pierced a lung."

"Rufus!" Kit exclaimed.

"Yes, my dear. Rufus and Henrietta. Our parasaurolophus friends punched and kicked this rex so mercilessly when they saved us from him, that he was forced to retreat to save himself. But clearly, the parasaurolophus attacks were much more damaging than Chase's bullets. The three cracked ribs are all unhealed—and furthermore, there is a small, fresh fracture in the parietal bone of the skull as well. No telling what sort of internal injuries might have accompanied those fractures. A ruptured liver? A perforated lung? A brain hemorrhage? I recall both Rufus and Henrietta landing solid punches and kicks to this rex's chest, gut, and head. And now we see just how deadly a parasaurolophus attack can be!"

Kit took Chase's elbow, hugged his muscular arm, and smiled at him. "I bet you're relieved."

"I am," he said, smiling at her. "My record's still good. I've never killed any large predator—mammal or dinosaur."

"Yes, Chase Armstrong," Ogilvey said. "You were, are, and

will remain the champion of wildlife, no matter how large or small."

"Or fierce," Kit added.

Will Daniels could be heard faintly, calling from the house. "Kit? Kit? Where are you guys?"

"Down here, Daddy," Kit called back.

"Well, get up here," Will hollered. "Gar is here. Wants to speak to Dr. O. And you and Chase too."

When they emerged from the woods, Gar was sitting in his fighter-walker, having hunkered the two-legged machine down in front of the house. As they approached and gathered around the gleaming silver quahka, he head-bobbed a Kra greeting to each of the three in turn.

"Trouvle," he said, in English that was inflected by his rows of theropod dinosaur teeth.

"Trouble?" Dr. O replied. "What sort of trouble?"

"Vad trouvle. Deelonga on the loose."

"Deelonga? Alamosaurs, you mean?" The professor's wooly eyebrows rose high above his thick glasses.

"Gah!" Gar affirmed, nodding his crested head again. "Alangosaurs walking long way."

"Walking? Where to?"

"Don' know exactly. Go to lay eggs. Go east."

"East? How far east?"

"Very pfar east."

"Ah," said the professor. "A migration to a nesting ground?"

"Gah."

A moment of silence followed as each tried grasp the new problem confronting them. As thoughtful Kra often do, Gar turned his long neck to preen the black feathers of his shoulder, which was no longer covered in battle armor in these times of truce.

"So," Chase began. "Are they headed toward human populations?"

"Gah," Gar said.

"I see the problem," Chase said. "What are we supposed to do about it?"

"Don' know, Chay-su. You talk with Suarez." Gar motioned for the group to come near, and they mounted the two hunkered-down legs of the fighting machine. When they were able to see into the cockpit, he turned on a video screen. Suarez appeared on a two-way video feed, his flight-helmet visor up and his tanned face a map of great concern.

"Hi, you guys," he said. "Glad to see you. Look at this." He reached for a button in front of him and the view shifted to a gun-sight image from the helicopter. It tracked a huge sauropod splashing across an oxbow river bend, followed by a dozen others.

"They're moving awfully fast," he narrated. "They came south down the Humptulips River to Hoquiam. Headed right into town, but they ran into some electric telephone lines that sparked when they broke them. That caused them to turn east. You should have seen people running and hiding in their houses! Driving their cars into ditches! These things really move! I'm estimating about thirty miles per hour at top speed. And they seem able to keep it up indefinitely."

Ogilvey leaned near the monitor, observing the animals intently. "They're not so fat as I expected. Rather lanky and long-legged. Thin bodied. They don't plod. They almost bounce along!"

"Well," Suarez said, "they're bouncing into trouble."

"Where are they now?" Chase asked.

"They've already passed Aberdeen on its north side. Forded the Wishkah River at Young Street Bridge Park."

Kit interjected, "That's where Kurt Cobain camped when he was down and out, isn't it?"

"Yeah," Suarez said. "Now it's full of muddy dinosaur tracks and dinosaur poo. They really leave some calling cards wherever they go."

"Ahh," Ogilvey said. "I would like to make a close-up inspection of that!"

"I wouldn't," Suarez replied. "Now, they're following the Chehalis River upstream. We held off the entire Kra army on the banks of the Chehalis, but these babies are only knee deep in water that would have sunk a fighter-walker. This is a whole 'nother problem. I don't know how we can stop them—without killing them."

"Easy, Suarez," Chase admonished. "We'll think of something."

"I hope so," Suarez replied. "Or else. We've got to think of human safety first."

"Of course we do," Chase agreed.

"My, my," Dr. O said. "This is a completely unexpected development."

"No," Gar said firmly. "I warning you."

Ogilvey thought a moment. "Ah, yes!" he said. "You did indeed. Now I recall everything. You told me alamosaurs were instinctually imprinted to nest in the riverbed sands of what was then the predecessor to the Columbia River. But you were not sure where exactly they would go, were you? Given that there have been sixty-five million years of changes to their home nesting area."

"Gah," Gar affirmed.

Ogilvey went on for the others' benefit, "The Kra had intended to hold the alamosaur herd within the Olympic National Park until next year. But their migration instincts are too strong."

"Gah," Gar said. "Treaty say Kra no can go south of Arran Tarr."

"South of where?" Kit asked.

"Arran Tarr," Ogilvey repeated. "The new Kra city on the Olympic Coast. 'Tarr' means 'west,' and so Arran Tarr means 'Western City.' Then, as now, it was a coastal city on the edge of the 'Taggassogh.'"

"The what?" she asked.

"'Tagga,'" Ogilvey explained, "means 'huge,' and 'sogh' means 'ocean.' Just as is true today, the largest body of water on earth during the Cretaceous Era was the Pacific Ocean. In fact, it was even wider than it is now—nearly half the planet's circumference. So it was called Huge Ocean by the Kra. Taggassogh. Have I got that right, Gar?"

Gar bobbed his head in confirmation. "Gah, Ogil-vee. You got right."

The doctor went on. "Arran Tarr, on the shores of the Taggassogh, was the Kras' second city after Arran Kra. It was actually farther north in those times, perhaps near present-day Juneau in the Alaska Panhandle. But in the warmer world of the Cretaceous, its climate was like the present-day Olympic Peninsula coast—cool rainforest. So the Kra intend to re-establish it farther south in our colder world."

"Isn't there any trace of it left?" Kit asked. "Maybe it was buried like Arran Kra was."

"Not likely, my dear. The Kra have already dispatched myriad small spy-drones—"

"Teezagoks?"

"Yes, indeed. And those small, hummingbird-sized flying photo-drones have already scoured the Alaskan coastal mountains for any sign of old Arran Tarr. But it would appear that time was not kind to the ancient city. The forces of erosion—rain, ocean waves, and worst of all, glaciers during the Ice Ages, have scraped and washed away every last trace of the place. But the Kra are resourceful, and soon we'll see a new city on the coast of Washington state—a new Arran Tarr!"

"Thank you for that, Dr. Ogilvey," General Suarez said. "Now, can we get back to the situation at hand? A bunch of big dinosaurs have decided to play hooky from the Kra reservation. So where exactly are they going?"

"Neekatonka," Gar responded.

"Neeka—what?"

"Neekatonka," Ogilvey said, scratching his wooly jaw, "translates as, 'inland'."

"That doesn't sound good," Suarez grumbled. "We've got cities and towns by the dozen inland of the Olympic Peninsula."

"A combined force of Kra fighter-walkers and our tanks

might stop them," Kit suggested.

"No can do," Suarez said firmly. "This is where my problem comes in. You see, the Kra fighting machines are constrained by treaty to remain on the reservation at Arran Tarr. It would take an act of congress to get them permission to leave their city to help control these beasts. But the U.S. Congress is notorious for not making decisions quickly. The situation is already tied up in politics. Getting Congress to quit bickering among themselves and approve anything—that's a real slow process. The Texans are opposed to any action at all until the rest of Congress agrees to put creationism study back in the grade-school curriculum. Congress is having a fight of, well, biblical proportions over this one. So, we can't get a vote, one way or the other. Treaty prevents us from killing dinosaurs without good cause, and the Kra can't help us without approval to move off their reservations. So our hands are tied by congressional inaction. We need somebody to figure out what to do before some people get hurt. Any ideas, Chase? You are the United States' official dinosaur-human relations specialist."

"Yeah. Sure, I am," Chase stammered, dumbstruck by what he was watching on the screen. Another huge beast was splashing across the river. "But it's all a little new to me. I guess I'd advise getting people out of the way and letting the dinosaurs go wherever they're going."

"Not possible," Suarez said. "But here's what I've been thinking. The Kra at the coast are constrained by treaty. But Gar has diplomatic credentials. He can travel anywhere he needs to go, right?"

"True," Gar agreed.

"So I'm thinking it would help if you folks there in Montana brought your fighter-walkers over here. We could use their sirens and electric bolts to help us turn these things back."

"Gah!" Gar cried.

"We're on our way!" Ogilvey concurred.

Gar leaned near the doctor and they carried on a whispered conversation in rapid-fire Kranaga.

"Er," Ogilvey said when they finished. "We'll leave early tomorrow, that is. Gar says he'll need to discuss this with Arran Kra's senior council and arrange chain-of-command for his absence. Things are, er, rather delicate, here. There is still some significant dissension in the ranks."

"Sounds like congress," Suarez grumbled.

"The Kra council is a bureaucracy in its own way, I suppose," Ogilvey agreed.

"Okay," Suarez said. "But these things are moving fast! Who knows where they'll be by morning."

"Heeh!" Ogilvey laughed. "I trust they won't be hard to find!"

***

Early the next morning Suarez, in field helmet and green camo fatigues, was Crom's passenger in an idling Humvee pulled off Interstate Highway 5 in southwestern Washington, south of the town of Chehalis in an area of forests and farmlands. Delivered by Demerest the previous evening, they now sat at the side of the freeway near where the Newaukum River, an upper tributary of the Chehalis, crossed under paired freeway bridges in full view of Mount Saint Helens' steaming volcanic rim. They had decided to make the north-south freeway their bastion against the beasts' eastward march. And they intended to turn the herd back by whatever means was at their disposal. That wasn't much, however, given the President of the United States' only stipulation regarding the situation, delivered by phone earlier in the morning. "Don't kill anyone, or anything."

Suarez had prepared his defenses the best he could on short notice. Searching for non-lethal solutions, he had requisitioned tons of fireworks from the nearby Chehalis Indian Reservation. With these, he hoped to frighten the beasts into retreat. He positioned truckloads of rockets, buzz bombs, and other noisy and smoky munitions along the highway near the bridge. And if they proved insufficient for the purpose, he had also spaced a dozen heavy Stryker tanks along the road, armed with blank shells. These could quickly converge on the alamosaurs wherever they might try to cross the freeway.

"Your strategy is to put up a tremendous wall of smoke and noise?" Crom asked. "Do you think that will be enough to do the trick?"

"It had better be," Suarez said. He looked to the south of the bridges. A quarter-mile distant, police patrol cars with lights flashing had blocked the freeway lanes. The same was true to the north. Behind the patrol cars, hundreds of trucks, motor homes, and automobiles were stopped and backed up as far as the eye could see. No doubt there were many hundreds of angry people in them.

Crom pointed to the west. "Here they come!" he exclaimed.

CHAPTER 2

Suarez snapped his head around. The Alamosaurus herd was coming up the valley of the Newaukum, long necks swaying like a forest of tall thin trees. They were wading along the river or walking beside it, and all were headed directly for the bridges. He snatched up the hummer's hand microphone and shouted, "All tanks stand by! Fireworks teams, prepare to light 'em up!"

Teams of Native Americans from the Chehalis Tribe had placed fireworks by the dozen at both ends of the bridge spans and in the center as well. As the long-necked herd drew nearer, drawn toward the bridges by their instinct to follow the river, Suarez commanded, "All right, Chehalis Nation, give 'em some rockets' red glare!"

At each firing position the tribesmen, some of whom had worn ceremonial clothing and feathers in their braided hair for the occasion, set off large rockets that left trails of sparks and arched toward the alamosaur herd. Bursting in the air over the dinosaurs' heads, munitions of various colors erupted into spheres, ovals, and sprays of red, green, gold, and blue sparks. The huge beasts reared and bellowed. Some turned in panic and stampeded back the way they had come. Others milled in a group, drawing together and lashing their long, striped tails defensively through the showers of sparks.

"It's working!" Crom cried.

"Don't be too sure," Suarez murmured. "Look at the biggest ones."

Two particularly huge alamosaurs had separated from the

rest of the herd. Positioning themselves on each side of the group, they pressed forward despite loud rocket bursts and sparks raining down around their heads. They came on with determination, taking long strides toward the bridges, one beast on each side of the Newaukum. Beside the bridges, two heavy Strykers pulled into position on the south, and two more on the north end.

Suarez commanded, "Stryker heavies, prepare to fire blanks." The gun turrets tracked the big beasts as they neared the bridge.

The alamosaurs came through the smoke and noise of the rockets until they were stopped by the bridge spans. Crom said, "We've got 'em boxed in by tanks on both sides. And, no way can they get under!"

It was true that none but the smallest of the younger alamosaurs could possibly have slunk under the bridge spans, but that was not the intention of the lead animals anyway. At the last moment, they made their intentions clear—they split and began to mount the freeway embankments on either side of the bridges.

"Strykers!" Suarez called into his handset, "make some noise!"

On both sides, the waiting Strykers aimed their guns at the beasts and fired almost point-blank. Heavy blasts of smoke and fire burst from their cannon, and both beasts reacted immediately. Rather than turning tail, they reared their colossal bodies high and, standing on their hind legs, flailed out at the Strykers with their front feet. Each of those feet bore heavy, hooked claws that looked like they could open up a tank like a can-opener. The tanks fired more rounds, but the noise and smoke only seemed to enrage the big alamosaurs all the more. Each one pressed forward, flailing, until the Stryker drivers wisely chose to pull back.

"What now?" Crom asked, staring incredulously at the melee.

"That!" Suarez exclaimed. He pointed at the herd, which had gained confidence as the big ones held their own against the tanks. They were on the move again, trotting along the south bank of the Newaukum and beginning to climb the freeway embankment, shielded from the retreating Strykers by the titanic, rearing body of the big adult on that side. One Stryker turned its turret and fired a blast at the herd, but instantly paid the price. The big alamosaur nearest it turned its body sideways with almost cat-like grace and lashed out with its forty-foot-long bullwhip tail. The blow struck the Stryker solidly along one side with a resounding *kathump!* Despite the war machine's tremendous weight, it flipped over onto its side like a child's toy. The crew clambered from hatches and ran for shelter under the bridge, encouraged along by several near-miss snaps of the big beast's tail.

The herd was now at full stride, moving like stampeding elephants. Diverted farther south along the freeway by the noise and commotion, they crossed the road by moving directly through the halted civilian traffic. They threaded their way between trucks, or stepped clear over passenger cars from which men, women, and children gaped at them. One of the police officers sounded several short blasts on his siren. *Whoop, whoop, whoop!* In response, a medium-sized alamosaur turned toward, not away from him. It stepped onto the hood of the car, crushing it and sending out a blast of radiator steam. Its next step fell on the flashing lights. As the car's roof crumpled, the trooper dove out his window, rolled on the ground, and scurried away between vehicles to safety. The alamosaurs' next step, onto the car's trunk, completed its demolition of the vehicle into scrap metal. Scarcely pausing to turn its lofty head and look at its handiwork, the animal rejoined the herd as it passed through the traffic snarl and moved into the green and pastoral landscape of the upper Newaukum valley, unimpeded.

As the noise of the ineffectual cannon and fireworks died away, Suarez sighed. "So much for that bright idea. I wonder where they're headed from here? The Cascade Mountain Range is in their way."

Crom pointed at a map on the Humvee's computer screen. "They can get across if they follow the river valleys," he said.

"From here, if they follow the south fork of the Newaukum east to the town of Onalaska and on to Cinebar and Morton, they can reach the Cowlitz River valley and head east past Randle and Packwood."

"That looks like the way they're headed."

"If they go up the Cowlitz and Ohanapecosh river valleys, they can get over Cayuse and Chinook Passes. From there, they can get through the rest of the mountains by going down the American River Valley to the Naches."

"Complicated," Suarez said. "But do-able, I guess. Then where will they go?"

"Once they're in the open desert country east of the Cascades, it's anybody's guess."

"Look at that!" Suarez cried.

"Now what?" Crom asked, but he quickly saw what Suarez had seen. Far above and beyond the alamosaurs and the immense traffic jam they had caused, a great billowing, white, mushroom-shaped cloud towered on the southeastern horizon. It was a steam eruption rising miles above Mount Saint Helens' craggy vent.

Suarez murmured, "It seems like the forces of nature have the upper hand today."

***

Two quahkas were parked in front of the ranch house. Will Daniels watched from the front porch as Kit, Chase, Dr. Ogilvey, and Gar shuttled from the house and the barn, loading storage compartments below the tails of the quahkas with supplies for a lengthy road trip. They packed tents, sleeping bags, camp kitchen supplies, and coolers of food amply stocked from Will's freezers and Kit's garden. As they worked, the professor kept up his habitual stream of chatter.

"Strictly speaking, these fighter-walkers are confined by treaty to the Arran Kra area. But Gar's is a diplomatically licensed vehicle. If we had asked the U.S. Congress for permission, they might have forbidden us to leave, just as they did the Kra on the Olympic Peninsula."

"Sometimes it's best to take action now, and apologize later," Will said.

"Exactly," Dr. O agreed.

"One thing I don't get," Chase said as he tucked a sleeping pad into what was becoming an overstuffed back compartment. "Why all this is happening in the first place? What's gotten into those alamosaurs?"

"Ever wonder," Ogilvey answered with a question, "how the Kra can hope to create herds of big animals without the continued use of their lunar cloning vats?"

Chase closed the hatch of the overstuffed back compartment with some difficulty. "They could set up some cloning vats here at Arran Kra, couldn't they?"

"Good thought son, but I'm afraid that would be impossible. You see, the Kra can only grow sauropods, rexes, and other huge animals in vats under lunar gravity. Earth gravity makes the task impossible. The largest animals would crush themselves under their own weight as they grew. In fact, the entire process is just barely viable on the moon."

"So, how will it be done?" asked Kit, who had climbed aboard the quahka to tuck a big leather purse and daypack into the back of the tail space. "I hate to think such magnificent creatures would go extinct again when this generation gets old."

"That would be tragic," Ogilvey agreed. "But we needn't fear that eventuality. Sauropods, you see, have no trouble creating new sauropods the old-fashioned way, by hatching babies from eggs!"

The quahka's radio made a scratchy noise. Then a man's voice came through loud and clear. "Suarez here. Anybody on the other end?"

Kit flipped a toggle on the quahka's console and replied. "We're all here, getting ready to leave."

As Chase, Gar, and Ogilvey gathered around the cockpit, Suarez said, "Good! I hope you'll get moving pronto. These things are unstoppable—short of shooting one."

"Oh!" Kit exclaimed. "You wouldn't do that! Would you?"

"Not unless it's absolutely necessary."

Ogilvey leaned over the cowling. "We are duly approved by the Kra Council to come and assist you. Where are they now?"

"They got past us. They're heading up the Newaukum River Valley. We're, uh, stuck in traffic."

"Traffic?"

"There hasn't been a traffic jam like this on Interstate Five since Mount Saint Helens exploded in 1980 and shut the freeway down. Trucks and cars are backed up for twenty miles each way. And we're stuck in the middle of it with no way out until traffic gets moving again."

"Did anyone get hurt?" Kit interjected.

"Negative, Kit. Fortunately, the dinos could care less about hurting anybody, as long as you keep out of their way. But the people up front did get quite a show. Meanwhile, nothing we've tried has turned 'em back."

"Back from where? Kit asked.

"Wherever they're headed. East, we know that. It's as if they've got a roadmap in those little pea brains."

"Pea brains!" Dr. O interrupted. "You underestimate them, General."

"Maybe so. But they can't be too smart, tangling with my tank troop."

"It seems they have prevailed in match one," Ogilvey muttered, sounding as if he had been personally insulted. "Alamosaur brains may set no record for size, but with a good fifty cubic centimeters of gray matter, they're as well off volume-wise as most dogs. And as we have already learned from the Kra, dinosaur brains are much more densely wired than mammalian brains. And, furthermore, let me point out that alamosaurs have twenty times the brain size of crows, which are known to use tools, anticipate the actions of others, and make plans for the future. Twenty times that much brain power! Mark my words, you should not underestimate their animal intelligence!"

"Look, Doc. I didn't call to argue with you. I called to tell you where they're at, and to see if I can get your help. Maybe those fighter-walker sirens and electric bolts can turn them back."

"Duly noted," Ogilvey said, calming down. "We'll be on our way shortly. Right, Gar?"

Gar, who had listened to the exchange with keen interest—turning his crested head left and right birdishly—nodded in response to Ogilvey's question. "Gah!" he affirmed.

Within minutes, the quahkas were loaded. Gar piloted one, with Ogilvey sitting awkwardly behind him in the space normally reserved for a Kra's long tail, brushing tail feathers aside and sneezing as if he may have developed an allergy to them. With a wave to Will Daniels, Gar lowered the quahka's canopy glass, stood his machine on its two legs, and started a smooth ostrich-like run down the ranch drive.

"This is exciting!" Kit said as she settled in behind Chase in his quahka. "Goodbye, Daddy!" She waved and he waved back as Chase lowered the canopy and piloted his machine down the drive after Gar's. She put her arms around Chase's midsection like a motorcycle passenger, and kept them there despite the smooth motion of the quahka once it was striding along behind Gar's on the county highway heading for the interstate.

Chase put his machine on automatic pilot to follow the tail of Gar's machine. He keyed the commands into the quahka's console, then turned and smiled at Kit. "So, your father's okay with you running off and sharing a campsite with me for a week or two?"

"He'd better be." Kit smiled.

Chase glanced at her thoughtfully, and then nervously cleared his throat. "Have you thought about… my question?"

Kit's smile faded just slightly. "Your… proposal?"

"Yeah. That would be it."

"I've thought about it a lot."

"And?"

"I… haven't decided."

"When are you going to decide?"

"I don't know."

"That's not very encouraging. Anything I can do to speed things up?"

"No. Can't we just live in the here-and-now for a while? After all, here-and-now is pretty exciting, isn't it? We're off on another dinosaur adventure!"

"Sure. Okay. I suppose."

"I just need more time to think, Chase. How about a moratorium on discussing 'us' until this trip is over? Agreed?"

"Agreed." Chase sighed resignedly.

***

Seven hours later, moving at 90 miles-per-hour on Interstate 90, the quahkas had crossed the western half of Montana and moved into the Idaho panhandle, where they paused at a roadside overlook of Lake Coeur d'Alene. Its cold waters shimmered in late-day sun as the humans ate sandwiches for dinner and Gar swallowed a pair of raw beefsteaks, bone and all.

When Suarez came on the radio, they gathered at Chase's quahka to listen to his update. "They stopped awhile to graze on the forests east of Packwood. But now they're crossing White Pass right below Mount Rainier. Have a look on video."

The quahka's small video screen showed the spectacular sight of long necks moving against the snow-clad mountain backdrop.

"They're moving toward Cayuse Pass, like we thought. They'll be heading down the east side of the mountains overnight."

"We've been traveling pretty fast," Chase said. "Where should we meet you?"

"I think you folks might as well hold up to the east, at Moses Lake maybe. Get a good night's sleep and be ready to hit the road early. We'll radio the herd's location then. If they head down the Naches to Yakima, we could have a major panic on our hands. Dinosaurs and a couple hundred thousand people aren't going to mix very well."

***

Suarez' morning report came as they were loading luggage aboard their quahkas in the parking lot of the Best Western Moses Lake Motel, having just finished breakfast at the motel dining room, where Gar's capacity to pack away raw pork sausage patties had astonished the waitress.

"Lost them?" Chase exclaimed to the radio. "How do you lose a herd of hundred-foot-long giant thunder lizards?"

"Our spotter helicopter had to land overnight. Thunderstorms came up. And the herd didn't go down the Naches. That's all we know right now. At least there is no imminent threat to Yakima. I'll get back in touch when we find them. Meanwhile, keep coming west. They're around here somewhere."

Several hours later the quahkas crossed the mile-long span of the Columbia River Bridge, pulled off the freeway at the small river-gorge settlement of Vantage, and stopped at the Petrified Forest Museum. They ate sandwiches in a parking lot that looked out over a grand view of the upper Columbia River gorge while awaiting another update from Suarez.

"What a spectacular place!" Kit exclaimed, looking across the river at the stupendous, step-walled cliffs on the far side.

"A totally cool landscape for dinosaurs," Chase agreed.

"Amazing geological history here," Dr. O added. "And all of it came into existence after the Age of Dinosaurs! See how the cliffs are made of layer upon layer of dark brown basaltic lava? Almost the entire eastern half of the state of Washington was submerged in lava flows that spread from horizon to horizon. Dozens of them, over millions of years, during the Age of Mammals."

"If you say so, Doc," Chase replied.

"Indeed, I do," Ogilvey responded. "And after the inundations with lava, the Ice Ages brought additional trauma to the landscape. Glaciers moved south from Canada and dam-med the Columbia River with ice. When the ice dam broke, it released as much water as exists in one of the Great Lakes. The land was flooded again, from horizon to horizon, but this time with water carrying icebergs. These huge cliffs were cut into the solid lava rock in a matter of days!"

Gar sat in his quahka, eating a package of half-a-dozen foot-long Oberto peperoni sticks one after another, without the benefit of chewing. When a radio call came in, he turned it up so the others could hear.

"We're on their tails again," General Suarez said. "They went up Pine Creek and Milk Creek Canyons to Manastash Summit and spent some time wallowing in the little lake there. Then they went down Manastash Creek to the Yakima River, south of Ellensburg. We caught up to them on the flat farmlands and followed them up Trail Creek into the Colockum Wildlife Area. Rugged country. Now they're following Tekison Creek Canyon down to the Columbia River."

"Sounds like a complicated pathway," Chase said.

"It is," Suarez agreed. "Especially when you're trying to follow them in wheeled vehicles over desert canyonlands. But we're keeping up okay, now that we've found them."

"No doubt," Dr. O replied, "the herd is following some not-too-logical, but instinctually dictated program. There must have been a similar route sixty-five million years ago. Despite the resurfacing of Washington State by mountain building, volcanism, glaciation, and erosion, they nevertheless have found their way to the Columbia."

Chase studied a map Gar had pulled up on his quahka's console display. "Colockum Wildlife Area is not too far from here," he said. "Let's get moving." He stepped down off Gar's machine and hurried toward his quahka.

Ogilvey paused with Kit near the Vantage Museum's doors. "A pity we're on such an urgent mission," he said. "I could spend hours looking at the incredible agatized wood on display here. Just think. Whole standing forests were inundated by those lava flows. After millions of years buried underground, the wood was replaced with minerals so fine that the details of cellular structure are preserved in the stone. Even a primitive rhinoceros was buried by lava and preserved as a rhinoceros-shaped hole in the rock."

"Like a victim at Pompeii!"

"Very similar indeed, Kit."

Chase called from his cockpit, "Can we get going?"

"Coming," Kit said. "Keep your shirt on."

The Colockum Wildlife Area presented a rough countryside of hills, canyons, forests, and desert scrub brush. The two quahkas followed a back road up and over the central highland and down the long canyon of the Tekison Creek to the banks of a wide bend of the Columbia River. There, as their fighter-walkers moved along a dusty, rutted road, they came upon a spectacular sight.

"The alamosaurs!" Kit cried, putting both hands on Chase's shoulders to look around him and take in the sight of two dozen stupendous sauropods gathered where a wide, sandy flat met the smoothly flowing blue waters of the mighty Columbia River. Most of the animals stood calmly with their heads held high atop their tall necks. A few of the smaller subadults had waded into the river and were rolling in the waters, enjoying what might have been the first full-immersion baths of their lives.

Gar piloted his quahka to a place partially hidden from the colossal beasts by a rocky rise and a dozen tall cottonwood trees. Chase followed and as soon as the canopy lifted, Kit was on the ground with Dr. O and Gar.

The professor was grinning from ear to ear. "Would you just look at them?" he half-whispered, even though his voice could not have carried over the hundred yards between their hiding place and the congregation of giants.

Kit did as he suggested, and Chase joined her, putting a hand on her shoulder. "They're beautiful!" she exclaimed. "Look at those colors!" The animals' leathery, scaly hides were mottled with giraffe-like geometric markings, which were not as bold as those of giraffes, but instead ranged through muted tones of tan and brown, reminiscent of desert camouflage.

Ogilvey turned to Kit to exclaim something more, but she

couldn't hear a word he said—just as he spoke, a loud droning sound overwhelmed his voice.

It was the song of the alamosaurs.

Emanating first from the largest alamosaurus at the center of the group, and then taken up by the whole group, came a sound unheard in 65 million years. Starting deep in the lungs of the huge chests, rising along the upright throats and issuing out the domed nasal cavities atop their heads, came songs like big thunderous didgeridoos. "Wwllrrrllrrrllll," sang the first animal, and the others joined in with a chorus of similar sounds that made the entire canyon of the Columbia reverberate with a near-deafening but glorious, song.

Ogilvey raised field glasses and observed as the sound continued. He shouted over the uproar, "I see how they do it! They hold their necks high like trumpeter swans. The sound vibration comes from the chest, just as birds use a syrinx in their chests rather than the larynx we mammals use in our throats. After traveling up the trachea within the long throat, the tone enters their domed head. Vibrating flesh of their nostrils modulates the sound. They close one nostril and then the other to make that *wwrrll* sound. Amazing!"

As suddenly as it had arisen, the group's chorus stopped, leaving echoes reflecting off the canyon walls.

"That must be their assembly call," Ogilvey mused. "Intended to guide any stragglers to join the herd."

"Gah!" Gar agreed.

"What an awesome sound!" Kit exclaimed.

"Sauropods really are thunder lizards!" Chase said. And then he pointed off to one side. "Hey," he said. "Look who's here already."

Two flight-helmeted soldiers trotted toward them from a military helicopter set down on the river side of the rocky rise.

"Good to see you guys again," General Suarez called as he approached, followed by his pilot, Demerest. "I guess now we know where they were headed! I wonder what they'll do next?"

"I doubt you'll have to wait long to find out," Ogilvey said. "In fact, look!"

The beasts began to mill around as a group, at the same time spreading out across the sandy area, which was longer and wider than two football fields. "Look at those males!" Ogilvey exclaimed. "Is that some sort of... dance, they're doing?"

Now spaced widely across the sandy field, the big males started a series of slow pivots in place, with necks stretched forward and tails outstretched to the rear. As they turned, they jostled and sparred with other males until they had adjusted their locations to avoid contacting the other dancers with nose or tail tip. "That's their way of separating nests by a full body length between pairs of males," Ogilvey explained. "To avoid trampling neighbors' eggs. Have I got that right, Gar?"

"You got right."

After suitably spacing themselves, the males paused their dances and their mates came near. In pairs, they began a slow, rhythmic swaying of their necks. Then they twined necks like giraffes sometimes do, and each pair began to sing. The females sang in a slightly higher but still deep register, while the males, with longer necks and more prominent nasal chambers atop their heads, made much deeper, truly thunderous sounds. As the pairs' necks twined and their heads orbited each other, their motion imparted an added, Doppler-shifting modulation to their *wwwrrrllll—wwwrrrlll—wwwrrrlll* sound.

"Like nothing the world has seen or heard in the last sixty-five million years!" Ogilvey bubbled.

"Beautiful!" Kit exclaimed. "And romantic, in a colossal way!"

"No-no!" Gar suddenly called.

As they had admired the alamosaurs, Ogilvey had led the others down from their rocky hiding place and they had strolled onto the sand flat, approaching the herd.

Gar stopped completely behind them. "No!" he called again. "Come back. Get away from dis place. Deelonga now very teetseetonka."

"Very what?" Chase asked. He had stopped in his tracks along with the others.

"Teetseetonka," Gar repeated.

"Er," Ogilvey said, wearing a thoughtful look. "Um. Teet-see has a meaning not unlike our word, 'testy.' It means irritated, aggravated."

"Gah!" Gar agreed.

"And tonka means, um—land. Am I right Gar?"

Gar nodded.

"So teetseetonka means, um, well—"

"Territorial," Chase concluded. "Like bull elk in the rutting season."

"That's it," Ogilvey agreed. "Gar says they get very territorial and we had better make ourselves less conspicuous."

"Uh-huh," Gar said. "Or we get deelonga-tuka."

Ogilvey cocked his head owlishly. "I'm afraid I miss your meaning."

"Tuka," Gar said, "mean very thin, flat, like paper."

"So deelonga-tuka means?"

"As flat as you can be," Kit guessed. "Trampled by a sauropod!"

"Good Kee-tah," Gar said. "Dey crush you flat like paper. Deelonga-tuka. Very bad."

They retreated to their rocky bastion, which was a low butte of basalt with vertical walls about 20 feet tall, with a central flat area ideal for a campsite. It was accessed by a narrow path between jutting outcrops and ringed by concealing cottonwood trees.

Ogilvey said, "We can set up our tents here and observe the beasts from cover, with no worries they'll climb the straight columnar-basalt cliffs to get at us."

Suarez excused himself and Demerest. He wanted to get aloft and make sure there were no unaccounted-for alamosaurs in the area, and make visual contact with Abercromby, who was leading a group of Humvees in the backcountry.

As their helicopter's whining engine warmed up, a big male separated from the herd. When the bull alamosaur approached the aircraft, Demerest quickly engaged the rotors for takeoff. But the *whup, whup* sounds agitated the beast. It made several bluffing charges at the chopper, trumpeting loud honks that were quite different from the sauropod song of a few moments previously. These were warning calls like long, solid, train-whistle blasts.

"Oh my," Ogilvey cried. "Gar has explained to me that dosokoti, the big, flying, quetzalcoatlus pterosaurs, are mortal enemies of baby alamosaurs. So of course they are attacked on sight by the adult alamosaurs. If this bull alamosaur has mistaken the flying machine for a quetzalcoatlus, it may not end well for our friend, General Suarez."

Demerest had seen the danger coming. She revved the rotors and lifted off. But the alamosaur wasn't interested in letting the aircraft get away. As the chopper rose from the ground, the behemoth turned its flank and lashed out with his tail, smacking the bullwhip-like tip on the fuselage. The chopper spun out of control, careening away from the beast, tipping at crazy angles and blowing black smoke from its turbine engine. Another smack from the bullwhip struck the tail off the machine, sending it into a faster spin. Demerest, using every bit of skill in her training, somehow kept the chopper upright and brought it down in the river shallows. Upon impact, its rotors flew into pieces and the engine burst into flame.

While the behemoth reared and bellowed at the smoke and flame, Suarez and Demerest quickly jumped from the wreck and splashed away in waist-deep water. But the alamosaur wasn't cowed for long. It lashed its tail at them as they ran, cornering them among some huge boulders at the river's edge just below the camp mesa.

Suarez drew a pistol, held it straight up, and fired several shots in the air. The loud sound of the discharges had little effect on the angry sauropod, which drowned them out with a louder bellow of its own. Suarez crouched to avoid a tail swipe that went inches over his head, making a bullwhip-like *snap* in the air.

"We've got to help them!" Ogilvey cried. "Or they'll be—deelonga-tukaed!"

Chase and Gar were already mounting their quahkas. Kit

jumped in behind Chase, and he stood the machine up, lowered the canopy, and dashed off, following Gar's machine toward the fight. Without hesitation, they engaged the giant animal with parasaurolophus-sirens blaring and electric bolts crackling from their weapon arms. The siren noise and the irritation of electricity crackling over its hide clearly bothered the alamosaur, but neither was sufficient to turn the colossus from its attack. Instead of retreating, it turned broadside to the quahkas and leveled a swipe of its tail that tripped both machines at once, sending them tumbling to the ground.

"You okay?" Chase asked Kit as they untangled themselves inside the fallen quahka.

"Yeah, fine," she said as he grappled with the control joysticks and stood the machine upright. "Try ducking next time!"

"I don't know how to make this thing duck!" Chase exclaimed. He turned the machine and retreated at a run. Kit screamed when another tail swipe hit them from behind and sprawled them face-first onto the rocky ground. "Jeez," she grumbled as they sorted themselves out again. "If you can't duck, then at least get us out of here!"

"I'm trying!" Chase said through gritted teeth as he wrangled the quahka to its feet again. Gar got off an electric bolt that drew the beast off them momentarily and allowed Chase to charge away, eluding a third tail swipe by inches. Chase and Gar got their quahkas a safe distance back from the bellowing, rearing behemoth, and then fired a combined barrage of electric bolts that convinced it to halt its attacks. Kit looked around and said with relief, "Looks like Suarez and Demerest got away."

The two soldiers had fled from the boulders and made their way back to the mesa while the quahkas had confronted the alamosaur. The bull seemed content that there was no longer a threat to the herd, so he turned his attention to inspecting the smoldering wreckage of the chopper.

Back behind the mesa again, Chase and Gar hunkered their machines down and opened the canopies. Kit was shaking as she climbed down from the machine. "Whew!" she said. "I don't ever want to go on *that* ride again!"

"I don't blame you," the professor agreed. He was closely inspecting a yard-long dent on Chase's machine through his thick glasses. "Gar says the tip of that tail can deliver a megajoule of energy in a single strike."

"How much?" Chase asked, looking over the damaged spot.

"A lot, however much it is," Suarez said as he rejoined them along with Demerest. Both were dripping wet.

"Thanks for the help," Demerest said.

"You are most welcome," Ogilvey said. "Although I was not personally along for the ride. Are you two okay?"

Suarez looked at Demerest. She nodded in the affirmative. "Yeah, I'm fine. Just a little embarrassed to lose an aircraft under my command."

Ogilvey looked beyond Demerest. "Oh my!" he said. "I believe that loss will be total!"

The group turned and watched the alamosaur wade into the river and rear up, flailing out with the hooked claws of its forefeet. It came down on the chopper wreckage with both claws, tearing huge gashes in the fuselage and crushing it down lower in the water. After several repeats of this rearing, slashing assault, the helicopter was not much more than a ripple in the river with a few jagged pieces of metal protruding from the surface. Finally satisfied that no possible threat remained, the big male turned and went back to be among his companions.

"Deelonga-tukaed!" Ogilvey exclaimed.

CHAPTER 3

By this time, a change had occurred at the nesting ground. All the males had left their dancing circles and the females had taken the males' places. While the males and younger animals watched from nearby, the females began their own dances, as if deciding whether or not to accept the locations the males had chosen. Eventually each female ceased turning and aligned herself in one direction or another. And then each one lifted her right-rear foot and used the three massive claws to scratch into the sandy ground. Staying in the same place and repeatedly scraping, the females created long slots in the sand about two feet deep, three feet wide, and six feet long. They observed their own footwork by turning their long necks until their heads hovered over the holes. While they worked, Gar spoke rapidly to Ogilvey.

The professor translated for the others. "Note the precision with which each female crafts her nest scrape. This is by no means a random hole in the ground. Any imperfection in her digging invites disaster."

"Why?" Kit asked.

"You'll see," Ogilvey translated for Gar, who shrugged his shoulders and tottered his head from side to side—Kra body language for one who is amused and keeping a secret.

Ogilvey continued. "Gar says you should especially note that the nests are flat around the rim, not raised. The females have made the tops of the holes even with the ground. That is very important."

"Why?"

Gar remained smugly silent.

"Er, I guess we'll know soon enough," Dr. O said.

"Dah!" Gar exclaimed, pointing a clawed finger at one of the females near the center of the nesting ground.

"Watch her!" Ogilvey said.

The female moved so that her four feet were aligned along the length of the scrape and straddling it on both sides. She checked her positioning carefully with her head swung far around for a good view. Then she squatted downward and back on her huge hind legs until her rump nearly disappeared into one end of the hole and she raised her tail high. A white, spherical egg protruded from her rump and plopped gently onto the sandy bottom of the nest. Quickly, another egg followed, and then another. She took two short steps forward, squatted, and continued to lay more eggs.

"She'll work her way forward until the entire trench is full of eggs," Ogilvey said.

Gar murmured something more and the professor translated, "Note, again, that the eggs are all being laid low in the nest, with none protruding higher than the level of the sand around the nest. That's also very important. Now, Gar tells me the laying process may take most of the rest of the day and into the evening. I say we finish making camp and cook ourselves some dinner—er, those of us who like our dinner cooked, that is."

Gar nodded in agreement, with a few drips of saliva gathering on his fangs.

They arranged their camp in the flat area atop the mesa, placing tents in a ring around a central fire hearth built of blocks of basalt rock. Dr. Ogilvey, a lifetime master of campfire cookery, provided beefsteaks cooked on an iron skillet, fried potatoes, and salad greens for humans. Gar was content to gulp his steaks raw.

Sundown was approaching, and shadows were spreading from the tall canyon walls as the campers finished coffee for the men, tea for Kit, and a meat broth drink for Gar.

"Aha!" Ogilvey cried eventually. "The alamosaur males have rejoined the females at their nests. Another round of neck twining and duet singing has begun! Now, watch that male on the far left."

"What's he going to do?" Kit asked. "Cover the eggs with sand?"

"Hardly!" Dr. O scoffed. "You sound like my rival, Dr. Summerlin! Please don't parrot his ridiculous theory that these magnificent creatures abandoned their babies to hatch and grow without parental help."

"So, Summerlin is wrong, is he?" Chase interjected.

"As usual," Ogilvey replied. "Just watch the male. See how he stands at right angles across the trench? And now he has put his right knee down to the ground beside the nest. Next, he'll settle onto his right hip. There he goes! See how his thigh is laid along the ground paralleling the nest? Most of his colossal weight is now born on that huge thigh. Now he'll slowly walk his front feet forward, much the way elephants do when lying down. See? And, there! He's got both elbows down on the far side of the nest, spanning it like a bridge. The eggs, you see, are directly under his heart. Now he shifts his weight forward from his thigh, and his belly covers the nest, hiding it from sight, completely. And that's it! He's down on the nest, incubating the eggs with his body heat. Did you notice how gingerly he set his breast down over that flat-rimmed hole? The flat ground takes his weight evenly, and the eggs are in no danger of being crushed."

"Astonishing!" Kit said.

"Yes, my dear it is. It's as if a goose had been expanded to stupendous size, but had retained the ability to settle down over its brood with exquisite grace."

"But won't the ground be cold under the eggs?"

"Not at all," Ogilvey replied. "Gar says alamosaurus body temperature is hot, like that of chickens and geese, about forty-one degrees centigrade, or one-hundred-six degrees Fahrenheit. The sand underneath is a great insulator, so the eggs will be basking in warmth all night. Tomorrow, we'll see the males leave the nests, and the females take their turns. Alamosaurs never leave a nest uncovered for more than a few minutes. With so much constant heat, the embryos develop with incredible speed. The entire transformation from egg-white-and-yolk to fully formed sauropod occurs in record time. Just two weeks, give-or-take a day, and they'll be ready to hatch."

As the other males took to their nests, quiet descended over the valley. After darkness fell and the fire burnt down to embers, the conversations around the campfire tailed off. Even Ogilvey seemed at a loss for another lecture. Chase and the two soldiers began arranging sleeping bags inside their tents. Ogilvey followed their example. Kit laid her sleeping bag in the open in front of her tent, near the fire. As all were settling down, Gar went to his quahka and retrieved a guitar-like instrument from the rear storage compartment. He sat on a boulder near the campfire and began to strum and sing a song in Kranaga. It was a gargling, cawing melody, and was accompanied on the stringed instrument with a sound like someone plucking a set of sprung springs, *boing, boing, boir-oir-ing!*

"Ooh! Kit moaned, pulling her sleeping bag up around her ears. "He sounds like Scuttle singing in *The Little Mermaid.*"

"Or the Beatles playing 'Honey Pie,'" Ogilvey chuckled. "I believe it's some sort of sauropod herder's song, equivalent to our cowboy songs. Woopee ty yi yo, git along little dogies!"

"How long will he keep that up?"

"I don't know, my dear. Not too long, I hope. I've had a long day, just like you, and I'd like to get some sleep soon."

***

Kit awoke early in the morning, refreshed. But she was disturbed by rustling sounds in the cottonwood branches high above her. She sat up—and caught her breath. The long neck of a big alamosaurus arched above the camp. The beast was stripping leaves off the tallest branches of the cottonwood with its rows of peg-like upper and lower teeth.

"Quiet, my dear," Ogilvey whispered. He had stuck his head out the front flap of his tent and was squinting up at the big beast, adjusting his glasses with one hand. "The males have been relieved of brooding duty by the females. They're taking their morning meals. Watch this big fellow browse! Look how he uses his long, prehensile tongue to wrap around twigs and bring them into his mouth, to be sliced off by his teeth! Just the way our giraffes feed! I must make a note of that! Another example of my Exaltation Theory in action."

"Oh-oh," Kit said. "Here comes another theory."

"Yes indeed," Ogilvey said, grinning at her. "My Exaltation Theory has been scoffed at for years. But here we have proof of its first principle—that until one considers the highest functionality possible with a dinosaurian body plan, one's study is not complete. There is nothing primitive about this dinosaur—he's as deft at plucking foliage as any giraffe ever thought of being! Perhaps even more so."

Kit smiled. "I'm so lucky to have you as my teacher."

"Indeed you are."

Kit got out of her sleeping bag, already dressed in her blue-jean shorts and a yellow shirt. She had kept her clothes on to be prepared for an emergency in the night, which hadn't come. After Gar had ceased his caterwauling, the canyon had gone silent, except for chirping crickets.

Ogilvey, who had slept in a surprising getup of adult-sized, dark-green *Jurassic World* flannel pajamas with indominus rex heads all over them, got up and eyed the big beast overhead as Chase and the soldiers came out of their tents, dressed for the day. As Kit pulled on her cowboy boots, Gar arose from his sleeping-swan posture on the other side of the fire pit from her, naturally dressed in his covering of black feathers. He yawned, gaping a mouthful of fangs, and then shook himself from head to toe to un-ruffle his feather coat.

Kit stood, hugging her own shoulders against the cool of the early morning air, and looked around the nesting grounds. A funny thought struck her. "They must make a mountain of poo while they're nesting."

"Not so much, my dear," Ogilvey replied. "With their ultra-evolved digestive tracts, they actually produce very much less poo than an elephant. Though the piles are bigger, they are fewer."

"How can that be?" Chase asked, coming to wrap Kit in his arms to warm her.

Ogilvey pointed over their heads at the browsing alamo-saur. "That mouthful of cottonwood leaves, twigs, and small branches will be processed by the most sophisticated digestive system the world has ever known, so Gar tells me."

"Gah!" Gar affirmed.

"Their stomachs have six chambers—"

"Henn," Gar corrected.

"Er, yes," Ogilvey said. "Seven, counting the crop. In contrast to the elephant's single-chambered stomach and the giraffe's four-chambered stomach, the sauropod digestive system is a powerhouse food-processing facility. First, sand and gravel stored in the gizzard abrade the twigs into a fine mash. After that, each chamber digests the food in a different way. The fourth chamber is most remarkable. It contains a culture of white-rot fungus that breaks down lignin, the molecular glue that holds the woody parts of the plant together. The subsequent chambers, five through seven, have different bacterial microbes within them, which secrete different digestive enzymes that break down the other parts of the plant. The fifth-chamber microbes and their enzymes are specialists in breaking down the cellulose fibers to yield nutritious sugars. The sixth-chamber organisms attack the vitamin-rich green leafy material, and so by the time the food reaches the seventh stomach, it has been broken down into a gooey mass like brown, nutrient-rich yogurt. In the seventh stomach, the sauropod's own digestive enzymes—twelve varieties of lysozyme—dissolve the microbes as well, so they spill their nutrients, which are then absorbed by the intestines. This whole process is so effective that better than ninety percent of a sauropod's food intake is absorbed into its bloodstream. There never was a more efficient digestive system on earth than that of the alamosaur. Even our ruminant animals—cows, goats and sheep—with their four-chambered stomachs, rate only a distant second to this digestive ability. None of them have the critical, lignin-digesting fungus in them at all. But it is a fact that all the major groups of plant eating dinosaurs had similar highly efficacious digestive tracts. Lignin-dissolving fungus in their fourth stomachs was the single most important reason they could become giants!"

"Didn't you forget to mention the third stomach?" Chase asked.

"Er, yes," Ogilvey said, counting on his fingers. "I guess I did."

The alamosaur tore off another mouthful of leaves and twigs, and gulped them whole. Then he moved along to browse farther down the line of cottonwoods that edged the bank of the river, almost as if he had heard more than enough of Ogilvey's morning lecture. "Well, er, anyway," the professor mumbled, "the final product of digestion—white and black like bird poo—is shot out the rear end of the digestive tract with quite a substantial velocity."

"Thanks for all that," Suarez said. "That's a lot more than I ever wanted to know about dinosaur eating... and pooing."

"You're welcome, General. Now then, what shall we do for two weeks while their brooding and browsing routine continues?"

***

The arrival of a Kra fighter-walker in front of the Armstrong home in West Seattle brought quite a reaction from the local residents. Children buzzed past on bicycles, teens gathered in a group to get a close look at the glittering machine, and adults watched nervously from their doorways around the neighborhood. Chase and Kit dismounted and walked to the front door of the small, brown, two-story, older house and rang the bell. Chase introduced Kit to his parents, Edith and Edwin Armstrong—gray, pleasant people who wore expressions of astonishment on their faces at the unexpected visit, and at the crowd now encircling the fighting machine. Chase was glad he had put the canopy down.

"Come in! Come in!" Mrs. Armstrong cried. "Make yourselves at home. Well, of course, you *are* home, Chase!"

Chase followed Kit in, quipping, "Welcome to my hatching ground."

The house was a modest place, with small rooms and old-fashioned furnishings. "Cozy," Kit said, when she had been shown around. "I like it." She wore an amused smile when she was shown Chase's boyhood room, complete with a now-undersized bed and football hero photos on the wall, as well as a Yellowstone National Park poster and a large-format print of a wolf pack hunting in winter.

After the tour, they went to a roofed, raised deck at the back of the house and sipped happy-hour drinks while overlooking a vegetable garden that took up most of the back yard. It burgeoned with ten-foot-tall corn plants, several types of squash, potatoes, peas, cabbages, broccoli, carrots, beets, and pumpkins.

"It reminds me of our garden at home," Kit said.

"We've always had our own little patch of dirt to dig in," Chase said, "like the alamosaurs."

After an hour of conversation in which Chase and Kit astonished Ed and Edee with tails of what had become an almost routine succession of incredible events, Edee suggested that Ed should help her prepare a dinner of pork chops and fresh-picked vegetables. Kit excused herself to freshen up in the guest bathroom.

"So?" Edee asked Chase when they were busy in the kitchen and Kit had gone. "Anything you want to tell us?"

"About what?"

"You know very well. Are you two—?"

"In love? Yes, I guess we are."

Ed leaned near. "Are you going to… pop the question?"

Chase frowned. "I already did."

"And?"

"She's, um… not so sure."

As Edee cut up a big fresh carrot, she said, "Give her time, Chase. She's clearly a very special person with a lot of potential. But a young girl like her gives up a lot of freedom when she says yes. Isn't that right, Ed?"

"She sure is a pretty thing."

"Anyway," Chase said. "For now, I just thought I'd show her my home. Take her around town. Go look at the view from the Space Needle. Take a ferry ride. Go to Alki Beach. The usual tourist stops."

"Good plan," Ed said as he laid a chop in the frying pan. "That's the way I won your mother's heart."

"You old fool," she said. "I had already been to all those places."

"Not with me, you hadn't."

"Charmer," she said, smiling.

***

Days later, Kit and Chase were in the garden getting fresh vegetables for a breakfast omelet when a call came in on Chase's cell phone.

"The hatching has begun!" Dr. O exclaimed. "You had better hurry or you'll miss it."

"We're on our way!" Chase said. Then he glanced at two plump, perfectly ripe tomatoes Kit had just picked. "Right after breakfast."

Within hours they were back in camp with Dr. O and the soldiers, including Crom, who had driven his Humvee down from the hills to join them.

The female alamosaurs sat on their nests, or stood over them to provide shade from the hot noonday sun. The nearest pair of parents held their heads low, watching their babies hatch.

Kit and Chase perched on one of the highest rocks of the mesa, from which they could just see down into the nest with their binoculars. Two rows of a dozen eggs each were cracking open. Several eggs had long baby sauropod necks rising from them.

"The hatching process can take hours," Ogilvey called up to them from a lower position in camp. "Those eggshells are strong, and the little tykes have quite a struggle breaking out. They use the claws on their front feet to scratch a hole in their shells. Meanwhile, look what's happening across the way."

On the far side of the nesting ground, another female stood across her nest, shading her babies, all of whom had emerged from their eggs. The two-dozen little necks looked like a small garden of twigs rising from the trench. Near the female, the male had begun a peculiar, rocking motion, leaning his massive body forward and then backward, in a slow, repetitive rhythm.

"Ah," Ogilvey said. "Chase, you mentioned I had neglected the function of the third stomach. It is a peculiar organ, shaped like a cannon barrel. And right now it is being loaded with partially digested food."

As if on Ogilvey's cue, the big male lowered his head near the rim of the nest, opened his mouth wide, and regurgitated a fire-hose-like torrent of green, coagulated, slime-coated food onto the floor of the nest.

"Eew!" Kit exclaimed. "How appetizing."

"Yes, indeed!" Ogilvey said gleefully. "Very appetizing, if you're an infant alamosaur!"

"Like it was shot from a cannon," Chase added.

"And indeed it was, my boy!"

The babies thronged around the clotted mass and devoured it eagerly, making a chorus of eager goose-like honks as they gobbled down their shares.

As the group on the mesa watched the feeding spectacle, another male alamosaurus walked around the far edge of the nesting area. Chase noticed some odd shapes in the shadow cast by his long, outstretched tail. "Would you look at that!" he said.

"I am looking," Kit said, with her binoculars clamped to her face.

"Aha," Ogilvey said. "That alamosaur and his mate fooled

us. Their brood hatched yesterday, but they laid over them so persistently that we never suspected the hatchlings had arrived. Now, just a day later, the young ones are already able to leave the nest."

"They're lined up under dad's tail," Kit said with a look of utter amazement on her face. "And they're following him like baby ducklings!"

"That's the safest place for them in a world full of predators."

"They're so cute! Like Littlefoot in *The Land Before Time!*"

"Where are they going?" Chase asked.

"To have a swim, I'll wager," Ogilvey said. "That's a favorite pastime of baby alamosaurs, and adults too. Nesting grounds are always near whatever river laid down the sand beds. Hence, the animals have an inherent predilection for swimming. However, in Cretaceous times, the adults would always keep an eye out for deinosuchus, the huge crocodile that often came looking for a small snack. No such danger here, though."

The father alamosaur waded into the river and his brood splashed in after him. Instantly, they were romping in the shallows, play fighting, rolling on their sides, and all the while gabbling like two-dozen geese. Satisfied that his brood was happy and enjoying themselves, the huge male waded out deeper and rolled over on his side, sending a small tidal wave across the surface of the river.

Nearer to shore, some of the babies took on a new play tactic. They dipped their heads, drew water into their long throats, and then jetted it out again like squirt guns, dowsing themselves or their playmates with streams of water.

"What fun!" Kit exclaimed. "I wish we could join them."

"You can!" Ogilvey said. "We've got two kayaks hidden in the reeds of the river bank, just below camp. Shall we?"

CHAPTER 4

Within minutes they had launched the kayaks. Kit's was a single, pale yellow boat. Chase paddled a turquoise two-seater with Ogilvey in the bow. As they made their way out onto the wide Columbia's slow-moving waters, Ogilvey warned, "Just be sure to keep beyond tail's reach of the adult. If we stay well offshore and don't make any rapid movements, we'll be just fine. I've done it myself several times in recent days. And Gar swam beside me like a duck!"

They reached a place, a safe distance offshore, where they had good views of the babies and the big male, who rolled over on his back in the water with all four feet rising up on tree-trunk-like legs, with both his head and tail lifted up as well. He thrashed his tail about as if he were playing, too.

"Amazing!" Kit exclaimed as her kayak rode smoothly over a wave the splashing sauropod had made.

Several of the subadult sauropods waded into the river farther upstream and began taking in huge throatfuls of water and hosing down their backs, cooling off from the heat of the midday sun.

"What a gorgeous scene," Kit said.

"A river shore filled with rollicking sauropods!" Ogilvey agreed ecstatically. "Below towering lava cliffs. What a scene indeed!"

An odd sound made itself known. Far across the river to the east arose a humming noise like a distant lawnmower. As the sound drew nearer, Dr. Ogilvey groaned, "Oh, no! Not *them* again."

"Who again?" Kit asked.

"Thera McArty," Dr. O muttered disdainfully, "and that neighbor boy, Bobby Everett. They have shown up every day for three days now on that noisy contraption." He pointed at an object coming rapidly toward them at mid-river, crossing from Crescent Bar on the far side. It was a speeding jet ski, coming on at perhaps sixty miles per hour. "They have been such pests," Ogilvey growled, "buzzing around on that noisy, smoking, oil-spewing contraption!"

The jet ski came straight for the sauropods. Bobby, the pilot, was dressed in a garish Day-Glo green-and-black sport wetsuit, life vest, and black helmet. He slowed and stopped the glittering candy-apple-red-and-black machine not far from the kayaks.

Over Bobby's shoulder, Thera, dressed in a bright pink helmet and baby blue wetsuit, raised her fashion-model-perfect face to greet them with a smile. "Hiya, paleontologists!" she called out. "How are the big beasties today?"

"They're just fine," Chase replied with a note of irritation in his voice. "But I wouldn't get too close if I were you."

Thera grinned. "Thanks for the advice, Handsome. I'll keep it in mind. But I'm still looking for a Pulitzer-Prize-winning nature shot. Come to think of it, here's a great shot of a big hunky wildlife biologist right in front of the biggest beast of them all. She drew her camera from a waterproof bag, raised it, and quickly clicked off a series of shots of Chase in his kayak against a backdrop of splashing sauropods. "That might be the winner, right there. Mr. Rugged Good Looks in rugged country with monster animals everywhere!"

Ogilvey frowned at Thera. "How the devil did you of all people find out about this expedition?"

"Why don't you ask Ms. Cowgirl?"

"Who, me?" Kit stammered as all eyes turned to her. "The only person I told was Daddy... and Maddy Meyer."

"The biggest blabbermouth this side of the Mississippi,"

Thera smiled. "She told Beefy Boy, here." She patted Bobby on the shoulder. He blushed pink on his cheeks and down the sides of his neck.

Kit let out an exasperated sigh. "I've had enough of this!" She turned and began paddling back the way she had come. "Are you coming, Chase?"

Chase waved a quick farewell to Bobby and Thera and turned to follow Kit.

Thera snapped a couple more pictures and then said to Bobby, "Tally ho, Beefcakes! I want some real close shots this time." The jet ski roared and Thera laughed mischievously as they streaked away toward the alamosaurs.

As Chase paddled after Kit, who was moving speedily toward the campsite shore, Ogilvey muttered, "Abominable jet-ski yayhoos. Noisy heathens! Those machines disturb wildlife wherever they go." And, exactly as Ogilvey had implied, wildlife on and near the shore began to flee. Flocks of laughing gulls and shore birds rose into the air. Two wading herons flapped away on heavy wingbeats, uttering cries of annoyance, "Grrrock! Grrrock!"

"Jet skis create a wildlife exodus," Dr. O muttered. "They make a horrendous noise! I'm certain they'll frighten every alamosaur back onshore!"

"Don't be so sure," Chase said. He stopped paddling and watched as the jet ski raced between the adult and the cavorting babies. Thera held her camera to her face, snapping pictures as the babies abandoned their play and rushed ashore, panicking as if a real live deinosuchus had come to attack them.

"Aw," Kit exclaimed, turning her kayak alongside Chase's. "She's such a mood killer."

"Yeah, she is," Chase agreed. "But I don't think Bobby is paying attention to how close he's getting to daddy."

As the brood of babies took to dry land, the big male got his feet under him and stood up. The jet ski completely circled him as he did so. Bobby steered at high speed for open water, but his speed was not enough to escape the paternal wrath of the alamosaur. The male turned broadside to the retreating watercraft and leveled a prodigious tail swipe at it, swiveling at the hips and throwing every ounce of his tremendous weight into the stroke. The tail lashed like a bullwhip and its tip deftly snapped on the retreating machine, hitting its stern and sending it flying end-over-end. Bobby and Thera were jettisoned from the tumbling craft in midair, and all came down in a simultaneous triple-splash.

The male raised its long neck high and straight, and issued a deafening challenge honk that reverberated up and down the canyon. Then it lashed out again and Bobby Everett vanished in a wall of white water kicked up by the blow, disappearing beneath the surface.

The mangled jet ski was on its side and half sunk in the water. Its motor had somehow stayed on and it made pathetic, *wlub, wlub, wlub* sounds as it drifted on the current. Even this much noise seemed to enrage the alamosaur. It lashed out again and again with its tail. Scoring hit after hit, it knocked pipes and pieces of metal off the wreck until finally it turned nose-up like a sinking ship and went down at the stern, slipping quietly beneath the surface and leaving only a small shimmering oil slick to mark where it had been.

Satisfied, the male waded ashore and followed his brood. The babies raced ahead of him in a tight group, appearing from a distance to be a single many-necked animal scrambling in the direction of the nest. The little ones hooted and honked in fear.

"So much," Ogilvey declared, "for mixing jet skis and alamosaurs!"

A distressed, gargling call turned their attention back to the riders. Bobby Everett had surfaced. His black helmet was cracked and part of it hung down over his face, blinding him. Dazed, he splashed weakly with both hands but was making no progress trying to swim.

"I'll get him," Kit said, paddling swiftly toward him. "You guys check on Blondie." She quickly reached Bobby and called to him, "Grab the rudder as I go by. I'll pull you to shore." He did as bidden and soon was being towed behind Kit on a course back to the camp landing.

Chase paddled to Thera. As they neared her, Ogilvey said, "She looks pretty bad off."

Indeed, Thera was floating quite still, on her back, her head held above the water only by her blue life jacket. "You'd better help her quickly, son, or she'll be a goner!"

"Take my paddle," Chase commanded. He shoved the paddle into Ogilvey's hands. "And my hat." He took the green park service ball cap off his head and plopped it atop Ogilvey's field hat, making a funny-looking totem pole of him. Then he kicked off his sandals and slipped over the side of the kayak and into the water. A few powerful strokes took him to Thera. She was motionless. Her eyes were closed. He reached an arm over her chest and under her arm, and pulled her limp form to him. Then he started a strong lifeguard sidestroke toward shore, dragging her along like a limp rag doll.

As Ogilvey followed in the kayak, making slow progress with uncoordinated paddle strokes, Chase neared shore twenty feet beyond where Kit had gotten Bobby sitting up in the shallows and was helping him get his broken helmet unstrapped. When he felt beach sand under him, he stood and lifted Thera in his arms. She seemed unconscious as he waded ashore with her. But when he leaned to put her on the ground, she suddenly wrapped her arms around his neck and held him tightly, refusing to be set down. She drew his mouth toward her open, willing lips.

"Oh, you big beautiful man, you!" she sighed, her breath hot and moist on his mouth. "Kiss me! Kiss me," she begged, "or I'll... die!"

"All right, Blondie," Kit said coldly from behind Chase. "You can let go of him now." She had approached while they were locked together. Dr. O and bloody-browed, contrite Bobby Everett followed her.

Thera was suddenly revived and cool herself. "Oh," she replied, looking haughtily at Kit. "Is he spoken for?"

Kit stopped in her tracks. "Well, um, no. Not exactly." She

looked embarrassed and angry at the same time.

Thera seemed completely recovered from her swoon—if there ever had been one. "Rumor has it, somebody's proposal of undying love got rejected." She glanced at Chase with a smile. "Right, Mr. Tall, Dark, and Handsome?" She had kept her arms knit around Chase's neck.

Wearing a stern expression, he pulled her arms loose and walked away without a word. Smiling gleefully, Thera called after him, "So strong. And so fine-looking in wet ranger shorts!"

Kit growled at Thera. "I hope your pictures got ruined!"

Thera smiled and patted the camera still slung over her shoulder on its strap. "Waterproof camera. And the jet ski will go on my National Photographic expense account."

Kit put her hands on her hips. "I think you'd better leave."

"Who's gonna make me, Cowgirl?"

Kit knocked her cowboy hat back on her head and doubled a fist.

"Ea-easy now, Kit," Bobby said, stepping between the two.

Thera stepped back a pace, but quickly recovered. "No problem, Honey. You hang around here and watch the boring stuff. I've got enough action shots in this camera to do a dozen magazine articles. I think I even got one of Bobby getting tail-whipped. Thrills, spills, and excitement, that's my business. The job of babysitting these big dumb beasts is all yours, Honey. Oh! Here comes my ride."

A Humvee had driven down from camp to check on them. "Are you guys all right?" Crom called from the open window.

"I am," Thera replied. "But we'd better get this side of beef back to civilization and have his head looked at."

Bobby touched the welt on his forehead and winced.

"Sure," Crom said. "Hop in."

Back in camp, Kit watched the Humvee vanish around a bend in the road up Tekison Creek canyon.

"Oooh!" she fumed. "That woman really bugs me. What a... a harlot!"

Chase chuckled. "She's just following a story."

"Convenient, how it landed her in your arms again."

Chase put his hat back on. It was the only dry part of him. "I wonder how she heard... about you and me?"

"You mean our, um, relationship problems?"

"Yeah."

"It's not the kind of thing I would mention to anybody, except... Maddy Meyer! What a gossip!"

CHAPTER 5

The next morning, all the nests had hatchlings in them. Kit surveyed the scene with binoculars. "Are my eyes playing tricks," she asked, "or are they bigger today than they were yesterday?"

"Heeh!" Ogilvey laughed. "What would you expect from infants that eat half their own weight per day?"

"Then they really are bigger? My gosh!"

"As Gar tells me, they grow prodigiously at this stage of life. And the parents are kept busy, constantly feeding them what they need."

Kit kept a tight watch on a male returning from the hills. He approached his female, who stood and greeted him with song. The two twined necks and sang their *wrrll-wrrll* duet. Then the male rocked forward and back several times and barfed up another fire-hose-worth of green glop inside the nest. Immediately, the mass was surrounded by two dozen babies, all gabbling like geese, pecking mouthfuls of the mess, and lifting their heads high to gobble it down.

The male bridged the nest and began his slow process of lying down. Those babies that were romping outside the nest scurried to get under his lowering belly as he worked his way gingerly down onto the nest. One baby, left outside, began to squeal in a loud, shrill voice. The male nonchalantly leaned slightly to one side, lifted an elbow, and allowed the babe to slip in behind his armpit and vanish under him with its nestmates.

THOMAS P. HOPP

"Aw," Kit cried. "How cute is that?"

"The babies will keep gorging themselves, even while underneath their father's protective lid," Ogilvey said. "The vomited food is under there with them."

"Disgusting!" Kit said.

"Yes, yes," Ogilvey readily agreed. "But it is an ingenious system, and a very efficient one. The babies are warm, overfed, and have nothing to do all day but eat and grow!"

The adult female wasted no time hanging around. With her mate on the nest, she walked away, leaving him in charge.

"Sauropods are quite fastidious creatures," Ogilvey remarked. "After several weeks of watching them, I know just what she'll do next. First, a bath in the river, where she and her female cohorts will gather and socialize by trumpeting together. Then off to the surrounding countryside to forage among the trees. It seems ponderosa pine is a favorite. They can't seem to get enough of those big needles and twigs."

"Pine needles?" Kit asked. "That doesn't sound too appetizing."

"Apparently sauropod taste buds are quite different from ours."

"I guess so."

Ogilvey took a lecturing tone. "What we see here is the pattern of life in a sauropod rookery. While one adult sits on the nest, the other forages huge amounts of pine, cottonwood, and other tree foliage. Then the forager returns and the nest-sitter is relieved of duty and goes off on a foraging trip. The cycle repeats for weeks, until the babies are big enough to forage for themselves and join the herd for the return leg of the annual migration. By winter, they'll be nearly a quarter of adult size, and the entire herd will be out at the coast again."

"Won't they decimate the trees along the migration route?" Kit asked.

"A realistic concern," Ogilvey agreed. "But not necessarily true. For one thing, the return migration should take a more northerly course, which, according to Gar, will avoid their grazing the same forests on the way back to the coast. And furthermore, the Kra have planned ahead. Have you noticed what's going on a little ways upriver?"

Kit focused her binoculars where Dr. O indicated. About a mile away, three large, four-legged lunkoo walking machines stood in a group. Wide, flatbed truck-like spaces to the rear of their cabs bristled with tall trees, the huge root balls of which were wrapped in burlap-like cloth.

"The U. S. Congress finally voted to allow the Kra off their reservations, for essential purposes—and this is one of those trips. They've become horticulturists!"

"They're going to plant those trees?"

"Indeed. Those tall transplants are Cretaceous yanakaigo fruit trees, brought from the moon on Kra landing ships. It was always the Kras' intention to transport these trees inland and plant them in the stream bottoms of the Colockum area, and all along the shores of West Bar. Once established, they can produce tons of fruit per tree. They are ginkgo relatives that bear a sweet, oily fruit that tastes very good to humans, too. Like huge avocados, larger than a football, and possessed of a stupendously huge pit."

Kit shook her head in amazement. "Dr. O, it's impressive how much you already know about alamosaurs."

"Oh, it's really no great feat, my dear. Gar has been explaining it all to me in detail. And I have simply taken good notes for my planned monograph on the life history of the alamosaurs. Want to hear some more details?"

"Something tells me I'll hear them, whether I want to or not."

Ignoring the remark, Ogilvey raised a pedagogical finger in the air. "The secret to the incredible gigantism of the dinosaurs is two-fold. First, as I have explained, their digestive tracts are about ten times more efficient than those of cows, horses, or other large mammals. That's the result of their having optimized herbivory for not just sixty-five million years as mammals have, but for fifty million years in the Triassic Era, and then for an additional one-hundred-thirty-five million years in the Jurassic and Cretaceous Eras. Time favored dinosaurs much more than mammals. Mammalian digestion is nowhere near as highly evolved as dinosaur digestion.

"And, as if digestive efficiency were not enough, the Mesozoic plants cooperated. Fruits evolved bigger and bigger forms, supporting more dinosaurs, and larger ones. On the sauropod migration route, there once were four trees that fed them fruit, which the Kra are now replanting. The leaves, twigs, and needles of modern trees are poor fare, but sufficient for small numbers of hatchlings. On the other hand, adults eating summer yanakaigo fruit can produce more eggs and raise more babies. On the fall migration routes, the deekaigo tree produces copious bunches of fig-like fruits, sprouting out of their trunks from top to bottom and hanging in pendant stems like outsized bunches of purple grapes. The adults eat these on high by swallowing whole bunches of the uppermost fruits. Meanwhile, the young pluck fruits one-at-a-time from the lower portions of the trunk.

"In the overwintering valleys of the Olympic Coast, the tutukaigo trees now being planted by the Kra, will produce a copious crop of apple-like fruits, which are plump in the fall, but do not drop from the branches. Instead, they shrivel with the winter cold but retain their nutritious load of sugars, just as raisins do. They are a mainstay of the sauropod winter diet, supplemented by browsing the evergreen needles of firs, pines, and hemlocks, and several varieties of evergreen trees the Kra have brought back after sixty-five million years of absence. The forests of the Olympic National Park will soon have double the diversity of plant life, once the Kra re-establish their native trees alongside ours.

"The nonakaigo tree produces mango-like fruit, which it holds unripe over winter but which ripen quickly as the spring sap begins to flow. They are more than a foot long with huge pits. It is wise to avoid the rear portion of a large sauropod eating these, because the pits are tapered at both ends, and the points can penetrate the flesh of an unwary onlooker."

"Well," Kit said. "With all they've got to eat, I can see why they got to be so huge. And I suppose the predators got larger to match the herbivores."

"Exactly," Ogilvey said. "In fact, the gigantism of the carnivores is simply the result of having so much meat available. No matter how huge or hungry the predators got, there was always more flesh on the hoof than could be eaten—despite the fact that the predators of the Cretaceous were highly active, voracious, and constant eaters of the herbivores around them, just like modern-day lions and wolves."

Ogilvey raised his rhetorical finger higher and was about to continue his lecture, when a shout interrupted him.

"Hey!" Chase called from the far side of camp. "Look over there!"

They hurried to where Chase stood looking to the sagebrush flats on the inland side of the nesting ground. The sagebrush bushes shook where several animals were moving swiftly among them.

"What's there?" Kit asked as she raised her binoculars.

"Coyotes," Chase said, holding his own binoculars to his eyes. "And they're chasing…"

"A baby alamosaur!" Kit cried. The little one burst from the edge of the sagebrush and charged, bleating, toward the nesting ground. An instant later, three coyotes emerged from the sagebrush in hot pursuit. "Oh, no!" she cried. "He'll be killed!"

The baby, however, was not an easy target. It sprinted with astonishing speed, galloping over the ground with the nimbleness of a small dog. "He's as fast as Zippy ever thought of being," Kit said. "Go, Little Guy!"

The coyotes, however, were not to be denied. One caught up to the terrified youngster and nipped at a heel. It went down, tumbling on the ground and setting up a frantic, cackling cry for help. All three coyotes pounced on it, but somehow it managed to come up from among them and streak away with an astonishing burst of speed, running on its two hind legs with its tail out straight behind and its forepaws at its sides. Then it went down on all fours and continued its desperate gallop. The coyotes were instantly on its tail again, and closing the distance fast. The outcome seemed assured until—

Whuuutchaaah! The tail of one of the subadult alamosaurs snapped, catching the leading coyote across its flank and sending it tumbling head-over-heels. As the baby alamosaur made good its escape, the stricken coyote turned 180 degrees and raced off with its tail between its legs, crying, "Ai-yai-yai! Ai-yai-yai!" like a hurt puppy.

"Aw," Kit said. "Poor coyote! I hope there aren't any broken bones."

Chase chuckled. "It gives new meaning to the phrase, 'You're gonna get a tail-whipping!'"

The other coyotes followed their companion into the brush and the incident was over as quickly as it had begun. The baby trotted in under the belly of its rescuer and turned to watch the coyotes disappear.

"That little alamosaur is a bit older and wiser," Ogilvey said. "It has learned about safety in numbers."

"And size," Kit said.

"And tail-whacking," Chase said.

"Speaking of which," Dr. O said, "now we see why alamosaur tails are ringed with black-and-white stripes like an iguana's tail. It's a warning signal to would-be predators, letting them know they are facing a dangerous weapon. Those coyotes won't soon forget!"

As evening neared, Ogilvey cooked dinner for all except Gar, whose preference for raw meat was well known.

"I'll be taking my leave, now," Suarez said after the meal, standing by an idling Humvee. "It looks like things have worked out around here just fine. I'm sure there's another crisis waiting for me somewhere. A general's work is never done."

"It was good to see you again," Chase said, shaking Suarez' hand.

"Likewise," called Ogilvey, who was cleaning a skillet with

sand and water.

"G'bye General," Kit added.

***

Late that evening, the group sat around the embers of the campfire. A full moon cast shimmering light on the calm Columbia River. Crickets chirped, but their small songs were overridden by unearthly music not heard in sixty-five million years—a sauropod serenade. The females, taking their turns on the nests, set up a droning chorus of didgeridoo-like tones rumbling up from deep within their chests, somewhat like colossal cats purring to the babes beneath them. Meanwhile, the males stood near their mates, singing long, bassoon-like notes, almost like they were chanting the mystical word, "O-o-o-m."

"They sometimes sing to their babies like that until the little ones settle down," Ogilvey said. "It's a dinosaurian lullaby!"

"It's beautiful," Kit said.

"And look over there!" The professor pointed out a gathering of subadults between the nesting ground and the river's edge, dimly outlined by moon glow. "Sauropods tend to sleep on their feet, especially the larger ones, much like our elephants and horses. See how some have paired up? See how they stand shoulder-to-shoulder facing opposite directions, and then lay their necks and heads across each other's midlines? Cozy, wouldn't you agree? And not unlike horses putting their heads across each other's backs to doze. When the babies are larger, they'll interdigitate themselves within the groups of subadults and adults, nestling against their flanks for warmth and safety."

Kit shivered and wrapped her arms around herself.

"C'm'ere," Chase said to her. Sitting against a large rock, he raised an inviting arm. "Nestle against my flank."

"For warmth and safety," she said, scooting near him and letting him put his arm around her shoulders.

Ogilvey rose. "I'll, er, just go and see what Gar's been up to."

He walked a short distance to where Gar sat in the lit cockpit of his fighter-walker, tinkering with instruments. They struck up a quiet conversation.

Chase gave Kit's shoulders a squeeze as they listened to the sauropods sing. She nestled closer. He turned to her and they shared a tender kiss.

"I've been thinking," he said after a moment.

"Oh-oh," Kit said. "About... that question?"

"Yeah. As I recall, it was a proposal of marriage."

"Yes, it was, as I recall."

"And as I recall, I got down on one knee on your father's front porch with you on the swing, after you laughed off my first try in my quahka while we were watching the wolves."

"I didn't take you seriously the first time."

"Yeah. I know. That's why I got this emerald ring—so you would take me seriously." He took the black velvet ring case out of a pocket, opened it, and held the platinum band in front of her nose, where she could get a good look at the large dazzling emerald in the firelight.

"You were so handsome and gallant, on bended knee."

He whispered in her ear, just audibly, "And then I asked you, Kit Daniels, will you be my wife?"

She reached out and gently closed the box lid. "And I told you I had to think about it."

After a pause, he asked, "So, have you thought about it?"

"I have."

"And the answer is?"

"Maybe."

He laughed, and not in a comfortable way. "Can you be a little more specific?

"I really can't."

He sighed with perplexity. And then he grumbled, "Maybe I should withdraw the offer, then."

She made a small gasp, and then was silent.

"I've got to get on with my life," he explained.

Again, she was silent.

"Please, Kit. Tell me yes or no," he persisted.

"Okay then," she said after a moment more of hesitation, "if you must have an answer right now, then the answer is... no."

There was an almost deafening silence. Even the sauropods had ceased their song. After a long pause, Chase murmured, "Oh."

"It's not 'no' forever," Kit said. "It's 'no' for now. I'm not ready."

"Why not?"

"I'm too young."

"Too young for...?"

"For marriage. Starting a home. Kids. All that. There's so much I still want to explore."

"We could get killed," Chase resisted. "Don't you want to leave a child—or two?"

"Is that your motivation for wanting to get married?"

"Partly. We live in dangerous times."

"Well, if that's it, I don't want to leave any motherless children. Remember, I was one."

"That's not my only reason. *I love you, Kit.*"

"I love you too, Chase. But these things take time."

He thought awhile. "Maybe we could just live together in my new place at Arran Kra. It's almost half-built."

Kit sighed. "I think not."

"It's not like we would be getting married."

She shook her head. "I'm not ready to live together or get married. Sharing a home is a big responsibility. Just look at all the trouble alamosaurs go through."

After another long silence, Chase said, "So, are you going to see other guys?"

"I don't know. Maybe."

Chase withdrew his arm from around her, stood up, and walked away.

"Chase?" Kit called after him with a note of deep concern.

He didn't reply. He walked to the quahka where Ogilvey and Gar were chatting, put an elbow on the cowling, and stared back at her with anger simmering in his eyes.

"Chase, my boy!" Ogilvey exclaimed. "Gar says we can leave in a day or two. Our presence is no longer required. The alamosaurs aren't a threat to anyone, and they instinctually know their way back to the coast."

When Chase made no reply, Ogilvey glanced at his glum expression and followed his eyes to where Kit sat by the embers. She wore a similarly gloomy face.

"Oh," the professor said.

Chase sighed. "Why is Kit so hard to talk to?"

Ogilvey thought for a long moment. "Son," he said, "of all the creatures on this planet, the opposite sex is probably the most difficult to comprehend."

"How can that be?" Chase asked, still staring in Kit's direction. "We're the same species! We're made of the same arms and legs and brains."

"True. But consider this. We humans diverged from apes about five million years ago, and therefore much of their behavior seems familiar to us. But go father afield in the animal kingdom, to zebras, let's say, and then it becomes difficult to really know how they feel about herding, grazing, going to water holes, or escaping predators. It is just not a human experience."

"But how can a woman be harder to understand than a zebra? I'm not seeing your point."

"You see, son, despite time and evolution, you retain much in common with a zebra stallion. You want to be strong, protective, and dominating. On the other hand, a zebra mare expresses maternal instincts, nurturing and caring for others of her kind. She tends to be mild while you, the male, tend to be more aggressive."

"Sure Doc. I all know that."

"Yes, but you see, that male-female divide is more ancient and fundamental than the species gap between humans and zebras. Although zebras have been a separate genetic lineage from ours for sixty million years, males and females separated more than *half a billion* years ago. The dawn of gender occurred among wormlike creatures on the bottom of the primordial ocean. That's nearly ten times longer than the separation of zebras from humans. And that means males and females of any species carry traits ten times older than the differences between humans and zebras. Hence, a male zebra has more in common with you, Chase, than you do with Kit, at least where gender is concerned."

"Okay, Doc. I get it. I guess there will never be a time when males and females completely understand each other."

"Perhaps so. Perhaps not. But consider this. Isn't it a more interesting world for the mysteries that remain unsolved? Isn't the complex dance between males and females a central theme of human life? Would you really want it all explained? Where's the fun in that?"

Chase looked again at Kit, sitting just out of earshot with her pretty face outlined in the orange glow of the fire. He sighed. "I guess you're right, Doc."

The rumbling didgeridoo drone of the alamosaurs vibrated the night air once more. Ogilvey chuckled at the sound. "Would you rather be an alamosaurus?" he asked. "They are creatures of such powerfully ingrained instincts that gender matters are predetermined. They simply take the other gender's behavior as a given and waste no thoughts whatsoever analyzing or worrying over it."

Chase shrugged. "Kit is a pleasant pain sometimes, I guess."

"That's the spirit." Ogilvey patted Chase on the shoulder. "Don't give up the struggle to understand her, boy. It's one of the greatest tasks nature has set for us."

The professor and Gar resumed their chat in Kranaga, discussing a map of the state of Washington on the quahka's console with the return migration route shown on it. Chase went back to the fire and sat down next to Kit.

Nothing was said for a time. Then Kit asked, "Do you think I'm as pretty as Thera McArty?"

Surprised at the turn in the conversation, Chase thought a

moment and then murmured, "She's a made-up, self-centered hussy."

"You didn't answer my question."

"You're a natural beauty, Kit. You're ten times as good-looking as her."

"Well!" Kit let a grin spread across her face. "I guess I got my answer."

"It's the truth."

"Keep talking that way, Chase. I like it."

She wrapped her arms around his chest, and he put his arm around her shoulders again. He hugged her tightly, and they shared another tender kiss as the alamosaurs crooned their moonlight serenade.

PART TWO

RIDING
QUETZALCOATLUS

Maddy ran bravely, but she wore a look of desperation.

THOMAS P. HOPP

CHAPTER 6

Within a week, the adventurers had returned to Arran Kra and Twin Creeks Ranch. The late summer heat was high and crackling with energy, but it was not the sort of muggy, humid heat that people back east or down south might feel. It was almost pleasantly hot, if that were possible.

One fine, sunny morning, Chase pulled up in front of the ranch house in a new car. Kit came onto the porch when she heard him beep the horn. Her mouth dropped open in amazement when she saw the vehicle he had arrived in.

"How do you like my new Corvette?" he asked her as he got out of the sleek, shiny, gunmetal-silver machine. "It's a Z zero-six supercar convertible. The Kra just delivered it to me up at my house. This is the first place I've driven it to."

"How much did this cost?" Kit asked, her eyes wide with amazement and interest at the ultra-dynamic shape of the machine, which in some ways was the automotive equivalent of a streamlined quahka fighter-walker.

"It would have cost a hundred grand, anyway."

She gasped.

"But it's a gift from the workers and management of Chevrolet. They said it was a thank-you for saving the world."

"You'll destroy a car like that on the roads around here. It's so low-slung, it's almost touching the ground. You'll high-center it every ten feet on that bumpy old road to Arran Kra."

"Not necessarily."

"And, by the way, how did you get it down here without demolishing it?"

"That's just it. I took it down the new road from Arran Kra. It's as smooth as silk."

"What new road?"

"Come on. I'll show you."

She got in on the passenger side, sinking into the luxurious suede leather bucket seat, and glanced around at the impeccable interior as Chase drove out under the newly restored ranch gate with the car's powerful engine rumbling low. When he turned left at the county road, she said, "Aren't you going the wrong way? The road dead ends around the next bend."

"It doesn't anymore."

Chase floored the accelerator, snapping their heads back. He quickly reached the place where, just days before, the old county highway had ended with an orange-and-white caution barrier. Now the Vette breezed past the spot and onto a new, smooth, wide road that curved gracefully up the slope of a foothill. Where only four-wheelers dared drive before, there was now a sleek asphalt road leading into the high mountain country. Chase negotiated the smooth curves at 120 miles per hour, racing up the long sweep of a valley and around an entire mountain, until the Vette came out onto familiar high country —the plains of Arran Kra.

He let the machine roll to a stop with its engine rumbling.

"Wait a minute," Kit said. "I'm confused. Where are we, exactly?"

"Look to your left," Chase said. "That's where your old switchback road comes out at its top. We won't need to use that rutted, rocky, winding old thing anymore. Not unless we're looking for stray livestock or riding horses for pleasure. This new road was a human-Kra collaboration. Kra engineers cut the roadway with rock-blasting quahkas, and then our county highway department brought in paving machinery. By a team effort, they got the whole project done in a couple of days."

"Amazing," Kit murmured. "It used to take twenty minutes bumping uphill in a Jeep to get up the old road. Now you just got us here in, what? Three minutes?"

"More like two. Notice anything else different around here?"

Kit glanced around. "There used to be a crashed Kra lander here. Now there are just some scrapes in the prairie."

"The Kra salvaged it for scrap metal. Used it to make the beams for building my house and Dr. O's museum. Speaking of which—" Chase put the car in gear and raced ahead. In moments they had pulled in at a parking area in front of an imposing structure. "David Ogilvey's Arran Kra Natural History Museum," Chase said.

"It's huge!" Kit exclaimed.

"About two city blocks long," Chase concurred. "Finished with fine stonework of travertine and limestone. As good looking as anything the east coast has to offer."

As they got out, the professor came down the stone steps of the colonnaded front entry and greeted them with a nod of his head and a tip of his canvas field hat.

"Construction complete, as of this morning," he said, wearing a grin. "Now if I only had some specimens to house in it."

"I know of a T rex skeleton that's only about half crated up for shipment to Washington DC," Kit said. "We could always deliver it here."

"As much as I wish that were possible," the professor said, "the president and congress are looking forward to your arrival at the Smithsonian Institution's museum with that cargo. We'll have to look elsewhere for our specimens. Meanwhile, Gar and I have begun to put together a Kra culture and technology display that I am sure will draw admiring crowds of Kra and humans alike."

Inside, Ogilvey showed them a bare, echoing interior. On one side, a huge television screen took up a two-story wall. Playing on it without sound was The Watcher's film footage of the asteroid fragments of Kela the Destroyer, ending the ancient Kra civilization. As they paused to watch, the space scene vanished into a static pattern and then reformed into a view of General Davis at his desk.

"The screen doubles as the world's largest cell phone," Ogilvey explained gleefully.

"Ah, Doctor!" the general said in greeting. "I'm glad I finally caught up with you. I have a long-neglected item on my to-do list."

"Yes, good sir. What is it?"

"I want to remind you and your Kra friends to be careful as you clean up around Arran Kra."

"Be careful? Of what?"

"The plutonium nuclear warhead we lost when the stealth bomber was shot down."

"No problem," Ogilvey replied. "Our Kra friends found the plutonium several weeks ago."

"I which case, I'd like to offer storage in one of our nuclear waste sites."

"No need, General. The Kra engineers have already neutralized it."

"Neutralized it? What does that mean?"

Ogilvey shrugged. "Gar has tried to explain the process to me several times, but unsuccessfully, I must admit. It has something to do with kekuah. But beyond that, it overtaxes my humble powers of translation, or Gar's modest knowledge of English to explain. Apparently, exposing plutonium to kekuah rays is quite a simple process, at least to the Kra. They have long since neutralized the plutonium's radioactivity and converted it to a stable, non-toxic, sand-like material."

Davis said, "I sure wish I knew how they do that. There's plenty of dangerous plutonium we would be glad to neutralize around the world."

"I am sure the Kra will be happy to share their methods," the professor said. "Then nuclear waste cleanup will be quick, efficient, and complete."

After Davis signed off, the giant screen went back to its apocalyptical images. Kit and Chase briefly walked the echoing empty halls with Ogilvey, who expounded about all the displays of dinosaurian life and behavior he intended to build into them. Eventually, they excused themselves and went out to the Corvette, which Chase allowed Kit to drive to his now almost finished home.

When Kit had pulled the rumbling silver car into Chase's four-car garage between his new SUV and his quahka, both of which were one shade or another of silver, they got out and went in for a tour of the recently constructed house.

"Everything is so new!" Kit exclaimed. "And so posh!" She admired the gleaming woodwork of floors, cabinetry, staircase handrails, and fine wainscoting on the walls of the hunting-lodge style house, built on a grand scale and sparing no detail. A huge river-rock fireplace greeted her in the great room, and the dining room, parlor, and media room were appointed with the finest in furniture, fixtures, and entertainment equipment. When they entered the huge, U-shaped kitchen, Kit gasped at the fineness and gleaming perfection of the stove, oven, grill, range, and appliances, which were all of the best quality Kra money could buy from human suppliers around the world.

"Gar and Gana personally oversaw fitting this place out," Chase said. "Nothing but the best for the victor of the battle of Arran Kra."

Suddenly Kit stopped in the middle of the gleaming kitchen and put her knuckles on her hips. She glanced around again at all the opulent furnishings. And then she turned to Chase. She looked disconsolate.

"What?" he asked.

"They wanted to build something like this for my father and me," she said. "But Daddy said he wanted to live like he always has. So they said they would build me my own separate new home."

"And…?"

"And I said no."

"Why?"

"I realized I didn't want to live alone in a big empty house. Even if it was all fancy and new… like this."

She continued turning this way and that, looking over the opulent, brightly sunlit kitchen with a mildly distressed look on her face.

"You're welcome here anytime, day or night," Chase offered.

"Day or evening," Kit said. "Show me around the rest of the place."

Down a corridor from the kitchen was a wing that housed indoor exercise equipment, a sauna, steam room and beyond that a large space with a swimming pool under a retractable roof for indoor or outdoor swimming according to the season.

Kit clucked her tongue and shook her head. "Show me some more," she said.

Chase led her up a large staircase from the great room to the master suite, where she was greeted by a huge four-poster bed, a vast walk-in closet, and an opulent bath. Chase led on through a door into an adjacent suite that could serve as— "A baby room?" Kit asked, looking over a crib, bassinet, and other clearly suggestive furnishings. "Is that what this is?"

"I—" Chase began abashedly. "I didn't tell them to build it this way. Gana just naturally assumed—"

"And you didn't disagree?"

"Well, no, I didn't."

She turned and looked up into his face with a hardened expression. "So, you really are serious about getting married and having kids right away."

"I only know I don't want to wait forever to call you my wife. Is that so bad?"

She was tight lipped.

After a moment, Chase took a conciliatory but firm tone. "Why can't you see what the Kra can see quite well? We are a couple." He looked at her beseechingly. She could see the hope in his expression, and that made her scowl.

"I want to finish school first."

"You can finish while we live here together. I'll let you drive the Vette to class."

"I want more than a fancy car. I want to experience life!"

"There's plenty to experience right around here. Or haven't you noticed? I don't see why we can't—"

"But I do!" she retorted, her face reddening.

"What is it Kit? Why not?"

"I'm just not ready. I want... to have some freedom, first."

Chase looked genuinely confused for a moment. And then his expression hardened. "I think you need to grow up, Kit!"

"I don't want to grow up. At least not yet."

"Well, if you play Peter Pan long enough, maybe one or both of us will get killed in the meantime. Haven't you noticed how dangerous it is out there?" He pointed out a window where a herd of pachyrhinosaurs could be seen grazing on the prairie.

There was a knock on the jamb of the door by which they had entered the nursery. They turned, startled, and saw a man standing in the doorway. He was a stranger, a portly fellow with a bald head and a close-cropped white beard. He was dressed in a summer weight blue suit. He pointed a thumb at his stout chest.

"Jeffrey Miller," he said. "I'm looking for Chase Armstrong."

"You've found him," Chase said.

Miller extended at thick-fingered hand and they shook. "U.S. Government business," he explained. And then he looked at Kit significantly. "Top secret, I'm afraid."

"I was just leaving," Kit answered Miller's statement while looking at Chase coolly. She turned on the heel of a cowboy boot and headed for the door.

"Take the Vette," Chase called after her.

She turned to reply, but the keys Chase had tossed were already in midair. She caught them and, smiling despite trying not to, went out the door.

CHAPTER 7

The convoy of Kra transport walkers moved through the Montana high country in single file. The silvery transports, ponderous bus-sized four-legged machines best suited to carry-ing cargo or groups of travelers, contrasted with a pair of speedy two-legged quahka fighter-walkers accompanying them as protection. The quahkas' tight interior spaces limited them to solo piloting with at most one tandem-riding passenger while the slower but more capacious transports, or 'lunkoos' as they were called in Kranaga, could carry much larger crews and greater larders of equipment and supplies. Hence, lunkoos had been specified for the expedition. Half a day's walk out of the city of Arran Kra, the line of machines moved onto a parched intermountain flatland between the alpine heights of the Absaroka Range just north of Yellowstone Park. Great billows of white clouds towered high into the blue summer skies above the rocky summits.

The objective of the expedition, a quetzalcoatlus rookery, lay in the flats, covering an area as wide as half a dozen football fields. It was a stretch of barren ground where the high moun-tain snowpack had only just melted away at midsummer and the seasonal heat was now in full sway. Although the dusty ground was all but featureless, the rookery itself was an eye-jarring place to anyone who had never seen the animals in their brooding territory.

The adult animals were dramatic to behold. Several score of the colossal Cretaceous beasts had gathered in the rookery. Stupendous, four-legged pterodactyls—the largest of them bigger than full grown giraffes and shaped much like them—stood on four stilt-like legs with towering necks surmounting their bodies. Their legs were longer in front and shorter in back, again reminiscent of giraffes, but their front legs contrasted sharply from giraffes by bearing large, folded, leathery wings typical of the pterosaurian lineage. The heads atop the giraffe-like necks were not at all giraffe-like, either. Instead, they looked like stork's heads with extremely long and straight beaks, offset for balance by backward jutting crests covered in coarse, bristling black quills.

The lunkoos moved to a small hillock overlooking the rookery at about fifty yards' distance, and settled their ponderous bodies down on the haunches of their jointed metallic legs. The Kra drivers exited the front cabins of their machines by raising a canopy glass cover, while Kra and human passengers debarked out the side doors of the center sections.

Stepping down onto the dusty ground, Kit Daniels pulled the brim of her cowboy hat down to shield her eyes from the glare of the sun. She observed the rookery carefully. The quetzalcoatli seemed to loom from the landscape like a forest of tall trees. "They're so huge!" she exclaimed. "And there are so many of them!"

"Oh, not really so many," Dr. Ogilvey replied as he gazed through his thick spectacles at the impressive gathering of big pterodactyls. "In the Cretaceous, so I have been told, their rookeries could go on for miles, just as modern flamingoes can carpet an entire lakeshore with their nests, or nesting gannets can cover an entire small island. And, speaking of nests, I'm impressed with the scope of their prodigious construction activities."

Beneath each adult quetzalcoatlus, which stood with its four feet widely spread, was an area shaded by the wing membranes that stretched between fore and hind limbs like an open-sided tent canopy. Within each shaded area was a collection of small boulders that had been gathered and arranged into a circle by the adult to protect—

"Look at the babies!" exclaimed Maddy Meyer, Kit's friend,

who alighted from the lunkoo dressed impertinently for the day's activities in a black leather miniskirt, black tights, and a form-fitting black T shirt with a hot pink Zombie Princess logo. Her only remotely appropriate item of clothing was her pair of black patent leather waffle-soled combat boots.

"If you can call them babies," Ogilvey chuckled, his gray-bearded cheeks dimpling with a jovial grin. "They've already grown to human height on a diet of carrion meat and small animals that the adults gather in those great stork-like bills and bring back to the rookery." He adjusted his thick glasses and pulled the brim of his khaki canvas field hat down to get a better look through the heat shimmer. "Judging from the ratio of one adult to one chick, I'd say the dads are already away on the morning hunt, leaving the moms to stand guard."

"What's the difference between moms and dads?" Maddy asked.

Ogilvey chuckled, "Ah, my dear, I forget sometimes that you are a relative newcomer to the dinosaur-filled wilds of Yellowstone Country, having been at college in Bozeman when the invasion fleet arrived from the moon. Kit, on the other hand, was here from the first day of the invasion some weeks ago. She knows all the differences between the males and females, don't you my dear?"

Kit paused before answering. Dressed more appropriately than Maddy for a hot and dusty Montana afternoon in blue jeans and a western shirt, she dug a cowboy-boot tip into the dust. "Is this a test, professor? How about size?"

"Yes." Ogilvey smiled. "The males are a bit bigger. And I suspect we'll all see the other differences soon, when they come home with crops filled with meat for the babies. And, speaking of babies," he went on, "it looks like Gar was right. It's high time we capture some of those yearlings before they get too big to handle." He pointed off to one side of the rookery where a dozen intermediate sized animals milled in an odd, aimless way. "The yearlings are rather lost at this time of year, having just been dispossessed by their parents in favor of their recently hatched siblings. They'll soon be driven by hunger to fly off and find their own food. Before they disperse, its an opportune time for the Kra to acquire some new mounts."

"They look too big to handle already," Maddy said. "We're not in danger here, are we?"

"I understand your unease at the proximity of these notoriously foul-tempered creatures," Dr. O said. "But our Kra guides have assured me they can control, or at least divert the beasts."

"If you say so, Professor."

"Now, just look at the color variations," Ogilvey went on, assuming her concern had been appeased. "The babies are covered in heavy brownish-gray fuzz, not all that differently from many types of baby birds. The adults, on the other hand, are exquisitely colored, much like marabou storks, a mixed black and white coat on the back and wings, naked pink neck and a red- black- and blue-splotched head with a tan beak. The yearlings are of an intermediate coloration. And look how they all possess some rather striking dark scales on the feet and, er, hands, or forelimbs, or, well, whatever you call the front paws of pterosaurs. Wing-paws, I suppose."

"Tetoonahn," said Tekkana, the Kra in charge of the expedition, who had just come down from the lunkoo to join them.

"Oh, yes," Ogilvey replied. "The Kra word is probably more appropriate than any English translation, given your sixty-five million year old relationship with the beasts."

"Yes-s-s, O-gil-vey," the Kra scientist responded. Still learning English, Tekkana was a typical Kra—a carnivorous dinosaur seven feet tall at the cassowary-like crest atop her reptilian head and ten feet long from the tip of her fang-filled muzzle to the tip of her long, feather-covered tail. The only thing exceptional about her among the Kra was her rather unique coloration, rarely seen in her typically black-feathered associates. She was feathered much like a spotted owl, with small white dots on the tips of otherwise medium-brown feathers, which gave her a polka-dotted look over most of her body, head, and neck, with the exception of some white featherlets on her face, and the feathers of her forearms, which were fully developed to their foot-and-a-half lengths, rather than plucked out as was normal for Kra soldiers in wartime. Tekkana's forearm feathers were things of exquisite beauty. Normally kept folded tightly to her sides, they unfurled when she pointed or gestured, revealing alternating stripes of brown and white, again reminiscent of the wings of a spotted owl. She spoke English fairly well for a Kra, whose many-fanged jaws often caused them difficulty in pronouncing human words. "Those front feet for walking and flying," Tekkana said. "Back feet can kick you hard."

"You don't say," Ogilvey replied.

Tekkana cocked her head birdishly, and then responded in humorless Kra fashion. "I just did say."

Maddy chucked Kit with an elbow. "I'll bet Chase Armstrong is going to regret missing this," she said.

Kit gave her an odd look, but kept silent.

Instead, Ogilvey responded, "Miss Meyer, I happen to know that Chase and Gar are meeting U.S. officials at Arran Kra today. They would love to be here but couldn't possibly have come. They're functioning on a higher plain than we are, namely the realm of global politics."

"Still," Kit said wistfully, "I'll bet the wildlife biologist in Chase wishes he could see this place."

"Assuredly," Dr. O replied. "Only urgent matters like discussions of war and peace and the treaties between humans and Kra could keep him away, especially when the girl who is the apple of his eye is here."

Kit had been looking uncomfortable. Now she flushed bright pink. "Let's not talk about Chase anymore, okay?"

"Oh, yes, yes," Ogilvey said, looking chastened. "I had momentarily forgotten that your relationship with him has, er, come upon hard times."

"Is that a polite way of saying it's all screwed up?" Maddy needled.

Kit went from pink to red. She looked like tears might come next. "Just shut up, you guys."

A breeze blew up from the rookery and suddenly everyone except Tekkana was forcing back tears—and gagging as well.

"What is that awful smell?" Maddy choked. Her short, dyed-black hair was blown by a dusty whirlwind that wafted a pungent odor somewhere between a sour pickle and a dead animal.

"The aroma of quetzalcoatlus guano," Ogilvey coughed, flustered but not quite so much as Kit or Maddy. "Given the immensity of the makers, the guano accumulates around the rookery in huge quantities very swiftly once the spring rains go and the ground dries up and the temperature soars to near a hundred degrees Fahrenheit, as is the case today."

Maddy gagged. "I think I'm gonna throw up." She grimaced until the little sparkling amethyst stone set on a stud piercing her right nostril was all but lost in the wrinkled skin of her nose.

The breeze shifted away from them. Kit recovered her emotional equilibrium along with her breath. "I still can't imagine anyone flying on one of those things," she said.

"You don't need to imagine it," Dr. O responded. "The dosokotakkan will arrive very soon."

"Doso-what?" Maddy asked.

"The Kra word for the riders of these creatures," Ogilvey said. "It stems from dosokoti, their word for quetzalcoatlus, and takka, which means driver or pilot. Dosokotakkan."

"If you say so." Maddy looked at the animals dubiously. "I can't believe anything that big can fly at all. Never mind having a rider on them."

"You'll be a believer soon enough." Dr. O turned to admire the rookery once more. "Such a delight to see them up close," he effused. "They're every bit as feisty as seabirds in their nesting grounds. See the occasional pecking and wing-flapping squabble between the adults? These tiffs, I'm sure, represent a natural way of spreading out the rookery and assuring that the guano doesn't pile too deeply before the end of summer. Look at it! The ground is white for dozens of yards around the entire rookery. I wonder if that's how far they can, er, shoot it?" As if in answer, one adult lifted its stubby black-tufted tail and let fly a white glob that travelled quite some distance before splattering on the ground.

"I guess that answers your question," Kit said with a wry expression.

"Right at human head level," Ogilvey remarked thoughtfully. "A quetzalcoatlus rookery is a dangerous place in more ways than one."

The squabbles between neighboring quetzies, though minor events by dosokoti standards, nonetheless stirred tall billows of guano-ridden dust into the slowly moving air over the rookery. The dust, the odor, and the echoes of angry heron-like squawks and loudly clacking bills made the entire scene hellish but utterly fascinating.

Dr. Ogilvey assumed the lecturing tone he often took with his student and protégé, Kit. "The Kra invasion ships had room to bring only three tame adult quetzies from Illik moon base. But the flightless Kra take great delight in riding these creatures, so Gar has approved the capture of three new individuals. That will double the number of domesticated animals. Now, the safest way to approach a quetzy rookery is on another quetzy, and the Kra use a tactic much like our elephant mahouts, who ride tame elephants when herding or capturing wild elephants for domestication. Sixty-five million years ago, these great pterosaurs were bred by the Kra to be docile, but only just barely. If left to go as wild as these, they quickly revert to ferocity, especially where their young are concerned. Given that they're giraffe-sized animals with razor sharp, five-foot-long beaks, approaching them can be fatal for anything our size."

"I guess so!" Maddy exclaimed. "They look like they could bite you in half."

"Snip!" Ogilvey quipped, nodding his head in the affirmative. "As if you were cut by a large pair of scissors."

Maddy shook her head in disbelief. "If you guys go down there, I'm staying here."

"Look!" Kit cried, pointing up among the clouds. "Here

come the dosokotakkan!"

Overhead, three huge winged creatures the size of small airplanes descended toward them in lazy, slow-flapping spirals. Nearing the ground, these three quetzies made a long, slow, gliding pass over the rookery. On their backs, riding in leather saddles, were three Kra.

"That looks like Haneek on the lead animal," Ogilvey remarked. "His mate, Teesa, is on the second. And their friend, Kalachi, is on the third. Those saddles are very much like a horseman's saddle, Kit, not really that different from the one you strap on Lucky when you take her out riding. The stirrups fit more snugly, given that they have got to hold the rider in place even when maneuvering through a barrel roll or flying inverted—although that's rarely done and the quetzies don't care for it any more than the riders. Halters and reins work very much as for horses, although steering is accomplished primarily by the rider leaning and using knee pressure to convey directions. One little inconvenience for the quetzy though, comes from the interference of its wing membranes when fastening the saddle to its body. As you can see, the membranes stretch in bat-like fashion from its arms to its hind legs. In order to pass a cinch strap under the animal's belly, it's necessary to perform an operation on them to open small holes in the membranes at both flanks so the strap can pass around the midsection. The operation is minor, the membranes heal well, and the animals are none the worse for it."

While the professor expounded, the quetzy riders completed their aerial survey of the rookery and brought their mounts down for elegant, slow-flapping soft landings not far from the transports. As the quetzies folded their wings and settled onto all fours, the riders dismounted to the rear of their mounts. The contingent from the lunkoos and walkers went to meet them, exchanging the peculiar, head-bobbing greetings of the Kra.

Ogilvey, Kit, and Maddy joined in the greetings, making their own head bobbing helloes to Haneek, Teesa, and Kalachi despite the inadequacy of human anatomy to imitate the grace-ful S-curve of the long Kra neck.

"Ahh," Ogilvey exclaimed after the greetings. "At last, a close look at a quetzalcoatlus. Come Kit, let's inspect one."

"They won't bite, will they?" Kit asked. "My father's horse, Buck, has a bad habit of that."

"That tendency has been trained out of them."

"Or maybe they'll flap us to death?" Maddy asked timor-ously as they came near the beast Haneek had just dismounted.

"I certainly hope not," Ogilvey said. "At least not until I've had a close-up inspection!" The beast eyed him calmly as he moved around it, closely inspecting its fore- and hind-limbs, belly, and flanks as high as his short stature would allow him to gaze. "I finally see the true nature of their beautiful covering of hair. It is quite comparable to the hair giraffes and other Afri-can animals possess despite the hot climate of their homelands. Very fine hair, and beautifully colored, wouldn't you ladies agree? The fur of the underside is a very pale whitish-tan, while on the back it is a blackish-brown with white spots. The wings, in contrast, possess a very pure white, very fine fur on their upper surfaces, no doubt to keep them cool by reflecting sunlight. Notice, though, that the entire wing membrane is pinkish and nearly naked on its undersurfaces, with ample blood capillaries to radiate body heat downward in the shadows to cool the animal."

He went near one folded wing and inspected it closely. "I see there is a distinctly different coloration on the wings' outer-most segments, where they're attached to the long, stout fourth fingers. See how they are colored black on top and white underneath, with the black all but hidden when the ends of the wings are folded back against the upper arm?" He gently grasped and moved the wing tip to inspect it, which the animal tolerated docilely. "Could the two-toned tip be a variable heat absorber?" he wondered aloud. "It shows a heat-reflective white color when folded tightly against the forelimb, but shows a heat-absorbent black surface when extended to catch the sun." The old paleontologist moved the wingtip out and in again several times as he spoke, until the animal tired of his manipulations. It uttered a harsh squawk and flicked its wingtip to brush him off, sending him staggering back several paces.

With his examination of the quetzy disrupted, Ogilvey turned to Haneek, who had stood by watching the odd scientific survey. "Explain for Kit and Maddy how you intend to capture those young animals."

"With this," Haneek replied. He retrieved a coil of rope that was slung over the two-pronged saddle horn on his mount.

"It's a lariat!" Kit exclaimed. She extended a hand for it. "May I?"

Haneek handed the rope to her and she uncoiled the noose end and spun it up, neatly circling it in the air over her head, cowboy style.

"Very good," Haneek said. "I didn't know hoonahs—I mean, humans—could do that."

"Human cowboys," Ogilvey remarked, "and cowgirls like Kit, are very handy with such things. Roping cows is second nature to many Montanans, including Kit."

Kit continued spinning the lariat, circling it on one side of her and then the other and then in front and behind without losing the rhythm of her spin. Watching, Haneek, Teesa, and Kalachi made clucks of pleasure.

"She's quite accomplished," Ogilvey explained. "Twice state champion in horseback riding and roping competitions."

CHAPTER 8

The day's work began when Haneek and his two companions mounted their quetzies and walked them into the rookery on foot with the intention of lassoing three of the yearling pterodactyls.

"Let's follow as close as we dare," Ogilvey said.

"I'm already as close as I dare," Maddy said.

"Oh come on," Kit cajoled. "This morning you told me you were in the mood for a little adventure."

"I've already had enough," Maddy resisted as Kit pulled her along by one hand.

They paused outside the guano-marked perimeter of the nesting ground to watch the riders demonstrate their wrangling skills. Moving into and among the squawking pterosaurs, Teesa and Kalachi maneuvered their tame quetzies between the yearlings and the nesting animals in the main part of the rookery. The mounts seemed to understand what was required of them. They fended off some of the mothers, who rushed, flapping and squawking, to the aid their older offspring. Despite their maternal blustering, they were forced to concede to pecking and flapping counterthrusts from the ridden quetzies. Driven from the security of the rookery, the yearlings moved away as a group, uttering a chorus of nervous squawks and cackling calls to their mothers, who stayed near their nests.

Haneek whirled his lasso and tossed it at one young quetzy, which escaped by ducking its head while bawling a cry that was half lamb bleat and half vulture rasp. This made its mother frantic, and Teesa and Kalachi had all they could handle blocking her charges toward her offspring and Haneek.

"It looks like that mamma's beak could slice Haneek in half with one try," Kit murmured.

"Indeed," Ogilvey affirmed. "The sharp bill is meant to slice meat from bone almost effortlessly. Dosokoti wrangling is a superlatively dangerous task."

As it turned out, none of the three riders were particularly good ropers. Time wore on without success in anything except flustering most of the flock of yearlings and enraging their protective mothers. Finally, with a wobbly but well-placed toss, Haneek managed to get a noose around the long neck of one of the juveniles. He fastened his end of the rope around his double-pronged saddle horn to hold the startled and struggling quarry, while Kalachi intervened on his mount to drive back the enraged mother quetzy. Teesa then drew her lariat and roped the easily targeted stationary yearling. With Kalachi continuing to hold off the mother, Haneek and Teesa backed their mounts out of the rookery area and dragged, as much as guided, the juvenile to the rear of one of the transport walkers. There, other Kra opened a cage that constituted the last third of the vehicle's bus-like body. The quetzy was coaxed inside with much pushing by several armor-clad Kra. The captors were kept busy dodging its formidable beak until the barred cage door was closed, imprisoning the animal at the back end of the lunkoo.

"Let me assure you," Dr. O explained, "this effort would be infinitely more difficult if it weren't late morning, the time when the male quetzies are out foraging. You see, the males of the species are decidedly more nasty-tempered than the females, which are bad enough. On a typical day, the females are alone at the nest in the morning and the males are alone in the afternoon. In the evening or overnight, when both are at the nests, this process would simply be impossible."

The professor glanced at his watch, and then up at the dosokotakkan, who sat on their mounts nearby. "You know, Haneek," he called, "it seems to me that you and your fellow ropers are using up an excessive amount of time. The mothers have spent too much time away from the nests in defense of the yearlings. The new babies have endured quite some time in the hot sun without their mother's wing membranes overhead like parasols to keep them cool. I fear they might overheat and die. Furthermore, the males may return soon, making the remainder of the roundup an exercise in futility, if not fatality."

Haneek nodded. "What should we do, Ogil-vee?" he asked. "We have not so much experience as Kit in using the rope."

"Then I have an excellent solution to your problem," the professor asserted. A grin dimpled his gray-bearded cheeks. "Why don't you let Kit give it a try?"

"Oh, no!" Kit reacted immediately. "I'm not getting on one of those things."

"Come now, my dear," Ogilvey urged her. "I've seen you rope and tie steers in a matter of seconds at the local rodeos. You could have this little job done in no time."

Haneek looked at her expectantly and bobbed his head once to indicate approval.

"Well," Kit said uncertainly, "I suppose."

"Great," Maddy cried. "I'll take some cell phone videos and put them on the Internet. You'll be famous!"

Without more ado, Haneek offered Kalachi's quetzy to Kit. Kalachi, who had shown the least skill in roping, gladly showed her how to mount up by climbing a rope ladder that hung from the quetzy's short-tailed rump. Kit settled into the saddle, nervous about riding much higher on this mount than she normally sat on Lucky. But the saddle's high cantle kept her securely in place atop the slope-backed animal. Haneek briefly explained how to guide the animal with reins and knee pressure. "Do not say 'Eelah' too loudly or it will fly. If it does, say 'Yannah' very loudly and it will land."

"I won't say either one," Kit replied. Then she said, "Here goes nothing!" She snapped the reins and the animal walked forward in a giraffe-like, ambling stride. She felt comfortable in the saddle, despite its having been designed with Kra anatomy in mind. Although the stirrups were intended to be grasped by the three prehensile-clawed toes of a Kra, she found that the pointed toes of her cowboy boots could be jammed in tightly enough to get a secure ride.

She rode across the bare ground to the rookery in the company of Haneek and Teesa on their mounts, and was soon at her task. With the two Kra riding interference, she maneuvered her mount in and through the tightly knotted group of yearlings. Quickly, she found herself facing an isolated juvenile she had cut out from the herd just like a steer. She swung up her lasso and although the yearling ducked and dodged, she tossed accurately and encircled the squawking creature's neck. She quickly wrapped the rope around the double horn of her saddle and tugged the struggling beast to a halt, waiting while Haneek got another rope on it.

"Superb roping," Dr. O called from a distance.

"Yeah," Haneek cried. "Very good tossing!"

"Yahoo!" Kit shouted exultantly. "I hope Maddy got some good shots!" She looked around and spotted Dr. O by the nearest transport with some of the Kra, but couldn't see Maddy there. As she backed her mount out of the rookery, tugging the yearling along in concert with Haneek and carefully avoiding the angry mothers, she glanced around again for Maddy. Still no sign of her. *Where has she gotten to?* Kit wondered.

"This is going to look great on the Internet," Maddy exulted as she used her phone to make a video clip of Kit, Haneek, and Teesa pulling their captive toward the transports. She stood on a vantage point she had found atop a somewhat higher knoll not far from the convoy. Conceivably, it might have been wise to discuss her decision to move so far from the security of the staging area, but she figured Dr. O would have urged her not to go. So she had just skipped asking. And the strategy was paying off with good video shots of Kit's first quetzalcoatlus roping.

"After all," Maddy murmured to herself with an excess of confidence, "I'm not really in any danger way up here." Her own words gave her pause. She stopped filming. She *was* safe, wasn't she? Slowly, she turned and cast a glance behind her. *And then she screamed.*

When Kit heard Maddy's scream, she had just handed the end of her rope to a waiting Kra at the second transport. Quickly, she looked around in the direction of the sound and spotted Maddy a hundred yards away. "Oh, my God!" she cried when she saw what had made Maddy scream. She had been surprised from behind by—

"A tyrannosaurus!" Ogilvey completed Kit's thought for her.

Maddy was running toward the transports, but the tyrannosaurus was closing the distance to her faster than she could run for safety. The tawny hackle-feathers that ridged its head and neck stood as tall as a Trojan horse's mane, displaying aggression. Kit quickly could see that this grim footrace would end badly for Maddy, so she made a split-second decision. She snapped the reins, shouted "Hyahhh!" and drove both heels sharply into her mount's flanks. The quetzy let out a loud squawk and charged in the direction of the knoll. At it raced forward, it adopted a gait unfamiliar to Kit, which almost unseated her. It was a rolling form of gallop in which the quetzy strode forward first with both forepaws simultaneously, and then swung its entire body forward between the front feet, in a gibbon-ape-like move that placed both hind feet ahead of the forepaws, which then were lifted in unison to take another long stride. It was like riding a crazy tripod, as the body and hind limbs swung forward as a unit, and then the two arms took their next stride. Staying seated was a task Kit thought she might fail before she reached Maddy, given the herky-jerky movement and the unfamiliar saddle. But she lost all fear as she watched the tyrannosaur loom over Maddy. "Hyaahh!" she shouted again. The quetzy responded by charging forward even faster. Haneek, Teesa, and Ogilvey all shouted warnings, instructions and cautions at her simultaneously, all of which seemed of little help and as Kit watched the rex close in on her friend. Maddy ran bravely, but she wore a wide-eyed, wide-mouthed look of desperation on her face.

Knowing the rex was about to win this grim three-cornered race, Kit shouted, "Eelah!"

Instantly, her quetzy crouched and sprang off all four legs into the air, unfurling its wings and giving a mighty flap that raised it high above the ground. Still not knowing quite what she was going to do, Kit steered with her knees to make the quetzy fly directly at the tyrannosaur. Just as the rex leaned to grab Maddy in its jaws, the quetzy flapped directly in front of it and took one snapping bite at the carnivore's head. The rex dodged, forgetting Maddy for the moment. As Maddy made her escape, the rex, only too happy to try for larger prey, lunged upward at the quetzy. Kit screamed as the huge jaws rushed toward her, but her quetzy had already veered off to one side, anticipating the counterthrust of the rex. Now it flapped quickly away. The rex then resumed its original pursuit, thundering after Maddy with a fierce eagle-shriek roar. Maddy, who had gained some precious ground, began to lose it again. With a few giant strides the rex closed in. Maddy tripped, went down, and let out a shrill, terrified scream.

Her scream, however, was drowned out by a new and much louder uproar from the quetzalcoatlus rookery. A half dozen of the adult females charged out of the nesting grounds, running two-legged on their stilt-like forelimbs toward the rex. Voicing cries that sounded like the raucous cackling of a legion of cranes from hell, they covered the distance to the rex quickly. Their forelimbs pounded out ponderous thump, thump, thumping sounds while their smaller hind legs swung completely free of the ground between their forelimbs.

This rapid charge took the rex off guard. It was poised over Maddy, ready to take her in one bite, but it hesitated a moment to confront the oncoming mob of quetzies. Facing off against this new threat, it reared up and roared defiantly. But the gang of sharp-beaked adversaries closed in and half encircled it. One quetzy, standing on its forelimbs, swung both hind feet forward and struck the rex in the gut with a powerful double kick, the thud of which was audible to Kit as her mount circled in the air above the fight. The other quetzies pecked at the rex, their huge bills clacking and snapping with thunderous power that might easily have maimed or killed the carnivore. Kit was heartened to see the rex back away from Maddy. It seemed to know that one solid chomp from a huge beak might break its neck or behead it entirely. The rex roared and snapped back at its adversaries, but it was a foregone conclusion that it was being forced to abandon its human meal in favor of self-preservation.

Maddy got to her feet. She was safe from the rex but now a new danger threatened her. She was underfoot among thundering forepaws as the great pterodactyls surged forward and then retreated in their confrontation with the rex. She dodged left and right among the quetzies, but was confused by the swirl of giant bodies and legs, and unsure which way to run.

Kit saw that Maddy's greatest danger now came from her rescuers, any one of which might maim or kill her accidentally with a crushing footfall. She steered her quetzy to fly just behind the group, making up a plan as she went. While the other pterodactyls faced off with the rex, Kit brought her flying mount in close behind them. She unfurled a second lasso from a hook on the saddle and spun it up quickly.

With a deft flick of her wrist, Kit steered the whirling lariat neatly over one of Maddy's shoulders and under the other arm. She gave a quick tug to cinch the noose around Maddy's torso and then spurred her quetzy to rise high into the air. She looped the rope over the saddle horn and when the rope tightened it pulled Maddy off the ground. Maddy rose up and away just as one of big pterodactyls lurched backward to avoid a counter-snap by the rex, pounding a huge forepaw on the spot where Maddy had stood a moment before.

Ascending into the air with Maddy in tow, Kit guided her mount to circle back to the staging area. There, she cried, "Yannah!" The quetzy flapped lower, touching Maddy down gently near Dr. Ogilvey, who caught her in his arms. Once her feet were solidly on the ground, he undid the rope from around her.

The great pterodactyl set down smoothly itself, folded its wings, and settled onto all fours. Kit jumped down from the saddle and raced to Maddy, who had crumpled into Dr. O's arms, weeping like a child.

"Oh, Maddy, Maddy!" Kit cried. "Are you all right?"

Maddy stopped crying and raised her face at the sound of Kit's voice. She looked at Kit blankly for a moment, with tears streaking black mascara down her cheeks. Then she snapped, "I'm never going anywhere with you again!"

Kit was surprised at Maddy's anger for a moment. And then she said, "It's your own fault, you know."

"No!" Maddy grumbled. "I don't know."

"Who would ever have thought you'd be so dumb as to go off by yourself? In tyrannosaurus country?"

"Come now, Kit," Dr. O said, placatingly. Her put his arms around Maddy again and patted her on the back. "Give her a moment to recover."

"Give me a lifetime to recover!" Maddy groaned.

The three stood in silence for a moment. And then Maddy looked over Dr. O's shoulder at Kit. She smiled mischievously and held up her cell phone. "I somehow kept this in my hand the whole time. I think I might have got some good pictures."

They both paused a minute. And then they began to laugh.

Ogilvey released Maddy and turned to watch the ongoing dinosaur ruckus. "Look at those quetzies beleaguering that rex! They won't quit until they drive it all the way back to Tyrannosaur Valley." Indeed, the carnivore was sprinting away across the open country with quetzies pursuing it on the ground and in the air, pestering it by pecking at its sides and tail.

CHAPTER 9

After Kit and Maddy recovered from the shock of their misadventure, Kit was pressed into service again to rope a third yearling pterodactyl. As the Kra loaded the young one into the third lunkoo, Ogilvey called out, "Here they come, right on time by my watch!"

Everyone paused to observe a long flight line of huge pterodactyls coming in from the northeast. "They are the male quetzalcoatli!" Ogilvey asserted as the animals circled the rookery and landed with the ponderous wing beats of the largest animals ever to fly in the skies of planet earth. Ignoring the begging of the yearlings, which rushed as a group to greet them with a great cacophony of screeches proclaiming their hunger, the males moved into the nesting area and sought out their mates.

"Look at those greeting rituals!" Ogilvey gushed excitedly to Kit and Maddy.

The pterosaur partners clacked their huge beaks together, raised their mouths to the sky, and uttered cries halfway between a heron's rasp and a train's whistle. The noise of many combined male-female pairs was loud, even at fifty yards' distance.

"I can hardly hear myself think!" Kit called loudly enough to be heard above the din.

"It must have been positively ear-splitting when there were thousands of individuals per rookery," Dr. O shouted back.

Eventually the noise died down as the last of the pterodactyl couples were reunited.

"Now," the professor said, resuming his academic décorum. "Please note well the gender differences. The male quetzies are bigger than females, but notice also the bright blue patch on the forehead and the tall manes of stiff quills projecting a foot or more at the back of their head crests, not just black as for the females, but with a broad red stripe as well. Rather formal, in a woodpecker-ish way. The males are the dandies of this species—dramatically beautiful creatures! And look at their greeting dances!"

As each male found its female partner, it began a ritualized dance. It raised its head and tail high, and a red-and-black tuft on the tail seemed to counterbalance the red-and-black tuft on its head. It strutted stiffly on its stilt-like forelimbs with wings folded tightly.

"Look at the hind feet!" Maddy exclaimed. "They're entirely off the ground!"

"Yes, yes indeed!" Ogilvey crowed. "The forelimbs are much longer and more massive than the hind. Fossilized trackways of pterodactyls have been found that possessed nothing but masses of forepaw prints, and no hind prints at all. Now, I guess we see why. Those fossils were of dancing pterodactyls, strutting and spinning around on just their forelimbs—a feat only a pterosaur could manage. Imagine a tyrannosaur attempting the feat."

"Impossible," Kit said. "With those tiny T rex arms."

"But absolutely easy," Ogilvey said, "for an animal whose forelimbs are so much larger and more massively muscled, like our quetzalcoatlus, here. Now look! The females are joining in with parallel dances in the same posture! Dancing and spinning, while in a handstand. Astonishing!"

Although the females were somewhat smaller than the males, and possessed more demure coloration—shorter black head crests and smaller tail tufts—they were no less agile, and engaged in the dance every bit as vigorously as their partners.

When the whirling and spinning and strutting had gone on for some time, the pairs set their hind legs down and faced each other on all fours. They then began to tap their beaks together again, first on one side and then the other. They then raised their beaks high again and squawked out their loud love calls, "Grrronnnk! Grrronnnk!"

As more couples concluded their greeting rituals, the din reverberated loudly in the air. "I'd say its time to get going," Ogilvey shouted, "for our eardrums' sake, if nothing else. Our expedition mates have finished loading the third of our captives."

As they boarded their lunkoo, Ogilvey paused in the doorway and pointed back at the rookery. "Ah!" he remarked. "I believe it's time to feed the babies." Kit and Maddy joined him in watching a new ritual take place. Throughout the rookery, the males arched their long necks over their rocky nest circles. From within the nests, small heads, short of bill and lacking crests, rose up and began pecking at their fathers' bills. After each baby had pecked a few times, the fathers were instinctually prompted to regurgitate the contents of their crops. As the males' bodies and throats convulsed with vomit, the babies eagerly responded by thrusting their heads entirely within their fathers' mouths and greedily gulping the vomited meat as it came out.

"Splendid!" Ogilvey cried.

"Eewww!" Maddy cried simultaneously. "Gross!"

Kit made a sour expression, as if uncertain whose opinion she concurred with.

Ogilvey's enthusiasm, however, was stronger than Maddy's dismay. "What a prodigious feeding!" he exclaimed. "No wonder the young can grow to near-adult size and begin flying within a single year! Furthermore, if that's not enough to eat, the mothers will soon fly off to rustle up some more carrion meat while the fathers tend the nests!"

The adventurers settled into their seats aboard the lunkoo, and it rose and began slowly walking away from the rookery. Through the rear window of their passenger compartment, they could see into the cage behind them. The young quetzy would soon be a newly domesticated flying mount, but at the moment it angrily voiced a series of loud, cackling complaints.

"Poor thing," Kit said. "It misses its mother."

"Perhaps," Dr. O replied. "But remember—a yearling quetzy's life is tough. Rejected by mother and father, it must learn to fend for itself. Tyrannosaurs and other predators often take them off-guard. This one is about to become a pampered, well-fed, and beloved pet."

Kit smiled. "Not such a bad life, I guess. Sort of like our horses."

"Exactly," Ogilvey agreed.

After they had traveled awhile in the gently swaying lunkoo, the professor asked, "Now, Madeline, what have you learned today?"

"To think twice before going anywhere with you two again."

"Yes, well, perhaps. But beyond that you have learned that the parental instincts of quetzalcoatli are sufficiently strong that they will even protect someone of a different species, if that someone happens to be about the size of their offspring."

Maddy wasn't listening. She was staring at her cell phone. "Oh, my God!" she exclaimed. "Look at this! I kept the video running when the tyrannosaurus was about to eat me. Watch! He gets closer! And closer! And finally, all you see is his great big wide-open mouth! Then you see the quetzies attacking and he turns away!"

"That's gonna be a hit on You Tube," Kit said.

As the line of lunkoos began their trudging journey back to Arran Kra, the three dosokotakkan, Haneek, Teesa, and Kalachi, rode their pterosaur mounts into the air, returning to the city by the most direct route possible, high in the sky and across the craggy peaks of the Absaroka Range. In the front of their lunkoo's bus-like passenger compartment, Dr. O took up a conversation with Tekkana, chatting quietly in Kranaga about the day's events.

Sitting farther back, Kit turned to Maddy. "What a day,

huh?" she asked.

"What a day for you, you mean. You got to ride that flying monster. All I got to do was almost get eaten by a T rex! I thought Chase Armstrong was supposed to be taming those things."

Kit shrugged. "I guess he hasn't gotten around to all of them yet."

"Speaking of Chase," Maddy said, smiling impishly, "he's going to like hearing how you heroically saved your best friend's life. I'll tell him myself. He's got to be impressed with a feat like that. Maybe he'll even take you back."

"Take me back!" Kit was suddenly irritated. "I was the one who told him no, not the other way around."

"Yeah, and you've been moping around ever since. Why don't you just come out and tell him you love him?"

Kit squirmed uneasily. "Maybe I do love him. But I also told him I wasn't ready to settle down yet. And that's when he got that look in his eye."

"What look?"

"Like he wasn't content to be just friends. And then he looked kind of far away, like maybe he was thinking of another girl he knew." She paled until she was white as a ghost. "Oh, Maddy. Maybe I really blew it."

"You could try patching things up."

"No. I can't do that, either. It will just lead right back to the same question—are we getting married, or aren't we?"

Maddy looked out the window at the tall crags of the Absarokas going by on the right. "A lot of girls would like to have the problem you've got with Chase Armstrong."

"I know! That's what has me upset most of all. If it isn't Thera McCarty trying to horn in, it might be some other girl he meets."

"Sorry I brought up such a sore subject."

"Yeah. Thanks a lot, Maddy. You've got me feeling as scared about other women as you were of that tyrannosaurus."

They both stared out at the scenery for a long time.

Eventually, Kit murmured, "It isn't just about that. It isn't just about getting married. It's just, well, I'm twenty-one and I'm halfway through college. I've got my whole life ahead of me. I want to—"

"Kick up your heels?" Maddy prompted. "See other men?"

"That's right," Kit said. "I've only ever had two serious boyfriends before Chase."

"See what I mean? You need to get out and get some experience before you even think of getting married."

"Yeah, I guess so. I mean, I wonder if I would regret it all my life if I didn't raise a little hell before I settled down?"

"You sure would!" Maddy asserted. "I've had plenty of experience and all's I can tell you is I'm totally ready for a whole lot more! Men come in all kinds of shapes and sizes—and wants and desires, and needs and abilities, and, oooh, sometimes they just take you in their arms and you just... you just... scream! You know what I mean?"

"That's just it," Kit murmured. "I'm not so sure I *do* know what you mean. Still, Chase is..."

"What?"

"Chase is..."

"What? C'mon, girl, spit it out."

Kit let out a deep sigh that ended almost like a sob. "He's too perfect."

"Oo-oo-oo-ooh, girl," Maddy exclaimed. "You've got it bad!"

Kit's eyes filled with tears. "What if I let him go," she choked, "and I never see him again?"

"Oh, I don't know," Maddy demurred. "He'll be living right up there on the Plains of Arran Kra, won't he?"

"Yeah," Kit admitted through pain that was cloying her throat. "But what if he gets... another girl?" She let out a full-fledged sob. Maddy wrapped an arm around her and hugged her for a long time. And then she said, "Look. Even if something like that did happen, there are lots of other guys around. Bobby Everett, for instance."

Kit shook off her embrace. "That big clod? Now you're making me sick."

"What!" Maddy resisted. "Bobby's a hunk. You could do a lot worse."

They were both silent for a moment. Then Kit said softly, "I suppose Bobby's not so bad, but..."

"But what?"

"But he's not Chase Armstrong."

"You're hopeless, Kit."

***

Kit sat on the front porch swing of the ranch house, gazing at nothing in particular, and moping quietly over the many contrary choices confronting her. Zippy, the old, battle-scarred Border collie, lolled on his back, paws in the air. Lying near her feet, he pawed one of her cowboy boots as if he thought it was time to have his belly scratched. But Kit's mind was on other matters.

The late morning air was beginning to heat up with the warmth of the sun. Out in the pasture, the parasaurolophus family was stirring, snuffling around and nibbling on pasture grass. A group of small, gazelle-like orodromeus raced by in their graceful two-legged trot with a few dramatic arcing leaps thrown in now and then. Tiny chattering black-and-white pterodactyls raced by in the air, hunting for insects on the wing. Kit's eyes followed the movements of the sound makers, but she didn't really notice much about them. Her mind was set on the puzzles that life had offered her.

She stirred to take real notice when a big shiny black crew-cab pickup truck came up the driveway and stopped in front of the house.

"Maddy said I'd find you here," Bobby Everett said as he got out and stepped down from the big rig's high running board.

"That busybody." Kit muttered, showing little interest in Bobby as he came to the bottom of the steps. "What else did she tell you?"

"Mmmm," Bobby said with a smile and a flush growing on his cheeks. "She said Chase Armstrong was definitely not here.

Down in Mexico or somewhere like that."

"So?"

"So, I've got a proposition for you."

"Oh-oh."

"Seeing as you've got nobody to chill with around here, I thought I would come over and keep you company."

"That's very kind but—"

"I've got some sandwiches in a cooler." He pointed a thumb at the crew seat of his pickup. "And some chips. And a couple of beers. Anybody up for a picnic in the mountains?"

"Why not?" Kit replied without much enthusiasm.

"Well, come on, then!" Bobby said with a grin.

CHAPTER 10

A thousand miles to the south, a jungle path typical of the two-rutted, overgrown roads that lace the green hillsides of Mexico's west coast, the Costa Verde, was so overhung with trees and vines and palms and tropical foliage that it seemed to vanish into green as it wound tortuously down toward the Pacific. Two young men carrying surfboards wended their way along the seldom-used road. Overhead, hidden in the overarching green, they could hear the loud squawks of parrots, the buzz of insects, and the twitter of small unseen birds. Somewhere not far off was the roar of what they hoped would be story-worthy surf.

"Dude," the taller and blonder surfer said. "We've been hiking, like, forever. This break had better really be badass."

"Oh, it is, dude," the shorter and darker, though also blond, surfer said. "Every wave's a magic carpet ride."

"Are you sure we're on the right trail?" the taller asked. "We must have walked five miles and passed a half dozen trails cutting across this one. Like, when do we get there?"

The shorter surfer paused and shrugged his bare, sweat-beaded shoulders. "The dude in the surf shop in Sayulita told me, 'Drive south of Monkey Mountain, leave the car at the pullout, go around the locked gate, follow the road for—' Hmmm, was it two miles or three? I forget. I had some killer tequila and a lotta smoke in me at the time."

"Yeah. And I'm thinking you still do." The tall surfer rested his board on its tail end. It was a top-of-the-line long board, painted with apocalyptical designs of skulls, explosions, and blood spatters. "I think we're lost, dude," he said.

"No, we're not," the other said. He set down his board, which sported an image of a great white shark taking a bite out of the board.

"How do you figure?" the tall one said. "I mean, like, we're in the middle of nowhere, in the middle of the jungle, it's wet and full of mosquitoes and I'm getting bitten and I'm getting creeped out, dude!"

"Shhhh," the shorter one hissed. "Quiet! Quiet!" He peered in front of them. "I thought I heard something up ahead."

They had paused on a relatively straight stretch of road, but it was hemmed in so badly by overhanging foliage that it was impossible to see more than a dozen yards ahead. Something moved among the shadows.

"That's good enough for me," the taller surfer said. "Let's get outta here."

"No, man. The dude's already seen us. He's coming this way. Better stay put. Act nonchalant. If he says we're trespassing, we'll just clear out."

"That ain't no dude, dude."

"What? Oh. You're right. It ain't a dude. It's… a Kra!"

They were unable to keep from gaping as the Kra approached.

"I've seen 'em on TV," the tall one said in a shaky voice. "But I never met one in person."

"Well, you're going to get your chance," whispered the shorter one.

The Kra was a good seven feet tall from its three-toed dinosaurian feet to the top of its head, which like all Kra heads, bore a crest on top like a cassowary, this one striped orange and black. Black-feathered all over, with clawed hands and red-orange eyes fixated on them, it came to within twenty feet and paused to regard them silently. It couldn't—and didn't try to—hide the knifelike reptilian fangs in its jaws. Those fangs dripped saliva as it regarded them coolly.

"Hey dude, I mean, hey Kra," the shorter surfer began

nervously. "We— We were, like, just looking for some wicked surf they said was down this way. Know of any?" He laughed thinly.

The Kra remained silent.

"Actually," the taller said, "we were just leaving. He picked up his board and waved this free hand at the glowering Kra. "Bye."

As the surfers turned to go back the way they had come, the Kra called loudly, "Toa-kee!"

Immediately, heavy rustling came from the underbrush behind the two retreating men. Sensing that something big was coming at them, they turned to look.

"Oh my God!" the tall one cried as a pair of four-legged beasts emerged from the jungle issuing diabolical growls.

The shorter surfer appealed to the Kra. "Please! No! No-o-o-o!"

The jungle filled with sounds like the snarling of huge dogs on the attack, mingled with the surfers' blood-curdling screams.

***

"You've got parasaurolophuses, too!" Kit exclaimed as Bobby drove past the Everett Ranch's pasture bottomland. On the green pasture grass, a second giant duckbill family had taken up residence much the way Rufus and Henrietta and stationed their brood in the Danielses' pasture.

"They make an awful racket when they start honking," Bobby said.

"Don't I know it," Kit agreed.

"We've got dinosaurs all over the place till there's hardly room for cattle."

"Same with us."

"I guess that's something we've got in common, then," Bobby said. Beyond the nesting parasauros, he left the bottomland behind and drove up a graveled, two-rutted road into the mountain country on the opposite side of the valley from the Danielses' Twin Creeks Ranch. Along the way, they passed the Everett family's high prairie with 500 head of Black Angus grazing and mingling with a herd of huge, dark, wooly newcomers.

"Wooly iguanodonts," Kit asserted as they skirted the large animals, which grazed on all fours but rose to a two-legged stance to watch the pickup roll by.

"Iguana daunts?" Bobby said. "I knew they was probably wooly something-or-others."

He drove into the high, treeless country above the prairie, finally stopping at a ridgeline pullout from which the whole valley below could be surveyed. The entire Everett Ranch was laid out before them, and beyond that, nestled under the heights of Sandstone Mountain and the Absaroka Range beyond, was the Danielses' extensive property.

"The boy or girl next door takes on a different dimension out here," Bobby said as he shut off the engine.

Kit smirked provocatively. "My side of the valley is the one with all the dazzling towers of Arran Kra. And spaceships coming and going with jewels and precious metals from the moon."

Bobby was unfazed. "Yeah?" he said. "Well, my side is the one with the best winter forage. You just send your iguana daunts right over if they need a little extra to eat."

Kit let the comment ride.

"Speaking of which," Bobby said after a minute of silence, "wouldn't it be something if these two ranches were combined? That would make one humongous spread of land."

"Combined?" Kit repeated. "How do you propose to do that?"

Bobby smiled. "Propose?" he said. "Funny you should use that word."

Alarm bells were suddenly going off in Kit's mind. "Oh no," she said. "Don't go getting all serious on me. I just came up here for lunch. I'm not in a mood for any crazy notions."

"Okay," he agreed easily. "How about a small one then?"

"What?"

He put an arm around her shoulders. "Kiss me."

When he leaned near, she put up a hand. "Whoa, boy! You're coming on like a tyrannosaurus."

He drew her to him despite her resistance. When he opened his lips slightly, preparing to kiss her, she put her hands on his chest and pushed back hard. But now his strong arms were both wrapped around her and pulling her closer. As his lips drew near hers, she turned her head. "Bobby!" she protested.

When he persisted, she wriggled her right arm free of his embrace and slapped him hard across the face.

"Ow!" he said, letting her go and rubbing his cheek. "You hit hard, for a girl."

"I can hit a lot harder than that. Now, give me a sandwich or drive me home. Your choice."

Just then a shadow fell across the cab of the pickup. A group of three huge quetzalcoatli flapped by lazily, high above.

Bobby reached for a rifle slung in a gun rack in the back window. Kit waved him away from it. "They're big males," she said. "But they're no threat, really. They're headed in the direction of the rookery. Probably bringing home lunch for their babies. Let's have our lunch."

"Okay," Bobby said. "I guess you know your pterodactyls better than I do."

Over sandwiches, they watched a spaceship descend to the plains of Arran Kra.

"Probably the Doosta," Kit said. "Shuttling down from the Nkinta, which was due back in earth orbit today, fresh from the moon. I wonder what's on board?"

"Some new kind of dinosaur, maybe?"

"More likely a load of gold and platinum ingots. The Kra are making good on their promise to pay for all the damage they caused."

There was a long silence. Bobby broke it with a nervous cough. "Listen, Kit—" he began. "You didn't really let me say what I wanted to."

"Oh-oh," Kit said. "Here we go again."

"Now, come on Kit. Just hear me out. Don't get all fussy. I think maybe I... I love you." He said it in a small, uncertain voice.

She shook her head slowly. "You're getting to be as bad as Chase Armstrong."

"So, I've come up a bit in your opinion?" He forced a laugh.

Kit sighed. "Is it so wrong for me to want to try living my own life first, before I get all tied up in a relationship? Is it so wrong to want to explore the great big wide world all around me?"

"What world are you talking about, Kit?"

"The world of parties at the university, the world of excitement and adventure, of Kra, and dinosaurs, and Dr. Ogilvey, and paleontology, and my career, and…

"And what? Where is that all leading you to? Is it really going to make you happy? I'm starting to doubt anyone could make you happy."

She frowned at him. And then she thought for a few seconds. And then she sighed again, in a resigned way. And then she said, "Oh, what the heck. Shut up and kiss me!"

Bobby looked shocked. "Well, okay," he stammered. He put an arm around her shoulders, leaned, and kissed her.

Kit pushed him back slightly. "No, Bobby," she said. "Don't kiss me like you'd kiss your sister." She pulled him to her forcefully and whispered hotly in his ear, "I want you to ravish me! Smother me in your arms. Destroy me!"

Bobby held back. "Uh, Kit," he said in a confused tone. "You're acting kinda weird on me now."

"Don't talk to me anymore," she snapped. "Act. Grab me in your strong arms and kiss me like you mean it!"

Bobby looked genuinely confused. "I don't know what to think of you—acting this way," he murmured.

Kit shoved him away from her. "Get out of my sight, then!" She turned and stared out her side window. She could feel the heat of a bright red flush on her face. Whether it was from excitement or embarrassment, she wasn't sure.

"How can I get out of your sight?" he asked. "We're in my truck."

Kit wrenched the door handle and got out. "There!" she growled. "Now you can get out of my sight." She slammed the door.

"O— Okay, Kit," Bobby said through the open window as he fired up the engine. "But it's a long walk down from this mountain."

"I don't care."

"What if a dinosaur comes along?"

"I'll bite its head off," she shouted. "Now, go!"

He shrugged, let out a sigh, and drove away shaking his head.

When Kit had walked halfway down the mountainside following the gravel road, she suddenly stopped in her tracks. "Oh-oh," she murmured, looking at something not far ahead of her.

It was a T rex.

She held her breath and kept dead still, hoping it wouldn't spot her. It was a hundred yards away, moving slowly through a stand of willows and looking over their tops. When it paused and cocked its head in her direction, Kit knew she had been seen. When it moved toward her, coming out of the willows and onto the road ahead of her, she fought a tremendous urge to run for her life. But she guessed that fleeing would immediately provoke the predator's instinct to pursue. So she stood her ground. She silently asked herself, *What would Chase Armstrong do?* And she instantly knew what that would be.

"Hey!" she called out loudly to the rex, stopping the huge carnivore in its tracks. "You want some of this?" She half-turned, stuck out a hip, and slapped her own rump. "Come and get it!"

She had spotted the radio collar around the rex's neck and knew Chase Armstrong had already had his way with this beast. It had probably learned Chase's aversion lesson—that attacking tailless human creatures led to electric shocks, darting, and other humiliating experiences.

Indeed, the rex was quite well trained. Kit slapped her rump once more to draw the beast's attention to its taillessness, and the rex responded by cringing at the memory of past humiliation. It turned and disappeared into a stand of lodgepole pines.

"Huh," Kit said with great relief. "It really works. Thank you, Chase Armstrong." She resumed her trek down the road, but after a few paces she paused and put her knuckles on her hips. She shook her head slowly and asked herself, "Does everything have to remind me of Chase Armstrong?"

PART THREE

SOMETHING IN THE JUNGLE

"Ey! Torro!" Chase shouted.

THOMAS P. HOPP

CHAPTER 11

Chase Armstrong sat at a table in the shade of the wide, open-air dining area under the huge thatched roof of La Palapa, the famous old bar on Los Muertos Beach in Puerto Vallarta, Mexico. He and Dr. Ogilvey, his aging, bearded, and bespectacled companion were dressed for the hot and humid weather in floral tropical shirts and short pants. They sat sipping Pacifico beers in the large dining area under the palapa roof, and watching parasailers move to and fro over the placid aquamarine ocean while a brass-and-drum band rattled and blared farther down along the parasol-dotted seascape. The sun blazed hot in a cloudless sky, and the palapa's generous shade and sea breeze made the heat of the day bearable—but just barely.

"Perfect weather for dinosaurs," Chase remarked. He smiled as curmudgeonly old professor Ogilvey removed his sweat-fogged bifocals and cleaned them with a white linen napkin.

"What could you possibly mean by that, Chase?" Ogilvey asked irritably while rubbing his bifocals clear. "As we have seen abundantly in the last year, tropical weather is by no means required for dinosaurs to live in comfort. There are species native to anything from tropic heat to arctic ice."

Chase nodded, took a pull on his beer bottle, and kept silent. To reply would risk a lengthy debate against the vast store of dinosaur data within the prodigious brain that occupied the thin-haired cranium under the old paleontologist's crumpled tan canvas field hat.

The young Mexican woman looked like she came from money. Fashion model perfect in face and figure, a haughty expression in her dark eyes, she exclaimed, "Chase!" when she saw him, and hurried to sit her shapely butt on his knee. She was dressed in a two-piece bathing suit that hugged her curves tightly, and wore a floral patterned sarong wrapped around her lusciously flared hips. Sandals on her feet were lined with dazzling jewels. Her shape was exquisite—tall and curvaceous. Her sleek, deeply tanned skin, flawless and exposed over much of her body, invited the touch of a male hand. Instead, she stroked the line of Chase's jaw with an elegantly enameled long fingernail. "We go partying again tonight, no?" she pried. "Last night was so much fun. I theenk I am falling een love, Señor Dinosaurio Maestro, Chase Armstrong."

Chase shot an amused glance at Ogilvey, who stared back at him, perplexed.

"I see from where you got your name, Señor Armstrong," she said, caressing his bicep. "Your arms are... so strong! Will you take me in them again tonight? If so, I will lose my head again, as I did last night."

"Oh, my," Ogilvey murmured despite himself.

"Felina," Chase said by way of introduction, "Doctor Ogilvey. Doctor Ogilvey, Felina."

Ogilvey touched the brim of his hat. "How nice to meet you," he said rather coolly.

Felina nodded at the professor once and smiled sweetly, simultaneously making herself comfortable in Chase's lap by leaning against him and putting her arms around his shoulders. He didn't resist.

"Ah! There you are," a man called. He had just entered the palapa and approached the table. Jeffrey Miller was a heavy-set, balding fellow whose good-natured smile belied the seriousness of his mission and the deadliness of his interests. He was dressed in shorts and a tropical shirt, much like Chase and Dr. O, suiting the jungle heat and humidity of Puerto Vallarta. "Making progress on our little mystery?" he asked in a pleasant but insistent tone. He sat down, lifted his white straw Trilby hat, and daubed sweat from his domed forehead with a hand-kerchief.

"Not much progress, yet," Ogilvey replied, although the question had been asked of Chase. "We've only been here a couple of days."

"And I see you've had your hands full," Miller said, looking over Chase and the girl and giving particular attention to her long legs. "Give me an update," he said, his gaze returning to Chase' face. "And don't spare the details."

Chase took a long pull on his cold Pacifico and shrugged. Being a man who tended toward action, he wasn't given to long explanations.

"Let me," Ogilvey, the long-winded one, obliged. "As you requested," he began in a professorial tone, "we have been to a location in the jungle north of here where the latest human remains were found."

"Excuse me," Miller cut in, looking past Ogilvey to the girl. "I don't think I've had the pleasure of making your acquaint-tance, young lady. You're not Kit Daniels, are you?"

"No, Señor Bald Man. I do not know Keet Daniels from a hole in the ground. I am Felina."

"Felina who?"

"My father's name is not important. He sells, er, commo-dities across the border in the U.S."

Miller made a sour face. "I think you had better run along, honey. This conversation is—er, of a sensitive nature."

She stayed put. Toying with a lock of hair at the back of Chase's neck, she made a pouty face. "I don't have to go," she mewed. "Do I Chase?"

"He's right, Felina," Chase said. "This is serious business. I'll look for you later."

She stood up in a huff. "Maybe you won't find me later." She spun like a dancer and walked away quickly, but not so quickly that she couldn't swing her long legs in a model walk and accentuate the swaying of the sarong that hugged her hips.

Jeff Miller watched her go, all eyes and open mouth. Then

he turned to Chase. "A dangerous one," he said.

"A pussycat," Chase countered.

"Anyway," Ogilvey mumbled. "Where was I?"

"You were saying," Miller said, "the two surfers—they vanished in the same area where the previous disappearances have taken place, right?"

"Well, I didn't say that, but it's true, as you know. All the deaths have occurred in the jungle-covered hill country around Monkey Mountain, just a few miles south of the fishing and surfing village of Sayulita. It's a remote coastal area, well off the beaten path. Tourists sometimes like to hike there to reach some untouched beaches, and surfers venture there to try the fabulous surf breaks. The local rancheros run cattle out to forage on the jungle hillsides. In all five previous deaths, the only remains ever found were scattered bones on one or another of the mountain trails. By the time we arrived, what bones had been found had been recovered and taken for DNA and dental record identification by La Policia."

"Any other evidence?"

"Only torn bits of clothing, as if the victims had been ripped limb-from-limb, and some very indistinct traces of footprints, pretty badly degraded by the rains. We saw some of these at one of the sites, but even with all our experience with dinosaur tracks, Chase and I were not able to make a clear identification of the species that made them."

"Shame," Miller said. "What else?"

"La Policia have a DNA match on the first bones found. He's one of several local rancheros who had gone missing, matched with family DNA, since there were no dental records."

Miller said, "Was that the man who went out to round up some cattle and never returned?"

"Exactly. His horse came home severely bitten. A search party found him early the next morning. Er, found what was left of him, that is. There were animal tracks around the bones —plenty of them. And some of them were three-clawed, which led La Policia to suspect an attack by a Kra. But the authorities around here have never seen Kra tracks. So they weren't certain."

"I'm aware of all that," Miller said brusquely, irritated at the length of the professor's lecture. "That's why you two were called in. You are our Kra experts. What I want to know is, have you seen any identifiable tracks?"

"We certainly would have by now," Ogilvey replied, "if it weren't for the rains."

"They've been pretty heavy lately," Chase concurred.

"A fine understatement," Ogilvey said, chuckling. "By the time we arrived, rainstorms had washed out not just the trail where that first ranchero was killed, but the whole mountainside as well. The authorities are still digging out the area to re-open the road. Thank goodness the weather has cleared, but whatever evidence remained there has been covered with a torrent of mud. It's really the ranchero's own fault that his death can't be solved. Right, Chase?"

"Sure, Dr. O. Cattle grazing is unnatural in the jungle. Cattle eat the seedlings and young sprouts, and that kills off the underbrush and denudes the slopes of plants and their roots, which normally hold the soil in place. After that, the rains erode the entire landscape in some places."

"And so," the professor concluded, "the ranchero's own environmental destruction was to blame for the loss of signs of the perpetrators of his murder."

"There may be some justice in that," Chase muttered. "I've got no respect for anyone who wrecks an ecosystem to earn a living."

"Spoken like a true Yellowstone Park ranger," Miller responded. "But you two were sent here because there is something in the jungle that is killing people, and we have been asked to provide an answer. Now, you fellows know the Kra, and you know dinosaurs, better than anyone. But it sounds like you haven't made as much progress as we hoped." He glanced across the dining room to the bar, where Felina sat glowering at him. "Kra killing humans, and vice versa, that's the kind of thing that could escalate into an international incident. And that might destabilize the whole peace treaty with the Kra. We could have war again."

Chase toyed with his Pacifico bottle on the table. "The trail's gone as cold as it could get in this heat—not to mention as wet and muddy as possible."

Miller let out an exasperated sigh and raised an index finger as if about to begin a stern lecture. But a commotion arose at the street-side entrance to the restaurant. He paused, turning to see what was going on. It seemed that someone—or something—intimidating had just entered the palapa.

An individual of a sort most people were unaccustomed to seeing was moving among the diners, eliciting surprised gasps from men and women alike. He wove his way between tables of shocked faces until he reached the one where Armstrong, Ogilvey, and Miller sat.

The newcomer was a Kra. Like all Kra, his carnivorous dinosaur ancestry was evident in every inch of his seven foot height—the long neck, the crest-topped head, the razor-fanged jaws, the long-tailed body covered in feathers, the three-taloned feet, and similarly clawed hands. Unlike the many dark-feathered Kra Chase and Ogilvey had met, this fellow was colored much like a human redhead. Red-orange feathers on his back and paler feathers on his belly and the underside of his long tail, mingled with darker red-orange blotches that corresponded to freckles in a human. He was dressed, or rather undressed, as befitted a Kra businessman—more properly a businesskra—in nothing more than a satchel slung by a leather strap across one shoulder. His feathers served the nakedness-covering function that clothes provided to humans.

Keeping his feather-covered tail high with cat-like grace, he approached the trio and bowed stiffly. "Chase Arrrstrong," he hissed in a voice unusually cold and reptilian for a warm-blooded Kra. He paused as if awaiting a welcome, but got none. Instead, Chase exchanged dubious glances with Miller and Dr. O, but said nothing.

If the Kra sensed their lack of enthusiasm, he took it in

stride. He spoke a few words in Spanish to a dumbstruck waiter who hurried to bring a chair suited for a Kra to sit on. Lacking a chair back, it was shaped more like a hassock to better accommodate the tail of its occupier.

The Kra took his seat and said to the waiter, "Teenaka."

The man hurried off to fetch the drink favored by many Kra, bringing back a cup of red-brown liquid made from fermented blood with an alcohol content similar to wine. The Kra took a sip. Still met with silence, he nodded his tall, crested head to each of his tablemates in turn.

"Vuenos tardes," he said in Spanish that was only slightly impeded by the rows of fangs lining his reptilian jaws. In the months since the cessation of hostilities between humans and Kra, Chase had come to hear the peculiar Kra pronunciation of earthly words as simply another form of foreign accent, although in this case the foreigner had been hatched on the moon and his species had originated in a time and place 65-million years gone.

"I am Doolah," the Kra said. "You went to see the kill sites? No?" Like all Kra, whose toothy and lip-less mouths struggled with the human letters M, P, and B, Doolah approximated the sounds as "ng", "f", and "v", in a hybrid diction Chase and Dr. O had learned to comprehend without too much trouble.

Chase eyed Doolah carefully. "We've been up Sayulita-way."

"You should not go there again," the Kra hissed with noticeable strain in his voice. "You could get killed."

"Says who?"

"Are you familiar with the name, Karrik?"

Chase shook his head. "Never heard of him."

"Oh, you should have," Doolah clucked gleefully. "Great military leader. Commander of the 24th division of fighter-walkers. Many, many human kills to his credit. That was, of course, before hostilities ceased."

"You're saying he's behind the murders?"

The Kra gasped in feigned surprise. "Ngeester Arrrstrong!

Such language. Karrik is no murderer. But sometimes people die when they go where they should not be."

"And we should not go to Monkey Mountain?"

"In these new times, Kra are allowed to travel the world, to buy private property, no?"

"Yes, yes, of course," Dr. O chimed in, sharing Chase's immediate dislike for this unctuous, smooth-maneuvering Kra.

"Just like you hoonahs, Kra are now free to live where they please." He used the pejorative them 'hoonah' with relish in his voice. "And where Kra live, they want privacy. You can understand that, no?"

"Sorry," Chase muttered. "Your privacy stops when people start dying."

"Would these change your mind?" The Kra unfolded a three-taloned hand, and a pair of diamonds the size of hen's eggs rolled out onto the white tablecloth. Sparkling through hundreds of facets, they dazzled the eyes of all present, including Felina, who sat up tall at the bar to get a good look at them. "Jewels," Doolah said, "fresh from our mines on the moon. Perhaps your girlfriend, Kit Daniels, would like one."

"She would," Chase agreed. "But I can't be bought. Besides, Jeffrey here has me on a pretty rich expense account. Don't you, Jeff, old pal?"

The Kra looked long at Miller. "We are well aware of that Chase Arrrstrong now has his CIA handlers, with their weapons and their money, and their spying ways. But spies and thugs were the same 65-million years ago. Now you, Ngeester Arrrstrong. You are different. You are a hoonah of great character and courage. That is why these CIA fellows sent you here. You know us. You have fought us. And," Doolah leaned close and hissed softly near Chase's face, "you have killed us."

Chase looked at Doolah with distain for his oily obse-quiousness, the highhandedness of his approach, of the stench of the blood drink on his breath. He said, "If you know me that well, then you know I'll follow this case where it leads."

Doolah swept up the diamonds with one hand and slammed his drink down with the other, splashing blood-red, stinking liquid across the tablecloth. He stood. His orange reptilian eyes glared into Chase's. "You have been warned. Stay away!"

He spun on a three-toe foot and stalked off.

"He didn't pay for his drink," Chase muttered.

"Beastly behavior," Ogilvey concurred.

"CIA is aware of that character," Miller said. "As well as Karrik. Doolah is a former trooper in Karrik's division and a loyal subordinate these days. We wondered where they both had gotten to. Now we know."

"It's a good bet they're involved in these murders," the professor said.

Chase scowled as he watched the Kra hightail his way among the tables and leave via the street entrance. "I've got a feeling they're hiding a lot more than just murder."

CHAPTER 12

The strange warning cast a pall over the conversation until a Mexican huckster in a straw cowboy hat, sandals, and white cotton shirt and shorts came along the beach. His eyes lit up when he looked inside the palapa and saw Chase.

"Oye, Señor!" he called. "Don' you wan' to try some parasail? Two-feefty pesos only. Very cheap!"

"Yesss," Ogilvey hissed, mocking their former tablemate. "Why don't you try it, Ngeester Arrrstrong?"

"Sorry." Chase waved the Mexican off. "I've got an appointment with a dinosaur at Monkey Mountain."

Felina had witnessed the exchange. She came to the table. "Aw, Señor, Armstrong," she exclaimed. "You are beeg and strong. You are not afraid of our leetle parachutes, are you?"

Chase took another pull on his Pacifico. "Just not interested."

Felina went into her pouting routine. "Oh, please do. I have a cell phone right heer." She pulled it from her cleavage. "I will take the souvenir pictures you can email to the little missus back home."

"She isn't the little missus."

"That's good," Felina said, smiling. "I will keep them for myself. I will add them to my collection of dashing young men weeth broad shoulders."

Chase shrugged. "All right," he said. "I suppose I've got time to give it a whirl. After all, Señor Meeller here is paying for it. Right, Jeff?"

Begrudgingly, Jeff pulled a two-hundred-peso note and a

fifty-peso note from his wallet and handed them to the man, who had hurried up from the beach when he saw he could make a sale. Pocketing the bills, the huckster gestured Chase toward two men who were standing on the beach and rigging a parasailing chute. Felina followed Chase out to the edge of the surf where, as the two helpers rigged the chute harness to him, she said, "Smile, handsome!" She took a selfie image of herself beside him as he tested the tautness of the harness lines attached to the already fluttering chute. The chute bore a distinctive logo that made it stand out even among the other brightly colored chutes festooning the beach—a green-outlined emblem of a horned dinosaurian head, a triceratops-like creature.

Among the many small speedboats standing off the beach and awaiting their own parasailing clients, a huge dark hulk roared to life. The boat, built on the lines of a sleek, gunmetal gray yacht, was angular and warlike in contrast to the smaller, brightly colored boats around it. As it turned out to sea, drawing on the line that would lift him skyward, Chase saw on its stern the same ceratopsian logo.

"Be careful out there," Miller shouted. Before Chase had time to reconsider, the dark craft gunned its engines and roared away, snapping the towline tight and wrenching him off his feet and into the air.

"I'm getting some great shots!" Felina called after him as he lofted upward into the air on a course headed straight out to sea. Other parasailing boats turned to run parallel to the shore so their fares could see and be seen, but this ominous machine held steady for the blue curve of the horizon. On her decks seventy feet below Chase, two Mexican men busied themselves with chores. One checked the security of the knot that held the towline to the rear mast. The other washed away blood from the deck, hopefully just the result of a previous fishing excursion. Chase glanced over his shoulder and saw that the hotel-studded skyline of Puerto Vallarta was shrinking with alarming swiftness. The boat gained speed and turned to the north, fairly flying over the water and dragging Chase behind with the wind so fast it pulled water from his eyes. Chase looked at the deck again and his concern amplified a hundredfold. There, talking with the two Mexicans, was a Kra. This individual, darkly feathered and orange-crested, birdishly cocked his head up at Chase for moment. Then he went back below decks.

Chase's anxiety grew as Puerto Vallarta fell miles behind them. After perhaps twenty minutes at sea, in which they moved at high speed well to the north of the resort peninsula of Punta Mita, the boat turned toward shore. Dead ahead Chase could see from his high perspective the tall silhouette of Monkey Mountain, half-concealed under white and billowing clouds. At the mountain's base on the seaward side he saw a sandy beach, on which three stupendous driftwood logs were stranded. As the boat drew nearer, his eyes widened when he realized that these were not logs. They were three huge, fifty-foot-long crocodiles, lazing on the beach sand.

The boat slowed as it neared shore. The two deck hands activated a motor winch that began to reel in the chute. Chase got a sinking feeling to match his altitude, which was decreasing rapidly. Beyond the beach was a mangrove swamp with what looked like a newly constructed boat slip cut through it. Above that, Chase noticed a secluded seaside villa half-hidden by the surrounding dense jungle, sprawling across a rocky, overgrown, jungle promontory above the ocean. It looked like an old ruined hacienda homestead of whitewashed adobe-walled buildings and red tiled roofs, now newly reoccupied and under repair.

The Kra reemerged on the boat's back deck. As Chase was drawn down inexorably nearer to him, he laughed a clucking Kra laugh, and called out exultantly, "I am Karrik, killer of many hoonahs—before you."

"Well, I'm Chase Armstrong and I'm not accustomed to being hijacked."

Karrik replied mockingly, "Don't worry Ngeester Arrrstrong. You won't be with us verrry long."

Chase's pulse skyrocketed as he realized the desperation of

his position, tethered as he was to a line drawing him into the hands of a deadly adversary. He glanced around, swiftly assessing his situation. The boat was still a hundred yards offshore and coming in more slowly now. There was a small Zodiac diving boat sporting the ceratopsian emblem anchored near a rocky reef where the Pacific surf crashed. Nearby, he could make out two divers working underwater with blow-torches. The greenish flaring of their torches, deep under the clear water, illuminated a huge metallic structure that looked like a submerged mooring slip. *For what?* he wondered. *A submarine?*

As the yacht drew him past the dive-boat, Chase thought of a plan. He pulled out a sheath knife that was strapped to his thigh under the pant-leg of his shorts. He called to the Kra on the towboat's deck, "Sorry to cut out early!" Grinning, he quickly sliced the towrope.

The Kra screeched in exasperation as Chase neatly sailed down, tugging at one side and then the other of his parachute cords, and landed almost on top of the zodiac. Splashing down, he hastily shed the harness, swam the few strokes to the boat, and clambered aboard.

As the Kra cried out in astonishment and rage, Chase twisted the key and fired up the engine. As he shifted the engine into gear, the two Mexican welders rose on either side. They aimed diver's spear guns at him, but he shoved the throttle arm forward hard and the engine roared. He ducked to avoid their otherwise well-placed shots and the Zodiac raced away.

Behind him, the big boat quickly came around and followed in hot pursuit.

Chase piloted the Zodiac toward Puerto Vallarta as directly as he could, but the dark cruiser forced him to alter course if he intended to survive long enough to get there. It fell in on his tail, easily matching the Zodiac's speed and making repeated efforts to run him down. Chase wove back and forth in front of the gray goliath, desperately searching the smooth ocean ahead for any chance of escape. Glancing around the inside of the Zodiac, he found no weapon aboard with the exception of his knife, which he slipped back into its sheath. The yacht on the other hand, was more well armed than Chase had suspected. An automatic hatch opened on the bow and a weapon Chase knew only too well rose up on a mechanical arm.

It was a Kra light cannon.

Knowing one blast from the weapon could punch a hold through him, the Zodiac, twenty feet of water, and ten feet of coral on the ocean bottom, he steered a zigzag course into an area of rocks and promontories. The fortuitous appearance of these wave-washed obstacles was providential, because it was only a matter of seconds before the Kra came on deck to personally man the laser, sitting in an operator's seat that rotated with the gun barrel. As the Kra lined up a shot, Chase dodged left around a pinnacle that jutted from the ocean. The much larger cruiser was forced to bear right to avoid reefs that lay around it. Meanwhile, the Zodiac skimmed across the shallow light green shoal water. Thereafter, Chase steered from reef to rock, endeavoring to shake the big boat or make its progress so tortuous that the Kra couldn't get in a clear shot.

The strategy worked. The first shot from the light cannon went high and wide, blasting chunks of oyster-covered rock from a sea stack as Chase raced behind its cover. The big boat, though faster than the Zodiac, was unable to turn with the same agility. Knowing it drew much deeper water, Chase chose a course among the rocks that repeatedly forced the cruiser to slow or move offshore to avoid grounding or sideswiping narrow gaps he negotiated easily in the agile Zodiac. More fire came from the light cannon, but all were long shots. Although they dramatically boiled the ocean or scattered rubble off pinnacles, none came near their marks.

Ultimately the skipper of the big boat grew wiser. He moved offshore slightly, flanking Chase in clear water and biding his time. Scanning the seascape ahead, Chase understood that the driver's strategy was bound to succeed. The coastline he needed to pass to reach Puerto Vallarta was one long unbroken stretch of sand. It arced around Banderas Bay for miles with no rocks or sea stacks for cover. The big boat could hang back and wait until its Kra gunner could target Chase with ease as he crossed those last open miles between him and safety. He would need a better plan if he hoped to survive.

He glanced at the big boat and saw the Kra on the foredeck shake a three-fingered fist at him. He looked toward the shore and saw a small white-sand beach between two rocky head-lands. That beach gave him hope of salvation.

He turned the Zodiac sharply toward shore and raced at full speed for the sand.

Tourists at the Hotel Four Seasons, Punta Mita, were accustomed to elegant surroundings and pampering by attentive and well-dressed waiters, bellhops, bartenders, and stewards, as they lazed, played, or swam under the subtropical sun. Now, they were treated to a frightening sight as Chase roared toward the beach with his motor running at full speed. People sunning on the sand or sitting at the palapa bar gaped in astonishment. Waders scattered, screaming.

Chase targeted a stretch of sand where the population was thinnest and drove the Zodiac at full speed over a cresting wave, steering it straight onto the beach. Its momentum carried it far above the wave wash and it came to rest between two parasol-shaded tables where shocked beachgoers gaped, agog with amazement.

As soon as the boat stopped, Chase leapt over the gunwale and quickly mingled with the throng of hotel guests, guessing that the Kra would never risk a shot in such circumstances. Out on the ocean, the dark boat circled once offshore and then raced away to the north.

There were shouts of "Bravo!" from men, and more than one admiring glance from the bikini-clad beach beauties Chase passed as he walked toward the hotel. A white-suited Mexican waiter looked at him, dumbstruck, holding a tray of drinks shoulder-high. Chase walked to him, smiled, nodded, and took a cold bottle of Pacifico off the tray. He took a long pull, and then a deep breath.

"That's hot work," he said, inclining his head toward the Zodiac, now a curiosity to children.

"Si, Señor," the waiter replied, at a loss for other words.

Chase held up the bottle and grinned. "There's nothing like a cold Pacifico on a hot day." He took another swig. "I left my cell phone in Puerto Vallarta. Could you call me a cab, amigo?"

"Si, Señor." The man set his tray on a stand and hurried off to do as bidden.

"Am I impressed?" a feminine voice asked from Chase's rear and to the right. He turned to see an American woman, tall, blond, and fit tightly into a skimpy thong bikini that hugged her form and left little to a man's imagination. She was sitting alone at a small cabaret table with a parasol for shade. She had raised her sunglasses above her forehead to get a good look at him.

He eyed her up and down, made cocky by an excess of adrenaline and testosterone. "I don't know," he replied. *"Are* you impressed?"

"Oh, yes, I am. Have a seat, Handsome." She gestured with a fine, tanned hand at the empty chair opposite her.

He took the seat, to wait for the cab if for no other reason.

"I like a man who makes grand entrances," she purred.

He sipped the Pacifico and began to explain, "I really didn't have too many options—"

She cut him off, saying playfully, "Might I suggest dessert? With champagne? Right now? In my rooms?"

He thought a moment. "I haven't had lunch yet."

"Oh," she said breathily, "I'm sure we can find something for you to eat."

"Señor," the waiter said, having come back sooner than expected. "Your cab ees waiting."

"Let it wait a little longer," Chase said. He took another swig of beer, looking deeply into the woman's blue eyes.

CHAPTER 13

At La Palapa, David Ogilvey and Jeff Miller were looking out to sea, engaged in a worried conversation when Chase came up behind them. He sat down in his chair and startled them by saying to their waiter, "Uno Pacifico mas, por favor."

As the man went for the drink, Ogilvey exclaimed at Chase, "Where the devil have you been?" His wooly eyebrows nearly lifted off his forehead.

"If the devil is a woman," Chase remarked blandly, "then you've got it about right. And speaking of the devil, I think I may have located the entrance to hell."

"Talk sense, boy," the professor scolded. "What happened to you out there? And how did you get back—?"

"I'll explain as we drive north."

"North?" Miller interjected. "But I've got contacts I have to meet here soon."

"Then we'll see you when we get back," Chase said, taking the beer the waiter brought.

"I'm not so sure I want to go with you either," Ogilvey resisted.

"And I'm pretty sure you do."

"How do you figure?"

"Would a fifty-foot-long crocodile pique your curiosity?"

"Fifty feet long!" The professor looked more astonished than when he had first seen Chase. "Why, that could only be Deinosuchus, the largest crocodilian that ever lived. But they have been extinct since the end of the Cretaceous. You don't mean to say——?"

"I do mean to say."

Ogilvey plunked his Pacifico down on the table, frothing it as heavily as Doolah had frothed his blood-drink. "Well then my boy, what are we waiting for? Waiter! La cuenta! Señor Miller will pay."

***

Chase drove a rented white Mercedes Benz north on Highway 200 up the coast. He passed Nuevo Vallarta and turned just after Bucerias onto the coast highway, a small winding road that took them into the jungle country north of Punta Mita and south of Sayulita. He turned onto an even smaller, rutted road and, after having broken a chain lock on a ranchero's gate, he drove into the thick jungle on the south side of Monkey Mountain. He stopped the car on a muddy stretch where the road rounded a jungle bluff. Below was a mangrove swamp. Beyond that, where a jungle stream met the sea, was a sandy beach where several fifty-foot-long crocodiles were sunning themselves.

"What did I tell you?" Chase asked as the professor stared in wide-eyed astonishment.

"Deinosuchus!" Ogilvey exclaimed. "The fiercest predator any shore has ever seen!"

"I have a feeling they're kept as sentries."

"No doubt," Ogilvey agreed, his smile fading. "Only a fool would go anywhere near them. Er. Or, was that what *you* intend to do?"

Chase pointed across the swamp to the promontory on its far side. "The villa's behind those trees. We'd better walk from here or they'll hear our engine."

"This can't be safe," Ogilvey protested.

"I've got this," Chase replied, patting the holster of a Colt .45 he had belted on now that they were away from civilization.

Ogilvey shook his head and muttered to himself as he got out and followed Chase along the sandy tire ruts of the jungle road. The route curved back and forth among overhanging palm trees, strangler fig branches, vines, and other jungle verdure. Along the way, the forest seemed to close down on them like a wet green blanket. Chase paused to inspect two abandoned surfboards. "These look too good to just be left out here," he remarked. He kicked one over with the toe of a sandal, and the sight of some jumbled leg and rib bones half buried in the sand made Ogilvey gasp.

"Dangerous surfing around here," Chase murmured. He knelt to inspect some traces in the sand. "Look at these tracks. Odd shapes. What do you make of them, Doc?"

Ogilvey leaned near the tracks and adjusted his thick glasses. "Three-toed, yes, but not Kra by any stretch. Not really bird-like either. And they're mingled with tracks that clearly have four claws. I'm dumbfounded. This creature is nothing I'm familiar with, either dinosaurian or mammalian."

"So the killers may not be Kra at all," Chase said. "But who—or what—else could they be?"

"These are tracks of a tetrapedal creature," Ogilvey asserted. "See how some of the four-clawed prints overlay the three-clawed prints? That suggests hind feet overstepping front feet in a four-legged animal."

"You're not telling a wildlife biologist anything he doesn't already know," Chase said. "But *which* four-legged animal? That's what I'd like to find out."

Ogilvey straightened up and stared at the bones for a moment. "Judging from the fate of those surfer fellows," he said, "I think I would rather *not* find out."

"Maybe so. But we've been sent here by the President of the United States, and our orders are to find out. So come on." Chase led on until the road had circumvented the mangrove swamp and the enormous crocodilians lurking there. When they neared the compound at the far end of the swamp, Chase paused behind the cover of some low brush beside the main gate to look the place over. A three-storied, multi-terraced villa house was nestled into a notch on the headland that jutted seaward on the north side of the mangrove swamp. Numerous adobe and stucco walls on its perimeter and half a dozen outbuildings for staff and storage were situated among overarching jungle trees.

The buildings bore signs of old age. Adobe walls had cracked and roof tiles had broken, but there was evidence of prodigious repair and upgrading going on, including a dozen Mexican laborers busy on scaffolding around the house or working with shovels on the ground.

"Kra wealth in abundance," Ogilvey observed. "The treasuries of Arran Kra must be a godsend to poor Mexican laborers like those."

"No doubt," Chase agreed. "But I wonder how they've kept word of all this from getting out?"

"Maybe they keep the Mexicans from getting out," Ogilvey suggested. "This road doesn't look like it's seen a vehicle in years."

An odd barking noise came from within the compound's walls. When two dog-like creatures emerged from the main gate and trotted along the road, Chase and Ogilvey slipped into the concealment of the jungle brush. The cover was just sufficient that the animals trotted past them without taking notice, which allowed an opportunity to observe their very peculiar physical make-up. While they were extremely dog-like in behavior and general shape, these animals were clearly not dogs, and not even of a mammalian lineage. Instead, their crocodilian derivation was obvious. Their hides were covered with brown angular scales, not fur. Their heads lacked visible ears. And their jaws were lined with prominent, crocodilian teeth.

"Araripesuchus," Ogilvey whispered once the animals had disappeared along the road. "Cretaceous dog-crocodiles. Did you see how they walked tall on four legs, not sprawling like their more conventional cousins on the beach?"

"I saw it," Chase replied. "And I don't like it. I guess we've figured out what made those tracks."

"And," Ogilvey said in a spooked tone, "what ate those surfers!"

"I wonder if they're trained as guard dogs?" Chase asked. "I wonder if they'll pick up our scent?"

"The fossil record," Ogilvey pontificated despite trembling with adrenaline, "shows that the bones of their nasal passageways were much like those of modern canines. So I think we can safely assume as much."

"What do you mean, safely?" Chase asked.

Suddenly, a pair of hound-dog-like howls went up from the point along the road where the surfer's remains had been.

"Come on," Chase said, gripping Ogilvey's elbow and dragging him out of the brush cover. "They've caught our scent. It will lead them back here."

The animals' yelping chorus increased in volume as they came back swiftly along the road.

"Wh— Where can we go?" Ogilvey asked.

"I'll take my chances in here," Chase said. He pulled Ogilvey through the stuccoed arch of the main gate and into the space between two buildings, where they were momentarily safe from observation by the workers.

The hound-reptiles came through the gate a moment later. They sniffed at the ground like two bloodhounds from hell, but had not yet spotted their quarry. To avoid them, Chase pulled Ogilvey on farther into the complex. Ogilvey urgently pointed above them, where, on the second terrace of the hacienda, were two familiar Kra—Karrik and Doolah. They were conversing while looking out to sea, but turned to observe the howling hound-crocs, which were following Chase and Ogilvey's scent through the villa. Chase pulled Ogilvey through the doorway of a large building before either the Kra or the hound-reptiles spotted them. Inside, they moved through a large dining hall set up in Kra fashion. It lacked a dining table but instead had a large central open floor space surrounded by Kra sitting mats—the open area being the location in which live prey was killed and dismembered by the diners. Crossing the floor space, Chase led Ogilvey out the far side of the room. He closed a wrought-iron gate behind them to block the hound-crocodiles. The area ahead opened out into the white stucco-covered, stepped seating area of a moderately sized arena. It was the sort of place where a wealthy Mexican landowner might once have held private bullfights.

Chase looked around for a way to proceed undetected, but he was dismayed at the bright, whitewashed, sunlit, and barren nature of the arena. As he paused, still clutching the professor by the arm, the hound-crocs appeared at the wrought-iron gate and began barking savagely. They threw themselves against the iron bars, slavering and snarling. The latch held, but just barely. Chase took a few steps away from them, descending to the next lower level of the seating area. He drew his revolver and cocked it.

"So nice you could join us," a mock-cheery voice called from above. Chase glanced up and found that he had stepped into the sight the two Kra on the hacienda's terrace, which overlooked the arena as well as the sea. The Kra had been unarmed, but now each one held a tintza rifle covering him and Dr. Ogilvey.

"Toa-lah! Toa-lah!" the dark Kra, Karrik, cried. In response to his voice, the two dog-crocs sat on their haunches obediently, though growls still rumbled from their throats. A moment later, three Mexican men and several more Kra arrived with automatic weapons and heavy Kra tintza rifles at the ready. They surrounded and quickly disarmed Chase, while Ogilvey stood with his hands raised, moaning in fear.

CHAPTER 14

"So, Ngeester Arrrstrong, you have found your way back to our little hiding place," Karrik said, when he and Doolah had come down to the arena.

"Like some others have before us," Chase muttered.

"Yesss. You refer to the two men with long boards to play in the water. They unfortunately came too near our home here. It was necessary for my toas to eat them."

"Nowadays we call that murder," Chase challenged. "The war is over, or haven't you heard?"

"So I have heard. But a toa gets hungry, war or no war." Karrik patted the head of the nearest dog-croc, which he had summoned to him. It keened like a pit bull eager to be set upon its prey, and looked at Chase hungrily. "The surfer boys had much good meat on them. I must admit I tried just a few tastes of it myself. Verrry sweet. Young and strong hoonahs have the best meat on them. As I am sure you do, Ngeester Arrrstrong. Perhaps I will have a taste, once our koonooku has had his way with you."

"Koonooku?" Ogilvey puzzled. "That's a new vocabulary word for me. An animal?"

"Oh, yesss," Karrik hissed with glee. A thunderous bellow came from the far side of the arena, as if for emphasis. "A verrry large animal."

"Kra are prohibited from killing or cannibalizing humans," Ogilvey blurted angrily. "That's Article One of Section Two of the Terms of Armistice. Or had you forgotten?"

Karrik laughed throatily. "I have never read it." Drool dripped from his fangs. "Don't worry, old greelock. I won't taste your flesh. That gristly meat is fit only for my pets." He stroked the head of the other dog-croc, which whined and licked its chops.

"You won't get away with this," Chase growled. "My government knows we're here."

"And I am sure your government will mourn your loss, when what remains of you is found washed up on a beach near here. Accidents sometimes happen."

"Why do all this?" Chase asked. "What's the point?"

Karrik paused a moment in thought, then said in derogatory tones, "Because you will not live to tell, there is no need to withhold it from you. We will buy more land here, or kill the rancheros and take it. We will establish our own small city-state, with every convenience a Kra could wish—food, sport, blood. Any Mexican official who will not aid us will either have his mind changed with a fistful of diamonds, or have his entrails served to our pet toas. Soon, we will be joined by another who will come here by way of the submarine dock you, er, dropped in on today."

"Saurgon!" Chase muttered.

"Exactly," Karrik gloated. "The one Kra leader who refuses to submit to human rule on earth. Here, he will begin a new North American campaign. Here, he will challenge Gar's weak authority over Kra who foolishly live in peace with hoonahs. Here, he will restart—and win—the war of our homecoming."

"You can't possibly get away with this," Chase growled.

"Why not, Ngeester Arrrstrong? The local Mexicans will get rich helping us. They are loyal enough. Perhaps you intended to expose our little plan? But as I have told you, you won't be with us verrry long." He motioned to several of the men and Kra, who began shoving Chase and Ogilvey roughly toward the brink of the arena, the sandy surface of which was a six-foot drop below them.

Chase swung a fist and knocked one of the men down. Instantly, half a dozen guns were pointed at his face.

"Reluctant to go in?" Karrik asked with a reptilian laugh. "Maybe this will persuade you. Toa-kee!" The two dog-crocs charged forward, growling and slavering. As they approached Chase and Ogilvey, both men turned and dropped into the arena. Chase landed on his feet, while the old paleontologist fell heavily on his side, uttering a loud "Oof!"

They now found themselves in bare surroundings with nothing but sand and a circular stuccoed perimeter wall forty feet in diameter. Eager Kra and humans took seats in the stands above them. The crowd grew quickly to several dozen humans and six Kra. All chatted excitedly as if in anticipation of a great event.

On one side of the arena, two tall, rusty, steel-plated gates penetrated the wall. One of these opened. Chase and Ogilvey both gasped when they saw the creature within a huge, metal-barred stall behind it.

"Coahuilaceratops!" Ogilvey exclaimed. "Or triceratops, depending on which side of the border you inhabit. Just look at the size of those brow horns!" The beast, tawny yellow-brown in color and the size of a small elephant, was uninterested in the professor's babbling. It concentrated on slashing at the stall's bars with the three horns on its face, biting at the bars with its powerful, hooked beak, and even raking the bars with spikes along the edges of its bone-armored frill. All the while, it bellowed in rage.

"I don't care which side of the border he's from," Chase muttered. "All I want to know is what's making him so mad."

The answer came quickly. The barrel end of a Kra tintza rifle protruded from an opening in the back of the stall and a bolt of blue electricity leaped from it, playing over the animal's back and short tail and enraging it further. When the bars of the stall parted to the sides, the beast charged into the arena, bucking and bellowing. It paused, seemingly surprised to be free of its tormenter, with only the bare stucco walls and sandy floor around it, and absolutely nothing to vent its rage upon except—

"It will trample us!" Ogilvey cried out as the behemoth bellowed again and turned to face them. "With those elephantine feet! Or impale us on those colossal brow horns!" It lowered those horns and pawed the ground. "Oh dear!" the professor cried. "It's preparing to charge!"

"Shut up, Doc," Chase commanded. "Let me think."

"About what, Chase? About being smashed? About being impaled?"

"About this." Chase ran several paces straight at the beast, threw up his hands, and shouted, "Yahh!"

The ceratopsian stopped in its tracks, momentarily surprised by Chase's boldness. Then it pawed the ground and issued a rumbling snort that was much louder than any bull moose Chase had ever heard.

"Look!" Ogilvey observed. "The fleshy area behind his beak expands to produce that super loud noise. I have wondered why the nasal openings of ceratopsian skulls were so big. Now I know! It's to amplify their snorts!"

"I don't care how loud he snorts, Doc!" Chase called over his shoulder. "I just don't want him to…" The beast lowered its snout until its brow horns pointed straight at Chase.

"Charge!" Chase concluded just as the beast bellowed again and thundered straight for him. He jumped to the side, dodging just outside the reach of the right horn. He went to the ground as the animal thundered past but was on his feet again in an instant.

Now the monster had Ogilvey in its sights. The professor was not as fleet as Chase and though he ran gamely on his spindly legs, he had no hope of dodging or outrunning the onrushing horror. The beast closed in on him quickly and hooked its head. Its left brow horn caught Ogilvey a glancing blow to the shoulder and knocked him to the ground. The beast wheeled with incredible agility for such a massive animal and stood over Ogilvey, who lay sprawled on his back. The crowd roared in anticipation of the kill.

As the goliath took a menacing step toward Ogilvey and lowered its horns, Chase knew he had to act swiftly or the professor was finished. "Ey! Torro!" he shouted on an impulse, just like a bullfighter. The ceratopsian turned its massive head and glared at him with its beady eyes. The crowd hushed.

In the momentary pause that followed, Chase availed himself of the only matador cape he could find—he tore off his red-and-white flower-patterned shirt, popping the buttons in his haste. He waved the shirt at the animal the way a matador would, hoping its bright color would focus the beast's attention on him and away Ogilvey, who had begun back-pedaling on the sand with all fours, like a turtle on its back.

"Ey! Torro!" Chase shouted again. He took several strutting strides toward the beast, as he had seen proud matadors do, and shook the shirt out to one side as those matadors had done with their capes. "Leave the old man alone!" he challenged. "Come and try me!"

"Bravo!" a human voice hooted derisively from above. A particularly hideous cackling laugh came from Karrik.

The ceratopsian, angered by Chase's bold approach and taunting cape work, bellowed again. And then it charged. Chase stood his ground as he had seen bullfighters do. He waved the shirt in front of him. This enticed the onrushing creature to dip its horns in an attempt to pierce the object of its anger with a vicious head toss. Chase stepped aside at the last instant, pivoted, and drew the shirt out of the way as the colossal beast thundered past.

"Ole!" several Mexicans shouted, sounding more appreciative this time.

The coahuilaceratops pivoted to face Chase again, pausing to observe him with narrowed, rage-filled eyes. It seemed momentarily confused by its failure to flatten this puny opponent. It pawed the ground, bull-like, and let out another hellishly loud snort. But it hesitated to charge.

"Ole! Ngeester Arrrstrong!" Karrik mocked. "I think he will get you next try."

Chase watched out of a corner of his eye as Ogilvey, who had struggled to his feet and limped away, tottered to one wall of the arena, removed somewhat from the action. This allowed the germ of a new plan to hatch in his mind.

"Ey! Torro!" he called once more, this time running toward a place on the wall where a crack split the stucco from base to rim. As he expected, the animal thundered after him. With the crowd roaring in anticipation, he waved the shirt and the animal took the bait. This time, however, Chase had a new intent. He used his shirt-cape to guide the ceratopsian's charge straight into the wall. He flicked the shirt aside as the horned beast impacted the wall head-on at full stride. Huge chunks of stucco-coated adobe flew in all directions.

There were surprised *oohs* and *ahhs* from the spectators. The beast seemed stunned momentarily. Stopped in its tracks, it shook its head, gyrating the giant, horn-studded frill over its shoulders. Then it backed away a few steps and turned to look for Chase.

Forming a plan as he went, Chase ran a short distance along the wall, and then stopped and challenged the beast with another shout and flourish of his cape. After another shake of its massive head to clear its small brain, the ceratopsian bellowed and charged again. Again, Chase deftly led it into a collision with the wall. This time, a huge section of stucco peeled off the underlying adobe bricks as they rocked with the power of the impact. And then, as Chase had hoped, the entire section of wall collapsed, tumbling down into the space between the two impacts. The coahuilaceratops wasn't finished. It gored the pile of rubble, pushing through it like a bulldozer—and bolted out of the arena.

The crowd hushed. Men and Kra got up and ran in multiple directions, responding to the entirely unexpected threat of a huge beast running amok within their compound.

Ignored by those above, Chase rushed to Ogilvey. He shouted at the stunned old man's face, "Can you run?"

The old professor stood frozen in place with his back to the wall. He seemed too shocked by events to be sure of anything. "I— I think so," he said.

"Then come on!" Chase grabbed the collar of his shirt and tugged him toward the new opening in the stockade. "We're getting outta here!"

They scrambled over the fallen bricks and emerged into what appeared to be the central plaza of the compound. The coahuilaceratops was nowhere in sight. They ran together in what Chase guessed was the direction of the arched gate. But as they crossed the front of the hacienda, its twin wooden front doors opened wide.

Karrik stepped out and quickly leveled a tintza rifle at Chase's mid-section. "Nesooka!" he shouted. It was the Kranaga word for "Halt!"

Chase and Ogilvey froze in their tracks.

"Verrry good, Ngeester Arrrstrong!" Karrik hissed gloatingly as he sauntered toward them. "You have survived my koonooku. But you will not survive *me.*" He came near and thrust the tintza rifle's muzzle under Chase's chin, as the sound of other Kra and humans' running feet could be heard approaching.

"Keck! Keck! Keck!" Karrik laughed with savage glee. "Prepare to—"

A loud bellow announced the arrival of the Coahuilaceratops. It came suddenly around a bend in one of the compound's many lanes. If a Kra's expressionless reptilian face could register fear, Karrik's did just that.

The animal didn't hesitate. Already at full charge, it thundered toward the three of them as if intending to impale one on each of its horns. Chase pulled Ogilvey to the side, while Karrik stood his ground, confidently unleashing the rifle's blue electric bolt. The bolt struck the ceratopsian on its horned nose and beak, but rather than slowing it, only seemed to further enrage it. It leveled its horns at Karrik, who discarded his rifle and leapt for safety, but just a fraction of a second too slowly. Caught by a brow horn in the middle of his ribcage, the Kra was lifted off the ground and sent flying. He flew twenty feet away, smashed into the stuccoed front of his hacienda, and fell to the ground in a crumpled heap.

While this transpired, Chase dragged Ogilvey to his feet by one shoulder. He cast a quick glance at Karrik, who was no longer a threat, lying motionless and gushing blood from his mouth. "Come on!" he commanded, wheeling and dragging Ogilvey around the far corner of the hacienda as men and Kra came to Karrik's aid. As the two fugitives hurried away along a back lane, the new arrivals commenced firing tintza bolts at the beast, which continued its rampage, bellowing and snorting and thundering amok in the plaza.

"I've never seen an animal resist that electric bolt," Ogilvey marveled as they hurried down the back lane. "Even a T rex will run for its life."

"Why don't they switch to lasers and kill it?" Chase wondered.

"They keep some pretty strange pets around here," Ogilvey remarked. "Perhaps they don't want it dead."

The ceratopsian continued bellowing and the electric bolts crackled. Chase assisted the limping professor to the gateway they had come in by. Finding it unguarded, they hurried out into the jungle unnoticed by those inside, who were preoccupied with other more urgent matters. For its part, the enraged ceratopsian finally smashed through a perimeter wall. Scattering adobe blocks before it and uttering a final bellow, it thundered into the forest.

By now, Chase and Ogilvey had ducked deep into the brush, and fortunately so. The hound-crocodiles charged out the hole in the wall, baying and looking around. But the beasts were not interested in humans. Instead, they rushed at the enraged coahuilaceratops, which was laying about with its horns, bringing down palm trees and outbuildings with single impacts. One of the hound-crocs rushed forward and set its teeth into the ceratopsian's flank, but that only increased the horned beast's rage. Wheeling quickly, it drove a brow horn downward and impaled the croc through the gut, pinning it to the ground. It cried out, "Ai-ai-ai!" like a hurt pup.

Leaving it in its death convulsions, the ceratopsian swung around quickly and caught a Kra who had come out of the compound with tintza bolt crackling. Hooking him on its nose horn, it tossed him high in the air over its frilled head.

"Let's don't stick around to see how this turns out," Ogilvey urged. They turned and scurried off along the road they had come in on.

"I wish there was something I could do to help that Coahuila beast," Chase said as they ran.

"My, what a soft touch you turn out to be for animals, no matter how fierce," Ogilvey mocked as he hopped long on a gimpy leg. "Tarzan would be proud of you."

"You don't understand, Doc. I want to see this whole place leveled. It's got the stench of Saurgon all over it."

When it seemed they had safely left the carnage behind around a bend in the road, they slowed to accommodate Ogilvey's limp. When an unpleasantly familiar howl came from behind, they turned to face a renewed menace. The second dog-crocodile had chosen to pursue them.

"What'll do we do now?" Ogilvey cried in a quavering voice. "I can't possibly outrun that monster."

"How about this?" Chase pulled the knife from its sheath on his thigh. As the beast rushed to close with them, he knelt and launched the blade with a deft throw that sent it through the air end-over-end. It made one, two, three turns and ended in the throat of the araripesuchus. The beast tumbled to the ground, snarling a last, convulsive death growl.

"Thrown as well as Tarzan!" Ogilvey exclaimed.

Chase went to the beast, now lying still. He retrieved the weapon and wiped blood from the blade on some bushes. "I almost forgot I had that on me," he said.

"I'm glad you remembered before I was in that thing's stomach," Ogilvey chortled. "But what's become of your concern for animals?"

"My concern stops when they want to eat us for lunch."

They moved along the road without further interference. The sounds of the coahuilaceratops confrontation faded behind them as they made their way back to the car.

"Greelock indeed!" Ogilvey muttered as he got in.

"Greelock," Chase said as he started the engine. "I heard Karrik call you that. What is it?"

"A type of pterodactyl," Ogilvey muttered. "The closest modern equivalent would be a buzzard, I suppose."

"Buzzard!" Chase laughed. "He was calling you an old buzzard. Not far off the mark."

"Laugh if you will. But I resented his implication I was so distasteful."

"At least he wasn't sizing you up for his next meal."

Chase put the car in gear and negotiated a turn-around on the narrow road. As he drove back toward civilization, he said, "Speaking of meals, I'm getting hungry myself. Bullfighting is hard work."

***

In the late morning two days later, Chase, Ogilvey, and Jeff Miller sat at a table under a sun umbrella on the beach in front of La Palapa, sipping coffee and watching the waves of the blue Pacific wash the sandy shore. The parasailing boats were at it again, and gaily colored chutes were moving to and fro in the azure sky. But the dark cabin cruiser was gone.

Miller fished through a large briefcase he habitually carried. "Here's a new satellite phone, Chase," he said, putting what appeared to be a rather large cell phone on the table. "Try to take better care of that one. And here," he pushed a leather case across the tablecloth. "It's a new Colt .45, to replace the one Karrik's people took from you."

"What I would like to know," Ogilvey said as he fussily squeezed the last drops from a lime wedge into his Clamato-and-coffee drink, "is what they will do next, now that their little plan has been exposed? What can they hope to accomplish here on the Costa Verde now?"

"Maybe just a hideaway where they can feed their, er, appetites," Miller suggested.

"You mean their taste for human blood?" Chase asked.

"That, and their desire to stage animal versus human games."

"That doesn't quite explain the big crocs, or those nasty crocodile-dogs, does it?"

"What better way to discourage visitors than to surround

themselves with deinosuchid and araripesuchid crocs?" Ogilvey suggested. "The coastline in the Monkey Mountain area is legendary for great surf and beautiful hiking. But what surfer will go near a beach patrolled by giant crocodiles? And what hiker will brave a coastal trail where human bones keep turning up?"

"They've convinced me to stay away," Miller replied. "But now the Federales will be keeping a much closer eye on developments. And if Saurgon knows we're onto him, then he might not try any bigger schemes."

"I don't know," Chase said. "Knowing Saurgon is involved, I can't believe they will behave themselves for long."

"I'm with you on that," Miller agreed, his expression darkening. "I haven't mentioned to you yet that our agents in Sub-Saharan Africa have lost track of Saurgon. He seems to have disappeared from the continent completely."

"Do you think he could already be here?" Ogilvey wondered.

"No," Chase muttered. "I'd have recognized him if I saw him or got a whiff of him. He's got the smell of a snake."

"And a snake's treachery," Ogilvey agreed. "I'm sure I would have recognized him too. But he is obviously too devious to confront us himself. He lets his henchmen, or henchkra, be the middlemen, keeping his movements concealed. They were obviously preparing the way for him. But whether he will ever arrive now that we've learned as much as we have, is unknown."

"One thing I don't get," Chase said. "How does someone as important as Saurgon just disappear?"

Miller shrugged and took a sip of his coffee. "Last we saw of him, he was inspecting the new Kra wharves in their treaty lands on the Skeleton Coast of Namibia. The whole of their capital city there, Arran Deess, is a very hostile place if you're a human. It was hard to tail him in a seaport that's mostly Kra with very few humans. We think he developed a submarine of some kind. Gar confirms there are plans for such things."

"He built a submarine?" Ogilvey marveled.

"Yes," Miller affirmed. "And then promptly disappeared in it."

"So he could turn up in any corner of the world," Chase said.

"Anyplace with a coastline, like here. But we've had satellite surveillance on that underwater boat slip since you spotted it. So far, no U-boat. We're pretty sure he won't show up here, thanks to you. Where he'll go next, we don't know. The ocean is an awfully big place."

"And deep," Ogilvey concurred.

Chase shrugged. "What will keep him from coming here after we leave?"

"Nothing, perhaps. But we have asked the U.S. Consulate to demand that Mexico put a tight watch on the villa at Monkey Mountain."

"Let's hope they do," Chase said with a hint of doubt. "But the Federales haven't stopped the drug cartels, have they? And Kra agents like Karrik and Doolah have more money at their disposal for payoffs than even the drug lords. I would bet on the Kra to win that power struggle."

"True," Miller agreed. "But in this case we've got additional allies. Our satellite surveillance teams have been in touch with some interesting Mexican groups—the Ministry of the Environment, for instance. Our space photos show the Kra have damaged a mangrove swamp by building a surface boat-slip in part of it. And there's more. Any effort on their part to expand the villa will trigger a whole series of legal citations. Mexico has modernized its environmental laws. There are laws against the destruction of iguana rookery trees, land crab spawning estuaries, sea turtle egg-laying dunes, shorebird nesting sites, and so on. There will be enough potential violations of environmental regulations to entangle the entire development in red tape and mandatory inspections. Those inconveniences will make it hard for them to maintain a secretive operation."

"Maybe they'll just feed the inspectors to their pets," Ogilvey said.

"I suppose that's possible. But it would bring down even

more heat on their heads."

Chase nodded. "It's a pretty bureaucratic solution, but it could put a halt to their building plans. Maybe even that under-water boat slip. But there's still the question of how effective the Federales will be."

"We're worried about that too. But so far the Kra seem to be getting the message. Our twenty-four-hour, seven-days-a-week satellite watch already shows they've quit working on the place. The construction crews are gone. There's nothing much left, except a few big crocs and a certain very large, very angry horned dinosaur."

"Brilliant!" Ogilvey exclaimed. "Using the threat of environmental laws to ruin Saurgon's schemes!"

Chase was thoughtful. "So Karrik is dead, and Doolah's plans are ruined. But Saurgon has plenty more lackeys. There are dozens of other ex-military Kra all over the world. I have a feeling we'll be meeting their kind again."

"Let's hope you are wrong on that account," Miller said.

"Ola! Chase Armstrong!" Felina called, coming toward them across the sand, clad in an even skimpier outfit than before.

"Ola," Chase replied, with a hint of a smug smile.

"Weell you parasail again today?" she asked.

"Not likely," he replied.

"Weell you be at the dance club tonight?"

He nodded slowly in affirmation.

"Muy bueno!" she said. Her dark eyes glowed with antici-pation.

CHAPTER 15

Kit sighed heavily. She turned off the ignition of her little red Volkswagen bug, which she had driven to a parking area outside the gates of Arran Kra on the new, smooth highway. She got out and made her way into the city, ignoring the glory of its newly revealed architecture and grandness of its streets and passageways as she walked along them to the Temple of Love.

She had come to pay a visit to Gana, whom she knew would be in attendance there for a ceremony marking her child's third lunar month since hatching. She entered the temple, a small one by Kra standards. It was intended to be a dimly lit and cozy place suited to comfortable reflections of those celebrating quiet ceremonies in affirmation of love between males and females, and parents and offspring as well—for such loves were of a common source among Kra as well as humans.

She found Gana in a small chamber, sitting on a couch of sorts and watching as her child, Jonak, played with a toy duckbilled dinosaur made of a rubbery material similar to a dog's chew-toy, which the young one was using for much the same purpose.

Seeing Kit at the doorway, Gana motioned her to come in and join her on the couch.

Kit took the offered seat. After a moment, she sighed again.

"Chay-su Arrrmstrong?" Gana asked.

"How did you guess?"

"Kra act same way when… lovesick."

Kit smiled ruefully. "Lovesick," she repeated. "I suppose

that's it."

She turned to Gana and gestured with uplifted palms. "What am I supposed to do?"

"Ah!" Gana said, raising a clawed index finger. "You come to right person—er, right Kra. I tell you."

"Okay," Kit said uncertainly. "What?"

"First, when you love someone, you must get a big piece of very fresh, very bloody raw meat. Chew it many times, then feed it to him from your own mouth."

"What?" Kit cried in astonishment.

"This never fails to excite Gar's interest in me."

"Yeah, but, *raw meat?* That doesn't sound too romantic to me." Kit consciously tried not to offend Gana by shuddering at the thought of her idea.

"Okay!" Gana said. "Better idea! You catch small, live, hoonah rat. You bring it to him in your teeth, still squeaking. That is much more romantic!"

"Oh, Gana! No!" Kit shook her head in disgust. "That may be the Kra idea of romance, but I'm not going to run around with a live rodent in my teeth!"

Gana cocked her head and looked at Kit in surprise. Then she nodded thoughtfully. "Oh, yes," she said. "I see. But, too bad, Kee-tah. It work for me every time. Gar start the mating dance before he even know his feet are moving! And then we strut together. And then we flap our wings together. And then we—"

"But Chase doesn't have wings!" Kit protested. "And you don't need to tell me the whole Kra mating ritual. I've heard about it a dozen times. I've even seen it a couple of times—too many."

"Sorry, Kee-tah."

"Let's face it," Kit said with another sigh. "When it comes to love, humans and Kra just don't have the same instincts."

"Poor humans! You are such primitive creatures."

Kit got up slowly and turned to go. "Thanks anyway Gana, for the, um, advice."

"You welcome, Kee-tah. Goodbye."

PART FOUR

DINOSAUR WRANGLERS

She was a big rex, bearing a dark, lion-like mane.

CHAPTER 16

It was a brisk, cool, late September morning in Montana's high country. The big parasaurolophuses, Rufus and Henrietta, were acting strangely. Now that their babies were bigger, the little ones were ready to run. Their antics distressed Henrietta. She moved around the pasture, never wanting to be far from the ten fledglings, who raced after the older triplets, Huey, Louie, and Dufus, striving to keep up with them and create an expanded herd. The fledglings had attained sizes comparable to their human ranch-mates, fed a rich diet of regurgitated half-digested hay and grass by their constantly attentive parents. And the triplets had eaten enough on their own to increase to nearly elephantine size. All this flesh on the hoof made for a crowded space within the pasture, and threatened to demolish its white equestrian fence if one or another of the restless youngsters romped too close to it.

Rufus, the biggest of all and overseer of the action, had changed as well. He had recently begun making a new call, which seemed almost a summons. It was a long hoarse honk, repeated over and over. It seemed to amplify the triplets' and the babies' urge to herd-up and run around the pasture. They became the equivalent of a flock of flying geese, but on the ground.

Dr. Ogilvey, Will, and Kit Daniels had come to the fence to watch and wonder at the antics of their duckbilled neighbors. Chase came up the drive in his gunmetal Corvette with the convertible top down. He parked in the graveled area between the house and barn and shut off the rumbling engine.

Kit came to him, followed by Dr. O and her father. "Hello stranger," she said.

He got out. "Sorry I've been away so much," he said. "I just got back from DC. Had a meeting with the President. Now I'm on my way home from the airport in Helena. I'm late for a meeting with Gar and some Kra officials. I just thought I'd stop by and say hi. What's going on?"

At that moment, Rufus let out one of his long bellows.

Kit smiled. "That's what's going on."

"What a noise," Chase said. "It's even louder than the usual call."

Ogilvey said, "That odd call has been going on for days, now. It's particularly strident today. Gar says this may be the day."

"What day?" Chase asked.

"The day their migration begins. If not today, then perhaps tomorrow."

Another vehicle came up the drive. In contrast to Chase's rumbling machine, there was only a little putt-putt as Maddy Meyer pulled up on her pink Vespa. She dismounted and hugged Kit. "What's up?" she asked.

"It's Rufus," Kit replied. "He and his family are leaving us. And I'm going to be broken-hearted when they go."

"Don't get yourself too worked up," Dr. O said. "If things work out, I may be able to arrange for you to go with them."

"What?" Maddy said. "Kit can't go *anywhere!* She starts school next week. It's our junior year at Montana State in Bozeman. I'm the one who'll be broken-hearted if she's not there with me. What will I do for fun?"

"She won't be gone too long," Ogilvey told her. "But these extraordinary times call for extraordinary school scheduling."

"Anyway," Chase said. "I can't stay. Gar is waiting to discuss this very migration."

"What about it?" Kit asked.

"When I find out, I'll let you know."

He fired up the Vette and as he drove off with a parting wave, Maddy bumped Kit with an elbow. "What's up with you two?" she asked.

"When I find out," Kit replied, "I'll let you know."

***

The next morning found Kit and Chase on an unexpected mission in Tyrannosaur Valley, which had once been called the Stillwater River Canyon. They were on horseback, Kit on Lucky and Chase on Buck.

Kit smiled at Chase, eyeing approvingly just how tall he sat in the saddle.

"You look good in a cowboy hat," she said.

"When you're doing cowboy work," he said, smiling back at her, "you wear cowboy clothes."

They had ridden to a place near the center of the valley, where Dr. Ogilvey had located a pack of young tyrannosaurs. This year's fledglings, they were not so different from Rufus and Henrietta's brood, except for their sharp teeth and claws. Like Rufus's brood, the rex young were running in a pack, leaping and playing, while waiting for their parents to return from hunt with gullets full of food to regurgitate. These fledglings, like the parasaurolophus fledglings, were about human sized. They were fine sights to behold, their sleek bodies covered head-to-toe with lion-like feather fur of a pale tawny color all over them. Some were faintly spotted like lion cubs.

Dr. Ogilvey sat behind Gar in a quahka hunkered in brush beside the two horses. "One or two matriarchs usually stand guard while other rexes hunt," he observed. "I wonder where they are? Perhaps the chicks are old enough to fend for themselves."

Chase scanned the valley from cliff to cliff, carefully eyeing stands of birch trees that might conceal a threat. "Mom's not at home, I guess."

"That will make our job easier," Ogilvey concluded.

"I'm still not sure why we need to do this," Kit said edgily.

Ogilvey grinned his slightly bucktoothed smile. "We need to collar a fledgling rex to see if its path to the winter range follows the same path as the adults. This is expected, to be sure, but it has not been proven scientifically. Even the Kra aren't certain if their paths diverge or stay close."

"Gah," Gar agreed.

"Let's get to it then," Chase said. "I saw them do this in an old movie, *The Valley Of Gwangi*." He slapped Buck on the rump with a coil of lasso rope he was holding and shouted "Hyah!" The horse galloped toward the gathering of rexes and Lucky followed, carrying a reluctant Kit with her.

"If they're like most predators," Chase said as they galloped side-by-side toward the pack, "They'll fear us if we don't show any fear ourselves."

"And what if they're not like most predators?"

Chase didn't answer. He made straight for the nearest of the dozen young rexes, spinning up his lariat. He tossed the rope well, but the rex he had chosen ducked it and sprinted away faster than the horses were moving.

Kit, the more experienced cowhand, had anticipated the moves of the rexes. She cut one rex out from the pack, quickly spun her lasso, and tossed it with finesse over the animal's head. Chase got another lasso on the struggling creature as it tried to pull away from Lucky, who tugged back on the rope where Kit had lashed it around her saddle horn. When Chase coaxed Buck to similarly pull back on his rope, the rex was immobilized between the two horses. Though its struggles were prodigious, it was out-muscled by the two cow ponies.

"Gyak!" it cried like a distressed eagle. "Gyak!"

Kit dismounted and ran to the rex. Approaching it from behind, she grabbed a scaly foot in both hands and heaved up on it with all her strength, dumping the rex over on its side. It made a plaintive cry, almost like a sheep's bleat. Then it snarled and snapped at her, but its neck was constrained by Chase pulling his lariat tight and holding its head back. Kit swiftly hogtied the hind legs with a short length of rope. She stood straight when finished and held a hand high like a calf-roper at a rodeo. Instantly, she got snapped on the butt cheek by the rex lashing out with its tufted tail tip. Will Daniels, who had been stationed nearby on his four-wheeled all-terrain vehicle, rushed in to help her by holding onto the tail. Meanwhile, Chase dismounted Buck and pulled radio-collar gear from a saddlebag. As he knelt and prepared to fasten the collar on the yearling's neck, Kit asked, "Why couldn't we have just used a tranquilizer dart?"

"I don't know the exact dose to use. Too little and you could get bitten."

"Or butt slapped," Kit said, rubbing a sore hind cheek.

"Too much, and an overdose might kill it."

"Furthermore," Ogilvey asserted, coming to join them, "Rex babies play rough. All rexes have a pecking order, just like chickens in a henhouse. And they start young. So, if we left this young one drugged and helpless on the ground, or let him wander off half asleep, he could end up permanently maimed by a few bites from his, er, playmates."

Indeed, the fledgling rex pack was watching the restrained animal with keen interest, and edging nearer.

"Um," Kit said, "we're sort of—surrounded. Have you noticed?"

Chase was busy tightening the collar's bolt. Kit waved her arms at the rexes. "Hyah!" she shouted, scattering them.

A loud roar turned all heads. "Oh-oh," Kit said. A fully-grown female rex had appeared around a bend in the canyon and was coming on at full stride. The restrained yearling bleated again, "Gyak!" In response, the female increased her speed. She was a big rex, tawny on the flanks, but bearing a dark, lion-like mane of feather hackles on her head and neck that made her look unusually ferocious, even among the top predators of Tyrannosaur Valley. Her long tawny tail twitched side-to-side angrily, waving a dark tufted tip that again was reminiscent of the top predators of the African veldt. No matter that she was female—as Ogilvey had long-since pointed out, no outward distinction as between lions and lionesses existed between the genders of rex. And that apparently included ferocity.

Kit stood and watched, her eyes growing wide and her voice nervous. "I think maybe you haven't trained her in human aversion yet, Chase."

"In any case," Ogilvey said, "T-rex parental instincts may override the best aversion-to-humans training we could give. Here she comes!"

"Collar's almost on!" Chase said.

Gar had been waiting for this moment. He stood his machine and let loose its loud, threatening parasaurolophus honk. There was no effect. The angry mother continued her charge.

"She's determined to save her offspring," Ogilvey said.

"Or eat us," Kit said.

"Or both," Will said.

As the rex came near, Gar strode his machine to intervene and unleashed its powerful electric bolt. The arc drove her back, but she tried to circle him to get at the humans molesting her young one. Gar intercepted her again with another bolt. She stopped, growling and lashing her tufted tail back and forth. But she seemed to comprehend that she couldn't get past Gar. The other babies gathered around her, chirping worriedly.

"Collar's on!" Chase cried. He rose and moved toward Buck, keeping a hand on the tethering rope.

Kit undid the lash around the animal's feet and backed away as well. Will held the tail for a moment as the two riders mounted and shook their lassos off the rex's neck. Then Will let the tail go and ran behind his four-wheeler for safety. There was no need for concern, however, as the terrified yearling ran swiftly to the protected ground under its mother's belly.

"Let's hope she'll still accept him as one of her chicks with that new collar on," Ogilvey said.

The big rex bent and looked the baby over, paying close attention to the collar. She sniffed at it several times. The baby responded to the nearness of its elder as baby rexes always do. It made a small, begging whimper and nuzzled her nose. In response, the big female's sides heaved and she barfed up a glob of bloody meat directly into the baby's open mouth. It gulped mightily to get the entire mass down.

"Ta-dah!" Ogilvey cried. "No harm done!"

"I guess not," Chase agreed. "Mission accomplished."

"Now let's get out of this Valley of Gwangi," Kit said, "before another big rex comes along!"

THOMAS P. HOPP

CHAPTER 17

When they arrived at the ranch house, they found the para-saurolophus family had gone. Kit rode Lucky out along the fence line to the nest and then returned looking sad as Gar hunkered his machine down and he and Dr. O got out. "They left!" she said, red-faced. "Just like that."

"Did you expect them to say goodbye?" Chase's joke wasn't appreciated.

"Of course not," Kit said. "But—I'll miss them."

"Gonna be awful quiet around here," Will said as he dismounted his four-wheeler.

Ogilvey said officiously, "We must make immediate preparations to get on the road after them."

"What do you mean we?" Kit asked. "I've got school to think about—"

Ogilvey grinned. "Oh, that's quite simple, Kit. I have already spoken to the dean and some other faculty members. You'll be welcome in their new distance-learning program. You can get class credits by telecommuting via your fighter-walker's radio satellite link."

"I guess that would be okay, but—"

"You will also be eligible to take a special foreign language class—Kranaga."

"Kranaga? But how—"

"Taught by none other than Gar, the Kra, who has just been appointed an adjunct faculty member by the regents of Montana State University."

"I guess congratulations are in order for you," she said to

Gar, "but—"

"And finally, my dear," Ogilvey interrupted again, "you will earn a full biology course credit for observing the migration and writing mid-term and final reports—the course being taught by none other than, well, me!"

"Okay, Doc. You've convinced me."

Ogilvey grinned. "I can see your undergraduate thesis in the making, entitled something like, 'The New Great Dinosaur Migration From Montana To West Texas,' complete with research notes."

Kit smiled. "It's the kind of thing I dreamed about as a kid. Now it's all coming true."

"Chase and Gar will be our drivers in their quahkas. Our jobs will be to make observations along the way. Meanwhile Chase and Gar will share the duty of assuring the plant eaters don't run amok in towns and farms."

"What about the meat eaters? Aren't they worse?"

"Interestingly, the T rexes tend to shadow the herds and pick off strays, but otherwise don't tend to eat much. They like to eat light and keep moving."

Chase had been listening while arranging gear in the back compartments of his quahka. "Come on Kit," he said. "Get your stuff. I've already got the camping gear loaded, including a tent for each of us. All you've got to do is pack your travel clothes. We can leave first thing in the morning."

Kit hurried inside, and soon returned with two big suitcases, a backpack, and a duffel bag.

Chase smiled wryly. "A woman can't just pack one bag, can she? I don't know where all that stuff is supposed to go."

"You'll just have to make room," she replied.

"You're just like your mother," Will said. "She always needed just a few extra things. Then she came out to the jeep loaded down like you, Kit."

"I just want to be prepared to dress for… anything," Kit said.

"Yes, yes," Ogilvey agreed. "There may be some nights

spent in towns or cities, but other nights will be out under the stars. I expect the dinosaurs to avoid civilization, if for no other reason than their preference for food. The herbivores will find little of interest in town. They have already proven themselves to be much like modern mammalian herds. They love the same grassy forage as elk, bison, and antelope, but also love bushes and trees. Fortunately that includes many weedy and invasive species like Russian thistle and tamarisk. They'll be improving the land as they go."

***

The next morning, Chase and Gar drove their quahkas down from Arran Kra at first light.

Kit was surprised to see Maddy on the front porch as well, her Vespa parked nearby.

"You're up kinda early—for you," she said to her friend.

"I couldn't let you go without saying goodbye."

They hugged. "Goodbye," Kit said. "Do my share of partying for me, will you?"

"You can count on me. Be careful, Kit. A girl could get eaten out there."

They laughed, and smiled at each other with melancholy fondness.

"Come," Ogilvey said. "We must not delay any further. Gar warns me that dinosaurs travel overland at speeds that may surprise us. They can go very far, very fast, with little water, running constantly because of their generally light builds."

"Are all of 'em going south for the winter?" Will asked.

"Most, though not all," Dr. O replied. "The migrants will include the rexes, triceratops, pachycephalosaurs, and those spunky little orodromeuses, which have proliferated at a phenomenal rate. People will be glad there are rexes to eat up the excess herbivores before the land along the route is stripped bare."

Will hugged Kit. "It sounds like a grand trip, Little Girl. I hope it works out like you want it to."

"It will, Daddy."

Maddy got in one last hug. "Oh Kit!" she exclaimed, squeezing tears from the corners of her eyes. "Text me often. It won't be the same without you here on campus. Send lots of selfie photos with Chase and some dinosaurs. Come back soon —and in one piece."

With Rufus, Henrietta, and the young parasaurolophuses gone, the ranch was silent except for Nelda's insistent lowing. "Milking time," Will said. "I'd better go deal with that." As he walked toward the pasture, Kit and the others mounted the quahkas.

Will called over his shoulder, "Be careful out there. Them dinos is still about the orneriest beasts I ever seen."

"I'll be careful, Daddy."

Chase said, "Don't worry, Will. I'll keep us both safe. See you when we get back."

He and Gar closed their canopies and then strode off, heading up the old switchback road that led from the ranch house to the high prairie.

To make certain the migration was in full effect, they checked some likely spots where dinosaurs might linger. Looping just slightly out of their way, they headed west to Tyrannosaur Valley and followed it up into the mountains. There was no sign anywhere of the rexes that just days before were common on their nesting turf. Now the big adults and their broods were gone.

Ogilvey explained, "They will follow the herds, picking off any stragglers. A broken leg or any injury that makes one of the herbivores fall behind will quickly be fatal. But that is all in the balance of nature. All of the healthy and strong herbivores will arrive safely on their winter grazing lands in South and West Texas."

Ogilvey lectured on for a while, until they crossed the mountain pass and moved onto the high plain where the quetzalcoatlus rookery was still in full swing. When they stopped and opened their canopies, Kit exclaimed, "Phew! They still have that same ripe smell, only more of it!"

"Yes, yes," Ogilvey agreed. "But they will fly off soon, the last migrants to leave the area, after the adults have foraged the last remaining carcasses. Just look at how those new babies have grown! They are at least twelve feet tall! And look at them flapping their wings, practicing for the day they will take to the air. It's a beautiful sight to behold!"

Some of the young animals lifted entirely off the ground and flew in brief low circular flights that brought them quickly back to where they had started.

"They will be making much longer flights within days," said Ogilvey. "They are still being fed by the adults. The males are away now, seeking sufficient carrion to fill those growing gullets. But we must leave them here now. When they decide it's time to migrate, they will overtake the herds moving overland with just a few days of flying."

Leaving the high plain, the quahka drivers made their way down to the Lamar valley, where they paused with open canopies to observe scattered herds of pachyrhinosaurs that remained and showed no sign of leaving, as was the case with some ankylosaur families and a large herd of wooly iguanodonts.

Kit was dubious. "Can they really survive a cold Montana winter? They'll be frozen stiff when it's twenty below zero."

Gar replied, "Gnachana wahki-too-too."

"Wahki-what?" Kit asked. "I didn't catch all that."

Ogilvey interpreted. "Gar says their wool coats will keep them warm."

"The ankylosaurs are not-so-wooly," Chase observed.

"Indeed," Ogilvey agreed. "I have discussed that with Gar. He says the thick layers of horn covering their spikes, plates, and tail clubs act as very effective insulators. As long as they can keep out of the blizzard winds of winter, they are protected within a warming encasement of keratin protein, one of nature's best insulators when properly covering the animal's surface. So we see that the ankylosaurs' protective armor serves two functions, first to fend off hungry tyrannosaurs, and then when the tyrannosaurs have traveled south, to fend off the freezing wind. Ankylosaurs are notorious for curling up into a ball to protect themselves. In this case, that balling-up, as well as an ability to lie still for weeks in a state of hibernation, serves them doubly well. And with tyrannosaurs *in absentia*, they will be quite safe despite their torpid state."

"What about wolves?" Chase asked. "They'll still be here, and they'll be hungry."

Ogilvey laughed. "Wolves might want to make a meal of a sleeping ankylosaur, but that scaly and bony armor is well nigh impermeable to the likes of a canine tooth. It takes the size and strength of a T rex to flip an ankylosaur over and get at its soft underside. Your wolves, Chase, will be frustrated in any attempts upon the fortress that is ankylosaurus."

"I suppose so."

"Now, I suggest we keep moving if we hope to catch the migrating herds, which are nowhere in sight."

The quahkas moved swiftly across the broad highlands of Yellowstone Park. They passed Norris Geyser basin, where Chase and Neggok had had their fatal confrontation, and traveled up the Firehole River Valley, passing geysers large and small, boiling mud pots, and iridescent fountain ponds that shimmered and steamed in rainbow colors. But still, there was not the slightest sign of a migrating dinosaur. Eventually, having traversed most of the park in a north-to-south direction, they pulled their quahkas to a stop near Old Faithful. They got out to watch the mightiest of all geysers send up steaming jets towering into the blue sky.

As Old Faithful calmed and settled, Chase was surprised to see his old boss, Bill Wycoff, among the large crowd of tourists who had gathered to watch the event and now stood gawking at the quahkas and their motley crew.

Bill smiled up at Chase. "People are back in Yellowstone, in droves," he said, gesturing at the people around him. "Not only do they have volcanic features to watch, but now they've got dinosaurs as well. Can't beat that with a stick."

Ogilvey replied a little testily, "Well, it's dinosaurs we are after, and they seem to be in short supply."

Bill nodded. "Reports are, the migrants have left the park completely. They headed south down the Grand Teton Valley. If you hurry, you might just catch them there."

"We are on our way! Gar?"

As the canopies closed, Bill called, "Oh by the way, Chase!"

Chase paused his canopy's descent halfway. "Yeah?"

"You still haven't returned that National Park pickup to the motor pool. No hurry, of course, but our accountants and maintenance people are eager to have it in hand again."

Kit giggled, watching the exchange closely with an amused look on her face.

"What?" Bill asked, seeing her chuckling. "Am I missing something here?"

Kit hushed. Chase shrugged. "I guess now's as good a time as any to tell you."

"Tell me what?" Bill's face grew concerned.

"It—" Chase hesitated. "Well, the pickup... got—"

"Anaka-tukaed." Kit finished for him.

"Anaka-what?" Bill asked.

Gar, who had also paused his canopy, had overheard. He let out a Kra laugh, "Gahk-gahk-gahk!" He bobbed his head several times to express his wholehearted concurrence with Kit. "Dat right, Keetah! Anaka-tuka. Anaka-tuka!"

Ogilvey, sitting behind Gar, said, "Yes, Chief Ranger Wycoff. The pickup has been quite thoroughly anaka-tukaed."

Bill looked a little cross. "I don't know what you mean by anaka—whatever."

Ogilvey's amused smiled faded. So did Chase's.

"Er, yes," Ogilvey said hesitantly. "You see, Anaka is the name the Kra use for the pachyrhinosaurus. And tuka means—well, you see—that your pickup truck has—er, well—"

Chase finally voiced what needed to be said. "It has been crushed flat as a pancake, basically." Watching the stricken expression that came over Bill's face, he broke into a sheepish grin. "Well," he said. "Not quite as flat as a pancake."

"No." Kit agreed. "It would take a full grown deelonga to

crush it that flat."

Wycoff pulled off his ranger hat and scratched at the thinning hair on the top of his head. "I don't know exactly what you're getting at," he said. "But I take it I won't be getting the truck back."

Chase shrugged. "That about sums it up."

"Anyway," Ogilvey said, breaking the silence that followed. "You say the dinosaurs went thataway?" He pointed to the south.

"Yeah," Wycoff said glumly. "And not a minute too soon, some would say—including our accountants!"

***

"My goodness," Ogilvey said over the radio as the two quahkas raced south along winding highway 191 out of the mountainous park and onto the plains of the Teton River Valley. "Those dinosaurs are hard to catch if you give them a head start. At this rate, the migration from Montana to Texas will be over in a matter of days, and we will have missed it."

Kit ignored the professor for the moment. She was filled with the exhilaration of rushing down the highway in Chase's quahka, sitting behind him like a tandem motorcycle rider, and indulging the unnecessary expedient of wrapping her arms around his well-muscled chest. And Chase, she thought, didn't seem to mind in the slightest that her hands lingered there. Wanting the ride to last a long time, she murmured into his ear, "Aren't we going kind of fast?

"We've got to burn up the highway if we want to catch up. There's no telling what kind of trouble a bunch of unescorted dinosaurs might get into."

On the prairies of the Teton flats, they rushed past herds of elk, just down from the high country on their own migrations to lower and warmer lands. But there was still no sign of dinosaurs. They slowed a little as they moved through the town of Jackson, Wyoming, and raised their canopies to exchanged good-natured waves with crowds of citizens and tourists who came to the street corners to watch them pass.

"These Jacksonites have had quite a show," Ogilvey quipped over the radio. "The valley narrows here, and the herds have been passing quite close to town."

"Any trouble?" Chase radioed back.

"No, indeed," Ogilvey replied. "Quite the contrary. Tourism is up in this tourist town, and the local chamber of commerce is already talking of having an annual Dino Days event. It's bound to be a civic—and commercial—success."

They accelerated once they were out of town, and moved up into the Gros Ventre Wilderness and across a wide pass. They raced down onto the flat grasslands beyond at a rate well over the speed limit. But still not one dinosaur came in sight. However, they did spot prodigious piles of dinosaur poo, which Ogilvey pointed out—with too great a frequency— proved the herds had been there and moved on.

As the day came to a close with a glorious sunset streaking clouds above mountain peaks, they made camp high in the Gros Ventre wilderness, well away from the highway, in a box canyon. Over dinner, they discussed many things, including their elapsed mileage.

"Incredibly," Ogilvey said, "the herds are moving nonstop, sixteen hours per day. As Gar says, they only stop when the night becomes pitch black."

"But we've got more speed," Chase said. "I'm surprised we haven't caught them."

"By my calculations," Ogilvey replied, "we have traveled 180 miles today, from the north of Yellowstone Park to Jackson to the middle of the Gros Ventre Wilderness. To stay ahead of us, dinosaurs like Rufus, Henrietta, and their brood, must have covered at least that much distance in one day. Therefore, their average speed calculates out to, let's see. Hmmm hmm hmm. I'd say slightly more than eleven miles per hour on average. That is about the speed the fastest human marathon runners travel, but sustained for seven times twenty- six miles. And that is just the average. Assuming they stopped for grazing and drinking water, so actual running speed must be greater. I would guestimate it at well over twenty miles per

THOMAS P. HOPP

hour, which is about a human hundred-meter sprinter's speed. The journey from Yellowstone to Big Bend is about 1,600 miles, but at such speeds, the entire trek may take only nine days. What a grueling pace! I hope they stop along the way for rest."

"Do you expect them to check into a motel?" Kit asked.

Ignoring her, Ogilvey said, "Migrating birds fly at about twice that speed, forty to fifty miles per hour. But dinosaurs, constrained to the ground, are still pretty impressive. Their migration rate is quite comparable in speed to the great migrations of the fleet-footed wildebeest of Africa, and covers a much longer distance."

On the high plains, they were able to track the herds by their footprints and dung heaps. Doing so, they traveled off road for most of the way. But where the land became too rough, it was easier to follow the smoothed out road cuts of Highway 191 for some distance, and then move back onto the grasslands again. On one of these sojourns onto asphalt, Chase suddenly remarked, "Uh-oh."

"What is it?" Kit asked.

Chase looked at the side mirrors that gave the quahka a rear view. "We just passed a cop beside the road. What's the speed limit around here?"

"I don't know," Kit replied.

Chase looked down at his instruments, but where a speedometer should be was the Kra equivalent, reading their speed digitally in unfamiliar Kra numerals in base six math. "I think that was a radar trap. Can you figure out this speedometer?"

"Let's see," she said, looking around his broad shoulder. "Thirty-nine gokaks. That's. Um. Six-times-six plus three-times—oh, how many gokaks in a mile?"

"Doesn't matter. Whatever it is, it's too fast. Here he comes."

The cop hit his flashing red-and-blue lights and came onto the highway behind them. Chase pulled over, slowing his machine to a stop on the shoulder. Gar did the same ten quahka-paces ahead of them. The cop, driving a squad car marked Sweetwater County Sheriff, passed Chase's quahka and pulled in behind Gar's. Leaving his lights flashing, he got out and walked toward the fighter-walker.

"Hmm," Kit said. "This should be interesting."

Chase opened the canopy and hunkered his machine down. They got out and went to Gar's machine but the officer put up a hand to stop them.

"Stay back folks," he said. "I got this machine on my radar, not yours."

When Gar hunkered his machine down and opened the canopy, the officer, whose nametag read McKREADY, took a step backward. He stared in mixed awe and fear at Gar's toothy face.

"Uh, sir," McKready began, and then stopped. "Uh, K-Kra. Uh, whatever it is I'm supposed to call you—did you know how fast you were going back there?"

Gar blinked and thought a moment. "Sessekna gokakn?"

McKready turned to Kit and Chase. "What'd he say?"

Dr. Ogilvey, sitting behind Gar, cleared his throat. "He said, thirty-eight gokaks, or thereabouts. Which, in miles per hours is... er, ninety carry the er, eleven..."

"I got you at one hundred-two miles per hour," Officer McKready said.

"Yes, precisely!" Ogilvey exclaimed. And then his expression fell. "Oh. I see."

Gar hadn't gotten the idea of a speed trap. "Hundred two. That pretty good speed, yeah?"

"Pretty bad, you mean," the officer said sourly. He stepped nearer the quahka and reached a hand up toward Gar. "I'll need to see your driver's license and registration."

"Gwah?" Gar looked to Ogilvey for help with the translation into Kranaga.

The professor looked befuddled. After a moment of thought he said to McKready, "Well, er, I don't believe Kra carry any such documents. Their right to drive these vehicles is granted by a personal code of honor and a verbal promise never to abuse the privilege."

"I'm not interested in explanations," McKready said. He walked around the quahka, inspecting it. When he completed the circle, he put his fists on his hips and looked up at Gar again. "Driving without a license is a crime in this state, sir. And your vehicle appears to be unlicensed as well. I'm afraid I'll have to arrest you and impound the vehicle."

"Arrest!" Ogilvey cried. "But this is impossible! We are pursuing—"

"Oh, it is quite possible," McKready interrupted. He slipped his fingers into the back pockets of his gray uniform trousers and rocked back and forth on his heels and toes. Gaining confidence, he commanded, "Now, step down from the vehicle, Mr. er—"

"Mr. Gar, the Kra!" Ogilvey exclaimed. "For your information, he's the supreme leader of the Kra nation!"

McKready looked doubtful. "Leader?" he asked.

"Supreme leader."

McKready turned and walked to his patrol car. He sat in his seat and lifted a hand-held microphone. Nearly an hour transpired as he occasionally talked on his radio, with several bouts of quite animated conversation. Eventually, he got out of his car and came back to Gar's quahka, appearing rather abashed.

"All right, sir," he said. "I'll let you go this time. It seems like maybe you have diplomatic immunity. But you had better keep your speed down." He turned on a heel and headed for his car. As he passed Chase he grumbled, "You too. Watch your speed."

He got into his car, fired the engine, pulled a wheel-spinning U-turn, and roared away.

The four travelers were left gaping at each other in astonishment. As usual, Dr. O was the first to speak. "Meanwhile," he grumbled, "the herds have been getting away from us!"

Chase glanced at the sun, which had sunk nearly to the horizon. "We can't go much farther today," he said. "This time of year, night comes early. It will be dark by seven o'clock. If we chase the herds at night, we might run right past them and never know it."

"Indeed, Chase," Ogilvey said. "We had best make plans to spend the night somewhere hereabouts and take up the pursuit in the morning at first light. Now then, where shall we stay?"

They left the highway in rough country west of the irrigated farmlands of Eden, Wyoming, and moved onto open range-lands, stopping in a brush-lined gulley far from prying eyes. They prepared and ate a camp dinner and by 6:30 pm were watching a local TV news show on a screen in Gar's quahka.

In one segment, they saw a Texas congressman, Ted Crud, addressing the media at a podium with dozens of microphones. "I know the President of these United States and his special envoy, Chase Armstrong, have soft hearts for these monsters," he said disdainfully. "But not me. And there are plenty of other congressmen and women who share my view."

"He mentioned your name on TV!" Kit exclaimed.

"Yeah," Chase grumbled, "but I don't like the context."

Ted Crud went on. "Now, Governor Smallwood of the great state of Texas and me issue the following challenge. No dinosaurs are welcome in Texas. Not Kra, not other beasts. Their migration will be stopped at the Texas border by any and all means available to me and the Governor, including vol-unteers armed with guns."

When the news went to a question-and-answer period, Ogilvey turned to the others. "I wish this ultimatum had been delivered before the migration commenced. What are we sup-posed to do now? The leading edge of the migration is almost halfway there!"

Chase shook his head. "We'll have to work things out as we go."

Another news segment showed a female reporter standing in front of an old-fashioned revival meeting tent. She said, "There is to be a meeting of the Exact Word Gospel Mission tonight, here at the Sweetwater Events Complex in Rock Springs. They tell me it's the place to be tonight if you question the presence of dinosaurs in Wyoming."

"Why, that's just a few miles south of here!" Ogilvey exclaimed. "Why don't we go and say a few words in defense of dinosaurs?"

Chase shook his head. "It's not the sort of thing I usually attend."

"Sounds like trouble," Kit added.

"But it's too early to turn in," Ogilvey resisted. "And I honestly would like to hear their, er, take, on the presence of dinosaurs on God's green earth these days. It could be fun, don't you agree Gar?"

Gar had just eaten several rib steaks, which he swallowed with bones in. He swallowed hard once more and shrugged his shoulders.

***

The big-top tent was impressively large, a classic religious revival meeting space of tall upright posts under a huge white canvas cover, filled with many rows of folding chairs. A wide plywood stage at one end stood on steel risers. It had a lectern podium and a long banner hung in front declaring "Do God's Work—Make Dinosaurs Extinct Again." Overhead, another banner read, "The Reverend Dr. Harley Skinner."

When the four travelers entered at the back of the tent, Skinner had been lecturing for some time. He cried out, "Oh Lord, we beseech thee, grant us salvation from the terrible lizards. For that is what the name, 'dinosaur,' means. Indeed, Lord, they are terrible, for they are abominations on the land, and bearers of false testimonial." The preacher did not immediately spot the newcomers as they moved along central aisle and found four seats together in what was a near-capacity crowd.

"False is their word, for they refute the Holy Scriptures' statement that God created the world in six days, and on the seventh day he rested."

"False, too are their claims that those giant bones in the ground are real. No! Brothers and sisters, they are false shapes made of dirt, created by Satan as traps for the unwary. Satan has fooled the scientists, and they are trying to fool you, into believing their biggest lie, which is that the world is four-point-five billion years old. How can they know this? The only truth is written on the pages of the Bible, and there we read that the world was created in six days, six thousand years ago. Not a day longer."

Skinner paused his rhetoric momentarily when a hubbub arose in the rear of the tent, punctuated by several women's screams. The crowd had discovered Gar among them. Gar was finding it hard to arrange his tail on the folding chair, and his long neck raised his crested head well above the level of the crowd. The preacher looked as flabbergasted as his flock at the appearance of— "The demon in our midst!" he suddenly cried. "I see among us the very one of whom I speak!"

Heads turned until all eyes were upon Gar and his companions.

Kit murmured, "Maybe coming here wasn't such a good idea."

"Demon!" the preacher cried. "What evil purpose brings you here?"

Gar looked at Ogilvey and swallowed hard. "What— mean— 'demon'?" he asked.

Ogilvey rose and began uneasily, "Er, let me answer on Gar's behalf."

"Gar!" Skinner cried. "So the demon has a name!" He paused to look at Gar while the audience held its collective breath.

"See here!" Ogilvey shouted angrily. "My companion, Gar the Kra, is no demon! But he is from sixty-five million years ago!"

"You see, believers? He repeats the lies we have heard!" Addressing Ogilvey, he asked, "Do you deny that this—creature—is a creation of our present times, and not of the past?"

"Yes, er well, no. I mean—"

"As a creature of our present times," the preacher overrode Ogilvey, "but never mentioned in the Bible, is he not then something ungodly?"

"Well, er, no—"

"And are the other dinosaurs not the demons and dragons mentioned in Revelations as the bringers of the End Of The World?"

"Um, no, I would not say—"

"Would you say, sir, that they are indeed the spawn of the Devil, and this demon even now appears in our very midst?"

"No. I would not—"

"A demon who denies the Bible by saying his kind lived sixty-five million years ago?"

"Well, yes on that, but, er, no on the demon part."

The preacher paused. The crowd murmured volubly. Gar lowered his head and sank into his chair as if he wished to disappear.

"P-Please hear me out," Ogilvey said. The crowd quieted somewhat. "There is no conflict with the word of the Bible," he said, "if each of God's days is 750 million years long. Isn't that possible?"

The preacher chuckled. "If it pleased God Almighty, then each and every day would be 750 million years long. For He is all-powerful. And my flock," he grinned and gestured at the crowd with outstretched hands, "would have that much more time to worship each day."

"Yes," Ogilvey said as laughter rippled through the other-wise silenced crowd. "And if God's day were 750 million years long, then six such days could account for all the time geologists say has elapsed since the solar system was formed."

"Wha—?" the preacher was unprepared for Ogilvey's tactic.

"And furthermore," Ogilvey went on, gaining confidence as the crowd stayed silent, "the seventh period of 750 million years could have just started, accounting for God's long absence from man's sight. He is enjoying his day of rest!"

"Bah!" the preacher roared. "This is another lie! You, sir, are obviously a minion of these dinosaurian devils. A human who aids them in their dark mission to claim the world for

Satan! Well sir, I condemn your lies, and I pray the Lord will scourge you along with your scaly companion!"

"Actually," Ogilvey protested meekly, "Gar is rather more feathery than scaly."

That made the preacher pause. He wrote a note on a piece of paper on his lectern.

Ogilvey went on, "I am sure that if you got to know him better, you would find Gar to be quite a pleasant personality. He's really quite likeable if you give him a chance—"

Gar raised his head a little.

"A chance?" the preacher thundered, his loudspeaker-amplified voice echoing off the bluffs outside town. "A chance to lead us to perdition? To lead our children astray with movies and cartoons showing how friendly and cute dinosaurs can be? To lure us all to museums where Satan's false bones are displayed proudly for all to see?"

At a loss for further arguments, Ogilvey turned to the others and whispered, "Perhaps we should go."

"Perhaps?" Kit hissed. "I'd say for sure we should go."

The preacher was far from finished. "Oh, my flock!" he roared. "What shall we do with these false prophets who spread lies amongst us? How shall we treat them?"

"Kill them!" someone shouted as the four got up to go.

"Burn them!" another cried as they moved into the aisle and turned for the rear exit.

Skinner called out over the din, "I pray that someone will soon act on God's behalf and smite these devil creatures down. Praise God. Say Hallelujah, brothers and sisters!"

The crowd roared as one, "Hallelujah!" as the four hurried outside into the darkness. As they mounted their quahkas, "Hallelujah!" went up again.

Ogilvey muttered as he settled in behind Gar, "However much I might wish to stay and verbally joust with that demagogue, I believe a strategic retreat is now our best option."

Several tough-looking young men came out of the tent and peered into the darkness of the parking area, obviously looking for them. But by that time the quahkas were under way and moving out of the lot. Some of the young men ran to their cars and pickup trucks and fired up their engines in hope of pursuit, but to avoid being followed, Gar and Chase piloted their quahkas up a steep gully among the badlands that overlooked the Event Complex. They soon sped away into the rough, moonlit country without any sign of pursuit. Making their way back to camp, they hunkered their quahkas down behind some concealing brush and group spent the night in their own small tents, each one reflecting somberly about the events they had experienced under the big top.

CHAPTER 18

They broke camp early the next morning and resumed their pursuit, following the dinosaur herds' winding course along the Green River Canyon, first south and then eastbound into the northwest corner of Colorado. Here, the herds had forded the Green River in the Brown's Park National Wildlife Refuge and then proceeded south again on the west side of the river. As the travelers followed the tracks and traces of the herds, they came upon an unexpected and shocking sight. In a broad, relatively flat section of rangeland, a gathering of at least a dozen tyrannosaurs, large and small, were finishing off a grizzly meal. Strewn across acres of grasslands were dozens of cow carcasses, most missing large portions of their anatomy, and all obviously killed by the tyrannosaurs.

"Oh, dear," Ogilvey said as the team stopped side-by-side in their walking machines with the canopies raised. "This is just what we intended to avoid."

"I don't get it," Chase said. "The ranchers have been warned to keep their herds away from the main migration routes. But these cattle seem to have gotten smack in the middle of things."

"To their great misfortune," Ogilvey concluded.

"The ranch owner is going to be irate," said Kit.

"And send us a great big bill for this," said Chase. "But wait a minute. Look over there."

Not far from where they had stopped was a barbed wired fence, running across the rangeland between posts made from rough-cut, weathered timbers. A hundred yards from them, a wooden gate divided the fence line—and that gate was wide open. Chase drove his quahka slowly to the gate and passed through with Gar and Ogilvey tailing him. His eyes scrutinized the dusty ground intensely. "There are tracks of a whole herd of cattle, all heading straight into trouble. And look! The tire tracks of a vehicle, an SUV most likely, and it was driving them through the gate."

Ogilvey piped up, "A saboteur! Someone deliberately trying to aggravate ranchers against the migration!"

"Exactly," Chase agreed. "And look there!" Up a dry wash and high on a ridge above where they paused their walkers, was another barbed wire fence, and another open gate. "This is sabotage, alright! The herd would have been out of sight over that ridge and safe from any notice by the rexes. This disaster was caused deliberately by—"

Chase stopped in mid-sentence and threw himself over Kit to protect her. An instant later, a bullet ricocheted off of the metal skin of the fighter-walker.

At first Kit was confused. "Wha—?" she stammered trying to disentangle herself from Chase. Then, as Chase hit a toggle switch and the canopy glass snapped down just in time to deflect another incoming bullet, she understood. "Somebody's shooting at us!"

"Someone sure is!" Chase sat up at the controls again and piloted the quahka into a tight turn, and then a dead run. "And I saw him just in time." Charging through the open gate, Chase steered for a gully, from which another shot smacked squarely onto the nose of the quahka—harmlessly, thanks to the armored skin of the fighting machine. "There he goes!" Chase cried, "running for his SUV."

The rifleman jumped into a large black pickup truck and spun its wheels attempting a getaway up the ridge road. But his machine was no match for a quahka, either in terms of speed or armament.

As Chase raced after the fleeing truck, he raised the quahka's weapon arm.

"Now, Chase," Kit cautioned. "Don't do anything rash."

Chase aimed carefully with the heads-up display on the canopy glass in front of him. He squeezed off a single laser shot, which struck one of the pickup's rear tires and exploded it into black shreds of rubber and a puff of smoke. Nevertheless, the pickup rushed up the dirt road. Being a heavy rig, it had not two rear tires, but four in two pairs. With three rear wheels still turning, the truck's speed had not abated.

Chase easily kept up with the fleeing gunman while taking aim a second time. He fired a shot that took out a wheel on the other side. When that tire exploded, the pickup was still able to gain ground, but its speed was reduced to a crawl.

Chase slowed his machine to a walk, as did Gar behind him. Another laser shot left only one rear wheel intact. It spun ineffectually and the truck ground to a halt. But the driver was not finished. In desperation, he jumped out of his cab and lit on the ground with rifle in hand. He swung it toward Chase's machine and sent another bullet ricocheting off the canopy glass.

Kit shrieked at the nearness of the deadly fire, but Chase was cool. He raised the weapon arm and aimed at the gunman. He touched a button on the console and said into a microphone, "Drop it!"

When the desperado raised his rifle again, Chase was ready. He flipped a switch with his left hand and, with his right, pulled the trigger on his joystick. Out from the quahka's weapon arm leapt—not a laser shot—but a bolt of blue electricity, which crackled over the gunman and dropped him in his tracks.

Minutes later the four travelers gathered around the man as he slowly regained consciousness on the ground.

"You know who this guy is?" Kit asked the others. "He's Reverend Skinner!"

"You're right!" Ogilvey exclaimed. "The very preacher who stirred up the crowd last night. He's traded his fancy suit for blue jeans and boots, but he's the same man all right."

Skinner raised himself to one elbow and looked up at the quartet glumly. "What are you gonna do with me now?" he asked.

"Turn you over to them," Chase replied, pointing at a sheriff's SUV racing up the hill toward them. "I called them while you were, um, snoozing on the ground here. They'll fix you up with some nice handcuffs. And while you're doing jail time for attempted murder, we'll get the rancher who owned this herd to send you the bill for a couple dozen head of beef."

"Speaking of which," Kit said, looking out over the valley, "the rexes seem to have finished their meal. Looks like a lot of prime beef got eaten."

The largest rexes had resumed their southward travel, one still wolfing down an entire rack of beef ribs. Several young rexes dawdled, gnawing at the remaining carcasses, and then they too rushed off, following the adults.

"See how they swallow bones and all?" Ogilvey remarked. "They will, of course, regurgitate those after their digestive acids have stripped the attached flesh. That will make their trail easy to follow."

***

A trip that had begun in Yellowstone Country and progressed south through Grand Teton National Park and beyond down the Green River through Wyoming and into Colorado, now veered west into Utah, passing Dinosaur National Monument. The excitement of the park employees and visitors at having live dinosaurs in a park that had until now only presented fossils to the visitor, was thrilling for Kit and Chase to behold. However, the excitement was short-lived, as the migrants continued after only a brief pause to bathe and sport in the Green River before moving south and traveling cross-country to the Colorado River system in the Moab, Utah area. There, the streaming herds moved down through Arches National Park in the Salt Valley over grass- and juniper- and scrub-lands. Continuing over Willow Flats to Courthouse Wash, they stopped overnight to browse willows and take morning mud baths in ponds holding recent monsoonal autumn rainwater. Moving on again, the big beasts turned west up Courthouse Wash to Seven Mile Canyon and then paralleled the highway south into Moab, where the streams of animals plunged into the Colorado River, fording it and moving along the banks past Moab, as astonished citizens gawked at the spectacle.

The four travelers followed and observed the animals daily now, easily keeping pace with the herds and their docile, well-fed T rex shadowers. From Moab, the herds proceeded to the Dolores River Valley, returned briefly to Colorado, passed Mesa Verde National Park, and then crossed the wide, high plains and plateaus of Northwestern New Mexico. There, the land was filled with grasses, sage, juniper, and piñon pines, all of which were fodder for one variety of dinosaur or another.

Moving southeast into central New Mexico, they passed Chaco Canyon on high grasslands, and then crossed the Continental Divide at Star Lake. From there, it was a downhill run to the Rio Grande River just north of Albuquerque. The great herds passed through town in the wide river channel, leaving thousands of observers astonished and talking of making an annual dino festival of the event.

It was heartening that the general reaction to dinosaurs was one of pleasant amusement. Only rarely was there a protest group demonstrating opposition to dinosaurs. But the goodwill so much in evidence in New Mexico was not fated to last for long.

THOMAS P. HOPP

CHAPTER 19

Fifty miles southeast of El Paso, on the outskirts of the tiny town of Fort Hancock, Texas, a hunting blind of posts and brush had been set up in a low area on the edge of a dry wash that crossed a section of parched grassland. Near the cool shelter of the willow, tamarisk, and scrub brush along the side of the creek, there was a tent of camouflage fabric, a portable camp table, and four folding chairs. Sitting on the chairs, four men watched the grassland before them, and waited.

Texas Governor Virgil Walter Smallwood wore a red buffalo plaid hunting cap with loose earflaps. Beside him was a big-game hunting guide by the name of Dick Chimney, an older man with years of experience in Africa but originally from Wyoming, who wore a similar hunting cap, with the earflaps properly tucked in.

The Governor let out a hickish chuckle. "Hyeh, hyeh, hyeh. This'll teach 'em they better not mis-underestimate me!"

"You got that right," red-cheeked Dick Chimney agreed, chewing on a half finished cigar that had long since gone out. "They thought you were just boasting when you said if any dinosaurs crossed the state line, you'd make West Texas a dinosaur graveyard. Well sir, we're about to make that threat a fact." He spat tobacco juice on a horned toad that had strayed too close.

The third man was Senator Ted Crud, who had swapped his three-piece pinstriped suit for a khaki safari shirt and shorts, and an Aussie bush hat with its broad brim folded up on one side. He looked rather photogenic, as if cell phone shots of the proud hunter and his giant kill were on his to-do list for the day. His babyish face was bright with anticipation of bloodletting.

"I hope they get here soon," he said. "I cancelled a meeting with some, er, rather wealthy oil company lobbyists just to join you gents. I intend to announce my run for the presidency of these United States right after they promise to pony up the big bucks to support me."

"Don't worry," Chimney responded. "I been following them dinosaurs by satellite surveillance for a week. They'll be here."

"Say, Senator," the Governor said, smirking. "If you want to impress them oil men, tell 'em you're gonna blame global warming on dinosaurs."

"How's that?" the Senator asked.

"Y'know," said the Governor, chuckling, "all that dang dinosaur poo. Piles of it as big as a wheelbarrow load, so they tell me. And think of all the gas they produce with it. Dinosaur gas. Mesozoic methane. That's a greenhouse gas if I ever heard of one!"

Crud grinned at the Governor. "You're a pretty smart man, Gov."

"Well, thank you kindly, Senator Crud. You see, I wanna be known as the Education Governor. I figure there ain't no better way to teach kids about dinosaurs than to put a stuffed one in the capital rotunda!"

Chimney glanced at the fourth man in the group. "I don't know Gov, that sounds an awful lot like you're gonna be teaching evolution. I don't know how Reverend Skinner here is gonna like that."

"Good point, Dick," the Governor said. "What say, Skinner? Any reason I can't mount me a dinosaur in the state capitol?"

The Reverend thought a moment. "I didn't come prepared for preachin'," he said. "Otherwise I'd-a wore my Sunday suit instead of these blue jeans and ostrich-hide boots. But if you want my personal opinion, you can do anything you want with them godless creatures."

"Well, thank you mighty kindly for your blessing, Rev."

"And thank you," the Reverend replied, "for getting me pardoned before I even got tried, and for getting me outta the clink."

"Hyeh! Hyeh!" Smallwood laughed. "Don't mention it, Rev! Governor Zebediah Smallwood, up there in Colorado, he's my cousin. All's I had to do was call him and ask, and he had you pardoned in a minute. I told him it was you and your religious supporters that got out the votes to get me elected. For that, I am in your debt for all eternity."

"Hallelujah!" cried the Reverend. Suddenly he sat up straight and pointed toward the northern horizon. "Hey y'all!" he said. "What's that there?"

Ambling over a low hill among the badlands to the north of them, came a group of animals large and small, moving south at a fast four-legged walk. The largest animal, in the lead, was easily the size of an army tank. It was armored, too. It had a broad frill at the back of its head and three horns, one above each eye and one on its nose. Other large members of its species followed. Between the big adults, smaller juvenile animals pranced and frisked around with the boundless energy of youth. The adults moved much more steadily, as if migration was foremost in their instinctual minds.

"Is that some kinda brontosaurus?" the Governor wondered.

"Er, triceratops, I believe," said Chimney. "Wouldn't you agree, Reverend?"

"How should I know? I walked outta class when my grade-school teacher tried to teach us about 'em. Got a 'F' in dinosaurology."

"Whatever they are," said Crud, "they're coming straight at us."

"S—Sure are, aren't they?" the Governor said with a note of concern in his voice. "You guys sure those guns are big enough?"

Chimney hefted one of the four elephant guns the group had brought with them. "Yep," he said. "I'm sure."

The men took up their rifles and arranged themselves along the brush wall of the hunting blind.

The triceratops herd approached quickly.

Suddenly the Governor looked like a man who doubted his own resolve. "Sweaty palms," he remarked, holding the heavy rifle at an odd angle. "Makes it hard to aim good." He lowered his rifle and swatted at a horse fly that had bitten his neck, and then looked at the spattered blood on his hand with growing desperation on his face. "May—Maybe somebody else should take the first shot," he said.

Chimney looked like he was getting impatient. "That gun's got .50 caliber bullets in it. That's big enough to smash through an elephant's skull, but if you don't aim well, all hell could break loose. But you're the one who said if they crossed the state line, you'd exterminate them personally. Well, here they are."

"Hyeh, but—but maybe I mis-underestimated how big they was gonna be!"

"Come on," said Chimney. "Man up and take your best shot." He checked the action on his own gun. "Firing mechanism's dusty. The sumbuck might need a little more oil."

The Governor broke into a smart-Alec grin. "Well, you got plenty of oil haven't you, Dick? Didn't your company just make a big strike out in the Bayou Wetland Preserve?"

"I never thanked you for the executive order giving me those fracking permits. Danged environmentalists had me locked out."

"Just goes to show. The executive pen is mightier than the environmentalist sword."

Cruz said, "If you guys are gonna keep jawing, then maybe I'll take the first shot." He raised his rifle and sighted on the big animal in front.

"Wait!" Chimney hissed, but too late. The sound of his voice made Crud jerk, rather than squeeze, the trigger. The boom of the rifle was accompanied by a kick much stronger than Crud had imagined. It swung his shoulder around ninety degrees and sent him staggering backward. Meanwhile, the shot flew high, skipping off the rim the animal's neck frill, cutting a groove and throwing out a spray of horn-covered chips.

"I was going to say," Chimney went on, "let 'em get closer so you can't miss. Now look what's happened. They've all stopped in their tracks. And they're looking straight at us. From this angle, I don't see a single vulnerable spot."

The Governor giggled nervously. "How about them beady little eyes?"

"From this distance?" Chimney grumbled. "Even I'd be lucky to hit the mark."

The triceratopses had instinctually drawn together, the adults facing the threat and the juveniles interspersed between for safety.

"Well," Chimney said coolly as he raised his rifle and carefully sighted. "A fifty-caliber round might just get through the bone of the forehead. That's about my only shot." He stood straight, sighted carefully, and gently squeezed the trigger. The rifle boomed loudly, and a moment later and the lead triceratops dropped. "Right between the eyes!" Chimney exulted.

The big beast's front legs buckled and she collapsed forward onto some bunchgrass tussocks, while the other animals bleated and roared behind her, uncertain whether to stand or flee.

"Good shootin'!" cried the Governor.

"Praise the Lord," cried Skinner.

Chimney watched the animals with a practiced eye. "Maybe these things are like elephants," he murmured. "I was part of an illegal ivory hunting team in Botswana for a while. If these things do act like elephants, then I'll bet we can kill off the whole herd. The lead one that I just bagged would be the matriarch, an old experienced female who leads the herd. So, you kill her first and the others are confused. They're easy to pick off because they're afraid to leave her, but they're afraid to attack too. A nice setup for wiping them all out."

"God's will be done!" cried Skinner.

"Forget God," said Crud. "I'm gonna put a trophy head in the Oval Office!"

"We'll all get trophies, eh?" said the Governor. "Look at the size of them heads. With that big beak and shield, they gotta be three yards long. And look at them horns! They could stick clean through you and go through the next guy too!"

"I wouldn't worry," Chimney said. "If they keep holding still, this is gonna be a turkey shoot!"

"Oh my gosh!" Kit cried when the matriarch went down. The four wranglers had been following a large herd of orodromeus but had stopped to watch the triceratops group moving at some distance from them. They only noticed the big black crew-cab pickup hidden in the streambed, and the men in the hunting blind, when the puffs of smoke appeared and the sounds of rifle shots echoed to them across the badlands. When the matriarch collapsed they had all drawn a shocked breath.

"Quick!" Chase cried. "Canopies down! Let's get over there as fast as these machines can run!"

The Governor and the Senator and Chimney and Skinner came out from behind the blind to get clearer shots. Seeing them, the entire herd suddenly turned and ran back the way they had come, the small ones bleating, the large ones bellowing in rage and fear.

"Aw," the Governor cried. "I was gonna get me a big one and a baby too!"

"I wonder why they decided to run—?" Crud began, but he froze before the question was complete, looking behind and above Chimney.

All three of the others turned to follow Crud's gaze. And all three gasped in terror.

From above and behind them descended a huge tan form. For just an instant, all four men refused to accept what it was.

But as it came down, there was no mistaking that it was a huge, full-grown tyrannosaurus rex! It had come out of the willows behind them and taken them by surprise. All four froze in fear as the horrific jaws opened wide and closed over Chimney's body before he had a chance to react. He was chopped in half, and the rex tossed its head back and swallowed the bottom half of him whole. As it did so, Crud raised his rifle to fire, but the Governor stumbled backward with his finger still on his rifle's trigger—and accidentally blasted Crud in the knee. The Governor fell backward as the gun's recoil knocked him off his feat—but he never reached the ground. The rex took one stride forward and caught him in mid-fall. Again tossing its head high, it wolfed him down whole. Crud had been struggling to raise his rifle, but the rex stepped on him with one foot and crushed him lifeless on the ground. But the monstrous beast scarcely hesitated over Crud. It was after Skinner, who had dropped his rifle and sprinted back toward the pickup. Skinner cast a glance over his shoulder as he ran shouting, "Save me, oh Lord, from this demon!"

When it became clear the rex would reach him before he reached his truck, Skinner turned and raised his arms to cover his face. "Dear God!" he cried. "Spare thy servant—!"

But God apparently was not listening. Perhaps, as Ogilvey had suggested, He was enjoying a snooze on his 750-million year day of rest. The chomp of massive jaws and the crunch of bones ended Skinner's outcry. Like the Governor before him, he was tossed high and swallowed whole.

The fighter-walkers arrived at the scene moments later. By then, the rex had stalked off into the badlands and was lost to sight. But the grizzly scene it had left behind was still there. On the grassy ground lay Crud, and the top half of Chimney, both quite dead and surrounded by pools of blood. Four rifles were there to be counted, but no trace of the two other humans could be seen.

"He killed 'em all!" a voice said from behind them, startling them. "He killed 'em all!"

A young thin man in western clothes approached from the direction of the pickup.

"Killed whom all?" Ogilvey asked as the man stopped to look at the bodies and shudder.

"The Gov," the man said. "And Senator Crud. And Dick Chimney. And my brother Harley. Swallowed him whole, I'll bet!"

Ogilvey cocked his head. "You'll bet?" he asked. "You mean you didn't see?"

"No sir. I was sleepin' in the back of the truck until I heard gunshots. Then I hid down low when I seen that big lizard chasin' 'em."

Kit had gone to the downed triceratops. "Chase," she called. "You'd better come here."

As the group joined her, she gestured at the beast with the flat of a hand. "Listen."

"She's breathing!" Chase exclaimed.

"She's alive!" Ogilvey rejoiced.

The beast was unconscious, and heeled partially over on one side. A deep, elephantine moan issued from its throat. Chase looked her over carefully for a few moments. "She's just winged on the frill," he said. "But this shot to the frontal bone is what put her down. Right between the eyes."

"Poor thing," Kit said.

"You know," Chase said. "That's a massive ridge of scaly skin and heavy bone between the horns. I wonder how deep the bullet went in?" He climbed onto the huge head, drew a folding knife out of his pocket, and probed into the bleeding hole left by the bullet. "The blade touched metal," he said. "Maybe I can—" He twisted the knife and a blood-covered object popped out of the hole. He caught it in one hand. "Got it!" he said.

"Here," said Kit, who had hurried to the quahka while he worked and returned with a tube of antibiotic ointment. Chase took it and daubed a generous amount within the hole. "There," he said with satisfaction. "That ought to help her heal, if she—" Suddenly the matriarch tossed her head and

Chase went sprawling to the ground on one side. "—wakes up," he finished, backpedaling from her quickly. The triceratops drew in a deep, sighing breath and struggled to get her feet underneath her. Then she rose.

"I advise a hasty retreat!" Ogilvey cried. They all hurried back to their walkers, while young Skinner ran for his truck.

The matriarch was shaky on her feet for some time, but seemed otherwise unhurt. Eventually, she shook her head one last time and lumbered away to rejoin her family, now a hundred yards off and standing in a defensive group in a small arroyo, the horns of the adults bristling in every direction.

CHAPTER 20

The two quahkas set off following the rex's tracks, with Cole Skinner following in the pickup a safe distance behind them, monitoring their communications on his CB radio.

They followed the tracks out across the open grassland. "Just one set of tracks," Chase radioed, "but I don't see the rex. I guess he got too big a head start on us."

"Like I told you," Cole radioed. "That one big lizard got 'em all. How are we gonna get back their remains? My brother deserves a Christian funeral. I guess you'll have to shoot that monster and cut them out of him, like they do with crocodiles in Africa."

Chase radioed, "I'm not partial to killing any animal. None of this was the rex's fault."

"But there's gonna be a big stink around these parts if we don't get the bodies back."

Just then, Chase stopped his machine. Gar halted beside them. Cole came up behind and got out of his pickup. "What's that?" he asked when he saw what the dinosaur wranglers had stopped to inspect.

"An extremely large—" Chase began.

"Pile of barf," Kit finished for him. "Phew! What a reek."

"But— But, what's in it?" Cole asked, not wanting to believe the testimonial of his eyes.

Ogilvey said rather clinically, "I see arms, legs, and other body parts, all tangled together. Hmm. They are well chewed but not yet digested. Unusual for a rex to give up its meal so

THOMAS P. HOPP

soon."

"Meal!" Cole cried, still trying desperately not to see what lay before him in a six-foot wide, slime-covered pile.

"Let's see," Ogilvey went on academically. "Maybe if we count shoes. Er, one pair of fancy black leather cowboy boots."

"Them ones was on the Gov'ner," Cole confirmed.

"And one pair of fancy waffle-stomper hiking boots—by Gucci, believe it or not!"

"Thems's Chimney's."

"And one pair of ostrich-hide cowboy boots."

Cole cried in anguish. "Harley! Oh Lord! My brother's been eaten by a dina-sar!"

"Then all the missing bodies and parts are accounted for in this one pile," Ogilvey concluded. "It is a rather large pile, isn't it?"

"Well, if that's all of them," Chase said soberly, "then at least there's no need to shoot the rex."

Cole looked astonished. "Ain't you gonna kill it just to—"

"Just to what?" Chase asked sharply.

"Just to get even?"

"Get even for the lives of men who came here to kill dinosaurs illegally? I'd say things are about even right now."

"Not to mention," Kit added, "that your brother tried to shoot me and Chase the other day."

Cole hung his head. He let out a sob, but said no more.

Ogilvey continued to inspect the pile. "Curious," he said. "As distasteful as I found the Governor and preacher to be, they were obviously even more distasteful to the rex."

***

Leaving Cole and the remains of the others in the keeping of Texas Rangers who soon arrived, the four travelers resumed their journey. They pressed on along the banks of the Rio Grande River as it wound its way southward toward Big Bend National Park. After camping overnight just to the rear of the herds, they rose early and pressed on in the park until they

194

reached a rise that overlooked a wide, flat bottomland through which the Rio Grande wended its path toward the sea. As they sat with their canopies open, Ogilvey talked as he entered notes into a small notepad computer.

"The total migration took about two weeks," he murmured as he typed, "give or take a day or two, bearing in mind that some animals are still straggling in." Absorbed in his work, he seemed to scarcely notice the wonders in the landscape that stretched before them. Triceratopses were there in several family groupings. And pachycephalosaurs, by the dozen, both large and small. And herds of Orodromeus raced over hills and gullies, hundreds of them.

Chase glanced sidelong at Kit. "What are you looking for so intently?" he asked her.

"There!" she suddenly cried. "There's Rufus! And Henrietta! And their babies! They all made it safely! And there are some more parasauros, over there! And there!"

"The herbivores are pretty bunched up right now," Ogilvey murmured as he wrote. "But they will spread out. Vegetation is rather sparse down this way."

"What about the rexes?" Kit asked.

"They will establish colonies in several of the foothill valleys around here. And the herbivores have little to fear. Rexes don't eat much in winter. They sleep a lot while the weather is cool, snuggling in family groups like housecats and dogs sometimes do. It's almost like hibernating."

"Gah!" Gar concurred.

"The land does look pretty barren," Kit worried.

"Indeed, right now." Ogilvey set aside his computer and gestured with the sweep of an arm to indicate the entire broad valley spread out below them. "Soon this land will be entirely green!"

"How?" Kit asked.

"Just to the east of here, a new park annex is under construction. It's a combination of a new National Park visitor center from which people will be able to view the dinosaurs, and a pump station that will bring irrigation water up from a

Kra desalinization plant now being built near the Gulf of Mexico. The park will soon get fresh water for growing dinosaur forage, and this whole region of Texas will also be given ample water for human crops as well. I still can't believe the Governor and Senator opposed those wonderful developments. Perhaps it's better they became dino-chow."

"Tsk," Kit scolded.

Ogilvey was unrepentant. "Hard-line religion and politics was their forte. Sometimes I think those are the two greatest barriers to human progress."

"Kra progress too," Gar added.

A huge shadow passed over them. Looking up, Kit cried, "Quetzalcoatli! Just look at them all!"

It appeared that the entire rookery had migrated together from Montana. Huge wing beats filled the air overhead with sound. Loud cries of "Graaak! Graaak!" could be heard everywhere.

"Splendid!" Ogilvey gushed. "To see quetzalcoatlus arrive here with their young again as in Cretaceous times—it's truly a blessing."

Deeper still in the Big Bend that afternoon, the four sat watching a distant caravan of two white vans and one white SUV travel down to the Rio Grande.

"Campers? Or hikers, perhaps," Ogilvey suggested as they watched the vehicles wend their way through an almost trackless portion of the park and approach the river.

"I don't know," Chase said as he watched their slow progress. "This close to the Mexican border, they are as likely to be smugglers of illegal immigrants, or maybe gun runners. Not to mention drugs. They're probably trying to find a new route to evade immigration agents, or drug enforcement agents, or the firearms people."

"Not to mention homeland security," said Kit. "They make me nervous."

"No worries," said Ogilvey. "We're miles from them, and there are no roads at all between them and us."

"And we got laser cannon," Gar added.

"Good point," Kit said. "But I wonder what they're up to?"

"My guess is, a pickup or delivery at the river," Chase said, "if they get there."

"Why wouldn't they?" Kit asked.

"That family of triceratops, down in the river taking a bath."

"Coahuilaceratops," said Ogilvey. "I believe is the correct term."

"What's the difference? Those look like the very same group we helped escape the hunters yesterday. You called them triceratops then."

"Ah, but they were on our side of the border then. Today we find them literally straddling the boundary between the U.S. and Mexico in the middle of the river."

Indeed, the animals were lolling in the water and bathing in shallows that extended clear across the river channel to the Mexican shore.

"In their northern range," Ogilvey explained, "we call them triceratops. But that land right across the river, where I see several of the young ones have strayed, is the state of Coahuila, Mexico. There, the fossils that have been found have been termed Coahuilaceratops. So, as far as nomenclature goes, you are welcome to take your pick. The animal is obviously the same one. The only difference is its seasonal location north or south of the border."

Chase said, "Now what are those drivers going to try?"

It was obvious the vans intended to cross the Rio Grande at a shallow ford quite near where the big beasts were enjoying their baths.

"This ought to be interesting," Kit said.

As they watched, one of the small triceratopses became agitated and ran to its mother, braying so loudly it could be heard faintly even from more than a mile's distance. In response, the big matriarch—the same one, perhaps, that had been hurt by gunfire previously—uttered a loud bellow. Then it charged one of the vans and gouged into its side with all three horns, easily overturning it in the river. Several shots rang out from the SUV, but the matriarch turned and flipped that vehicle entirely over by hooking its nose horn under its front bumper. Then, with help from several other large beasts, it proceeded to smash and batter the SUV and van into scrap metal. While all this transpired, gunmen spilled out of both vehicles and splashed, swam, or waded until they emerged on the Mexican shore of the Rio Grande.

The second van, still on the U.S. bank, was pursued by several of the ceratopsians as it retreated northward along the route it had come by.

"The U.S. has some new Border Patrol agents," Chase quipped.

"Pretty effective ones, I would say," Ogilvey replied. "Better than anything Congress has authorized in years!"

The quahkas pressed on, paralleling the river's course, which changed from southward to eastward. They paused at each high point to look out over the Big Bend country and observe the dinosaurs that dotted the rugged landscape. On one of these pauses, they watched a contingent of Kra fighter-walkers and four-legged, freight-carrying lunkoos, which had arrived with many bales of hay and hundreds of cantaloupe-like fruits so huge they could be seen from more than a mile away.

"What are those things?" Kit asked.

"Deessakaigo!" Gar replied.

"The deessakaigo fruit," Ogilvey explained, "is a relative of our cassava melon. But this species grows fruit as big as basketballs—or even larger! Just one fruit can provide all the nutrients a fully-grown triceratops or parasaurolophus needs for a day. And yet the plants, which grow along the ground like any other melon vine, can produce dozens of them per week in the prime fruiting season, which happens to be mid-winter, after the plant has gown foliage all summer. Like cassava melon vines, the roots of this plant can reach deeply into the soil, in some places as much as one hundred feet, to get at the water flowing in subsurface aquifers."

"How can any plant grow roots that deep in one season?"

"Oh, they don't. Unlike our melons, these ancient vines are long-lived perennials. They can eventually be hundreds of years old, or in some cases thousands, with massive bark-covered main vines that spread over the ground for hundreds of feet, building truly massive thickets of greenery where otherwise there would only be desert."

"It surprises me such a highly evolved species could have been wiped out by the asteroid strike," Chase said.

"No doubt the vines survived the impact," Ogilvey agreed. "But without their huge herbivores to spread their seeds, they were ultimately doomed right along with the dinosaurs. Now, happily, they are back and I dare say, even humanity may find them useful in the desert parts of the planet."

"Taste good," Gar said, "for pflant-eaters like hoonahs."

"Will wonders never cease?" Chase murmured.

Ogilvey looked at him thoughtfully. "If you're asking for the benefit of my long experience, my boy—then the answer to your question is no."

Kit had been glancing around the landscape as they talked.

"What is it you are looking for my dear?" Ogilvey asked.

"Something's missing," she replied. "Where are the alamo-saurs?"

At that moment, a scratchy noise alerted them to a call coming in from a distance on Gar's radio. Gar answered, "Gah?" and a woman said, in urgent tones, "This is police dispatch, San Antonio. I was given this frequency and told to ask for Mr. Chase Armstrong."

"I'm right here," Chase replied.

"We are dealing with a situation," she said.

"What sort of situation?"

"A... um... a dinosaur situation."

"Yes?"

"You see, there are these big, long-necked animals—"

"The alamosaurs!" Kit exclaimed.

"Yes. Well. You see, they took a left turn at Del Rio and

moved away from the Rio Grande. They came east across some rangelands, took a bath in Medina Lake and now they're smack in the middle of our downtown business district."

"Oh my!" Ogilvey cried.

"We'll be there as soon as we can," Chase replied. "Meanwhile, whatever you do—don't make them angry!"

Moving at top speed of thirty-nine gokaks, the quahkas reached San Antonio within several hours. In that time the herd of alamosaurs, twenty-nine individuals, juvenile and grown, had moved just as the dispatcher had suggested. Following the winding path of the San Antonio River among the city's streets, they had already reached the center of town by the time the quahkas arrived. An amazing sight greeted the travelers as they disembarked their walking machines.

"Alamosaurs," Ogilvey cried, "at the Alamo!" Indeed, the herd had paused in the park where the famous monument to freedom was located, and they were grazing on the foliage of tall trees neighboring the old Spanish mission building. "And, by the way, Chase, do you see what kind of trees they are munching on?"

"Cottonwoods," Chase replied.

"Indeed," Ogilvey concurred. "And, do you know what the Spanish name for cottonwood tree is?"

When Chase hesitated, thinking, Ogilvey answered his own question. "Alamo, my boy! How about that? We are witnessing alamosaurs eating alamos—at the Alamo!"

After a short time, the big beasts moved on, paralleling the San Antonio River's course through town without further incident. As the tall beasts moved off, Ogilvey said with some dismay, "Oh dear."

"What?" Chase asked.

Ogilvey stared at the grounds of Alamo Park. "Oh dear, oh dear, oh dear."

"Come on, Doc. Don't keep me in suspense. What is it?"

"Where herbivores graze, they also, er, poo," the professor said.

Kit broke into laughter, as did Gar. And suddenly Chase noticed what Ogilvey had seen. "Oh-oh," he said. "The park maintenance people and street sweepers are gonna have their jobs cut out for them."

Where the big animals had paused, mountainous piles of poop had been dumped on the lawns and the flagstone paving of Alamo Plaza. More heaps had been left in the wake of the herd, which was already far to the southeast of the park, moving peacefully out of town.

"Hopefully," Chase said, "we'll be able to re-route their migration next year."

"Gah," Gar agreed. "We plant more trees for them to eat— somewhere else!"

"Where are they headed?" Kit wondered. "I thought all the dinosaurs would spend the winter at Big Bend."

"Not all," Gar replied.

"The alamosaurs," Ogilvey explained, "and a few other species, are headed for the coast. They prefer the sandier, flatter environment of the shoreline. And there are some relatively unpopulated coastal marshlands in the area between Corpus Christy and Brownsville."

"There are some wide open National Wildlife Refuges and National Seashores in that area," Chase said.

"Exactly," Ogilvey concurred. "Those will be refuges and seashores for alamosaurs and their friends, very soon!"

"It's pretty desolate country," Chase said. "If it weren't, people would have filled it with farms and towns long ago."

"Right again," Ogilvey said. "But Kra technology has the solution. Even now, they are constructing the world's largest-ever desalination plant down at Laguna Madre near the Padre Island National Seashore. They will draw seawater from the Gulf of Mexico in huge quantities and use kekuah power to remove the salt and make it into fresh water. They intend to irrigate wide areas of the coastal plain, producing the equivalent of a whole new ecosystem. Grazing will be abundant and the environment will benefit dinosaurs, mammals, Kra, and humans alike!"

THOMAS P. HOPP

"I'd like to see that," Kit said.

"And you will," Chase replied. "I'm not going to feel comfortable until I see those alamosaurs wallowing in the surf at Padre Island."

"Which reminds me," Ogilvey mused. "Gar has told me the invasion landers that touched down near the Louisiana coast brought more than fighting machines. They released dozens of Archelon—the biggest sea turtles ever to have lived! And Padre Island is imprinted into their instinctual behavior as the place where they will dig their nests and lay their eggs. Imagine! Turtles the size of automobiles crawling out of the Gulf of Mexico to build their nests among the dunes. It will be a spectacular sight!"

"Let's get moving then," said Chase. "A day trip to Padre Island ought to finish off our trip nicely!"

PART FIVE

SAVING
PACHYRHINOSAURUS

The pachy reacted to each move Kit made, flicking the point of its long but lightly built horn instantly to match her, move-for-move.

THOMAS P. HOPP

CHAPTER 21

Within hours they were watching the long-necked alamosaurs wade and roll in the surf at Padre Island. Offshore, they sighted several giant archelon turtles, which seemed to be waiting for nightfall to come ashore and lay their eggs.

Kit made observations of it all on a small computer for her class credit. She described a glorious sunny day in the warm estuary lands, with birds and pterodactyls overhead, other beasts familiar and unfamiliar foraging around them. Under the circumstances, she found herself truly enjoying Chase's companionship. On such a day she could easily forget her pressing life questions and just delight in being alive and being together with the person she loved most to be with. As she worked, sitting in the quahka while Chase roamed nearby observing a pack of coyotes that were observing the alamosaurs, a call came in on the radio. She answered it.

"Hi, Little Girl!" Will cried joyously when he heard her voice.

"What's up, Daddy?"

"Well, you see, winter is setting in early up here. I could use some help with the herd."

"We're just about on our way," Chase called, having overheard and approached the quahka.

"Just get here as soon as you can," Will said. "I got caught unprepared by an early snow. More snow is on the way. I got nearly five hundred Black Angus that shoulda been rounded up days ago and brought down off of the high prairies. If the snows come any harder, they might die."

Kit looked concerned. "I'm sorry Daddy," she said. "It's my fault the drive was postponed. Chase, how quickly can we get back to Montana?"

"Two or three days at top speed, unless the cops slow us down."

"Okay," Will said. "But just you be sure and hurry. There's a foot of snow already on the high prairie. Cattle ain't buffalo, you know. They don't have any instinct to scrape the snow and get at the grass underneath. They just nibble the tops of the grasses where they stick up. They'll starve in time, if we don't move 'em down to the lower pasture."

"We're on our way," Chase assured him.

***

True to their promise, they were at the ranch three days later and averted a near-tragedy by using their quahkas to gather the cattle onto the bare-and-wet asphalt road to Arran Kra, which the Kra had underlain with heat elements that kept it free of snow.

It wasn't hard to coax the herd down the new highway to the ranch, where the large pasture beyond the paddock was still free of snow. It couldn't provide enough forage for 500 cattle, but it would hold them until the spring thaw came and it was time to wrangle them back up onto the prairie again. Until then, hay from the big barn would keep them fat and fit. Elk and deer, down from the mountains by instinct, would filch some of the hay, but as far as Will was concerned they were welcome to it. He had hunted and put elk and deer meat on the table enough times to know that what's fair is fair.

***

With the cattle settled in their warmer home, life slowed down. Chase busied himself at his new home, which the Kra workers had completed to a state of weather-tightness, but had yet to finish off completely on the inside. Kit continued her studies, now actually able to spend some time in Bozeman at lectures, and socializing with Maddy Meyer and her friends. It seemed the time for adventures was over—but that was not quite true. When Dr. Ogilvey called her on her cell phone and asked if she would be interested in making some field observations, she readily agreed. But if she could have imagined the way they would turn out, she might have chosen the safety of the classroom over the excitement of the field.

Two days later, she found herself piloting a fighter-walker high into snowy Yellowstone Park, acting as driver and scientific colleague to Dr. Ogilvey. Although it was just mid-October, winter had descended on Yellowstone Park in all its furious glory. A storm had barreled down out of the Arctic much earlier this year than any on record. The mountains, plains, geyser basins, and lodgepole pine forests of Yellowstone all bore heavy mantles of white windblown snow that sparkled under a low sun. The chill blue sky was laden with threatening purple-gray clouds. Towering billows of steam rose from the geysers.

"It's wicked cold out there," Kit said, gesturing out the fighter-walker's canopy glass at the animals she and Dr. David Ogilvey had come to observe and make some scientific notes about. She had approached quietly in the two-legged, silver-metal-skinned quahka and hunkered its jet-fighter-like streamlined fuselage down near a bank of the Lamar River beside a stand of pines, trying to appear as inconspicuous as possible in the otherwise open and flat river valley. "I wonder how *they* like it?"

In front of them, scattered across the flats, were a half dozen big dark wooly beasts, just short of elephant sized, mingled among a herd of several dozen bison, but far outclassing them in bulk, wooliness, and horn coverage. To be sure, the bison standing knee-deep in snow were warmly covered in dark brown fur including thick curly wool that blanketed their shoulders and foreheads against the cruel wind that frosted their heads and shoulders with driven snowflakes. But the larger animals were even more densely wool-coated in a similar pattern, heaviest on the neck and shoulder hump, less dense at the rump. Nevertheless, there was no mistaking these animals as merely outsized American buffalo. They were—

"Pachyrhinosaurs," Professor Ogilvey said in his habitually lecturing tone, "were in some ways the dinosaurian equivalent of our buffalo, or I should say in scientific correctitude, *Bison bison*. Perhaps the wooly rhinoceros would be a more apt comparison, if it weren't extinct."

"Whichever example you choose, these beasties are just a bit bigger," Kit replied. "And fiercer."

"Yes, my dear," Ogilvey agreed. "No one knows better than you and Chase Armstrong just how fierce they can be."

"I'd rather not be reminded," Kit replied.

"Don't worry, Kit. I'm sure you and Chase will settle your differences someday."

"I didn't mean *that*," she resisted. "I meant the way one of these things flipped over Chase's pickup truck and smashed it to bits—with us in it! I thought pachyrhinosaurs had flat noses. But some of those nose horns are stupendous." She indicated the nearest large animal, which bore on its nose a dark brown rhinoceros-type horn the likes of which no rhinoceros had ever possessed. It was easily six feet long, angling forward from the top of the animal's beaked snout and towering almost as tall as a tall man like Chase. And making the animal look even more formidable was a bony frill at the back of its head covered in dark brown wool and fringed with smaller black horns that pointed in various angles up, down and sideways from its perimeter. Further compounding this formidable headgear were a pair of smaller upright horns aligned in the center of the frill. These were similar to, but longer than the secondary horns of rhinoceroses.

"Yes, my dear, of course you had a traumatic experience," the professor said in a sympathetic but somewhat perfunctory tone. "An attack by such an awesomely horned beast must have terrified both of you. But look how calm and picturesque these magnificent animals can be when not enraged by the roar of a truck engine. We now have our chance to observe details never before noted by human eyes. See how their frills, rather short for ceratopsians, are sunk cozily into the wool on their shoulders? I had wondered how they kept their frills from freezing in the cold of winter. Now I see the answer. The frills are protected by their woolly covering in front and some more nice wooly insulation behind. That must be sufficient to keep warm blood flowing through the living bone of the frill even in the face of the fiercest of winter storms. No wonder pachyrhinosaurs had shorter frills than triceratops. As we have seen, the long-frilled triceratopses migrate south for the winter while the short-frilled pachies bear the brunt of the winter cold right here, having adapted to the worst kinds of Arctic conditions."

The temperature reading outside the quahka was displayed in glowing green numerals on the fighter-walker's instrument panel in degrees of the Kra temperature scale. Though indecipherable to Kit, they had meaning to Dr. Ogilvey, who was the world's preeminent expert on the Kra numbering system and scale of temperature, called Klistohn. Sitting tandem behind Kit within the cockpit in a second seat fashioned for him in the workshops of Arran Kra and installed behind the pilot seat in the normally solo-piloted walking machine, Dr. O leaned around Kit, pushed his khaki safari hat back on his balding head and gazed through his thick spectacles at the gauge.

"Let's see." He scratched at a gray-bearded jaw. "Two hundred fifty-five degrees Klistohn is, er, minus two-sixty-eight times one-point-three-seven plus twelve. That would be, er, minus nine degrees Celsius or fifteen degrees Fahrenheit—if I've done the calculations correctly."

"If you say so, Doc," Kit replied. "All I know is, I'm glad this quahka's nice and warm."

"And well armored," Dr. O murmured. "Just in case."

"I still find it hard to accept that a dinosaur could be so well adapted to freezing weather," Kit remarked, never taking her eyes off the closest beast, which seemed near enough to be a threat.

"Believe the testimony of your own eyes," Ogilvey responded. "You're just reluctant to relinquish the fallacious notion of the Late Cretaceous Era as a time of tropical temperatures throughout the world. I, on the other hand, have been arguing with my paleontological colleague George Summerlin for years that although most of the world was indeed warmer then, nevertheless the farthest northern landmasses of the Late Cretaceous saw some bitter cold in the dark depths of winter, especially in the highlands. Does Summerlin truly believe that no large animals inhabited the mountain ranges of Cretaceous Alaska or Siberia? Those highlands were frigid in winter even in the warmest epochs of the Cretaceous. All we have lacked is fossil evidence proving this sort of cold-adaption. But that lack is only because those ancient cold uplands were all eroding rather than building up sediments, so no fossils were ever buried in the first place. It's just a trick of fate that no fossil beds have been found in what were high and cold environments sixty-five million years ago in the regions around the poles. Gar assures me that such places did indeed exist. And pachyrhinosaurs were prime inhabitants of those places, in just the way vast herds of bison and caribou have claimed them in our times. Indeed, Kit, now that dinosaurs have returned to the earth through the agency of the Kra, we can see for ourselves that pachyrhinosaurs are easily capable of tolerating sub-zero temperatures. I have noticed, however, that some of them tend to linger near the geysers and hot springs where the snow cover is thinner and they can get winter grass to eat. Some Yellowstone bison do the same."

Kit glanced at a nearby small geyser and its surrounding hot water pool. Dense white steam billowed off the geyser's fountain-like spray and rose from the surface of the iridescent blue pond. Glinting in the winter sun, it was an enchanting sight.

Ogilvey lectured on. "With the advanced degree of cold adaptation these animals possess, only the horrendous cold of the post-asteroid global winter was able to do them in sixty-five million years ago. Dinosaurs like these truly did not deserve extinction."

Kit settled back in her pilot seat. "You know, you're right," she said.

"Of course I am," Ogilvey responded without thinking first. And then he asked, "About what?"

"About the calmness of this scene."

"Hmm. Yes," he agreed good-naturedly, settling back as Kit had, to take it all in.

After they had arrived, coming cross-country from her father's ranch sixty miles away to the north without the need for roads, she had hunkered the two-legged machine down and retracted its arms to diminish its profile in the snowy landscape and allow the animals to behave in ways that came naturally to them. The view outside the quahka's glass canopy was idyllic in its frigid, snowy splendor. Just like the bison, the pachyrhinosaurs were idle, standing with their beaked noses into the wind, the wool on their humped shoulders receiving a blanket of white but protecting their bodies from the breeze's chilling effects. Some of them were, like the bison, chewing their cud. Others chewed grass freshly dug from snowdrifts. The movement of their jaws was their only motion, except when one or another of the big beasts scraped the ground with an elephantine forepaw to dig out more grass.

"And so," Ogilvey murmured, "let's resume our count. Twenty-seven bison, was it?"

"Yes," Kit replied.

Ogilvey duly noted the number on a clipboard. "And adult pachies?"

"Just two of the largest size."

"Males—or bulls, I should say," Ogilvey made another note.

"And four of the slightly smaller adults."

"Cows." He made another note. "And juveniles?" he prompted.

Kit did a quick count of the smallest pachies. "Seven approximately bison-sized ones."

"This year's brood," Ogilvey replied, making another note.

"And five of the slightly larger ones."

"Last year's brood, the yearlings."

"All accounted for," Kit concluded.

As Ogilvey scribbled more notes, Kit puzzled, "How do they manage to grow their babies as big as full-grown buffalo in a single summer and fall?"

While still writing, Ogilvey murmured, "It starts with a well-placed nest. A sandy area and a modest stretch of warm sunny days, even in the mid-summer Arctic was sufficient to get the embryos within the eggs to go through their final stage of development before hatching. If the weather turned cold, so Gar tells me, then even the most immense dinosaurs were able, in one way or another, to lie across their nests to keep them dry and warm."

"That would have been hard to believe," Kit said, "until I saw alamosaurs do it. They're so huge, I would have bet they would crush their eggs if they sat on them."

"Aha, my precocious student, you've made a good observation but I didn't say 'sit,' I said 'lie.' Perhaps we'll see how pachyrhinosaurs do it one of these days. According to Gar, the weight of the parent goes on the sandy rim of the nest, not on the eggs. The babies are safely covered under a lid formed by the adult's body and warmed by the parent's belly heat, but not at all subjected to pressure. And then of course, after hatching came hyperalimentation."

"Hyper— what?"

"—Alimentation," Ogilvey said, "is, essentially, overfeeding by the loving parents. Parent pachyrhinosaurs would forage near their hatching grounds, gathering huge amounts of grass, brush, and other plant matter, which they swallowed but later regurgitated and chewed as cud. The food was processed into a mushy, congealed mass that was vomited up at the nest for the hatchlings to consume, which they did greedily, growing to almost half adult size in the space of six months."

"Y-u-uck," Kit said with distaste. "I know about dinosaur vomit. Rufus, our parasaurolophus, upchucked plenty of disgusting wads of slimy hay for his babies—right next to our barn!"

"So he did," Ogilvey concurred. "And hence the growth rate of those duckbill goslings to horse size in their first year, big enough to join Rufus and Henrietta on their annual fall migration from Montana to Texas."

"I miss the whole family," Kit sighed.

"They will be back like oversized songbirds in the springtime. Now, look at how these pachy babies have grown. When they hatched this summer in their sandy nest on the banks of Eggshell Creek, they were no larger than the size of big guinea pigs and every bit as fuzzy and cute. But they have attained bison size in a single growth season! Amazing. That rapid development was due to the constant provision of processed food by their parents, as well as their own pro-digious grazing. They have been munching on every available bush, shrub, or blade of grass they could find on the high plains, foraging literally by the ton. I dare say a human child would grow that large in a year if provided regurgitated food by its parents."

Kit shuddered in disgust. "A lovely image, professor. But tell me, do the parents feed the yearlings that way, too?"

"No, my dear. The adults are so focused on fostering the hatchlings that they drive away any yearling who tries to mooch a bite of their cud-vomit."

"Phew," Kit exclaimed. "Dinosaurs sure do a lot of barf-ing."

"It's a way of life for them. Many modern birds do the same."

"Why don't pachies migrate south for the winter like the other dinosaurs?"

"Why should they? They've obviously adopted a strategy of sticking it out through the bitter winter by growing long coats of fur." He scribbled again. "I note that the winter coats of the young are longer and denser than those of their parents—as thick as the coats of musk oxen. The same is true for the young of that herd of wooly iguanodonts, which we see moving in the distance and which, by the way, I'll need to name, one of these days."

"How about Fuzzosaurus?" Kit suggested.

"Hmm. Yes. What is the Greek for 'fuzz'? Ah, well. Next,

some notes on habits. Let's see, cud chewing suggests a multi-chambered stomach as in cows and bison, to thoroughly ferment the food and aid in its digestion—"

"Listen!" Kit interrupted the professor's ruminations. "What's that roaring sound? Another strange creature?"

Ogilvey kept scribbling. "Sounds more mechanical than dinosaurian," he murmured.

"Now I recognize it," Kit said. "It's a snowmobile engine."

"Not likely," Ogilvey replied. "Park officials have suspended snowmobiling here until any threats the dinosaurs pose are fully understood. That's one reason we're here—to get a count as well as to observe the animals' habits."

"If the park is supposed to be closed, you'd better explain that to *them*." Kit pointed at a snowmobile with two riders that roared over a low hillside. It came to a stop not far from them on a low rise overlooking the river plain.

CHAPTER 22

Ogilvey pushed his glasses up on the bridge of his nose and squinted at the machine, which had stopped about fifty yards from them. "The driver looks familiar," he murmured. "He's bundled in a snow suit and ski hat but those pink, chubby cheeks—"

"Bobby Everett!" Kit exclaimed after taking a good look.

"He'll get a citation and a major fine if a park ranger spots him—Chase Armstrong for instance."

"No," Kit said in an irritated tone. "He won't get a fine. Not with *her* riding behind him."

"Oh, yes," Ogilvey agreed after taking a look at the tall, long-haired blond passenger dressed in a smart-looking, form fitting pale blue snow suit and ski hat. "I see he has brought a member of the press—Thera McArty."

"Oh, joy," Kit muttered sarcastically. "My favorite person."

Bobby and Thera dismounted their ride and Thera pulled an oversized camera out of a storage compartment. She began taking photos with a huge zoom lens that moved in and out as she framed shots of the animals.

"What we have here," Dr. O muttered, "is a meddler."

"If she disturbs these animals—" Kit began.

"She'll ruin our observations," Ogilvey finished her sentence.

"No," Kit corrected, "the pachies will ruin *her!* I hope."

"Tut, tut," Dr. O said with a smile. "What I hope is that she won't steal our discoveries and publish them before we make a full scientific presentation."

"I wouldn't put anything past her," Kit replied. "She's a man-stealer. Why not science too? But it looks like she's more interested in great shots for National Photographic than in animal behavior. If you ask me, she's too close to them."

"Yes, indeed," Dr. O agreed. "The whole herd have paused their eating to look at those two. If I were them, I would give a thought to personal safety."

Kit patted the dashboard of the quahka. "That's one nice thing about this ride," she said. "We're a lot safer inside a war machine, and warmer too."

"True," Ogilvey replied. "The heated comfort of the quah-ka has transformed the job of wildlife observation. Now it's almost as cushy as an office job."

Kit grumbled, "We're not going to observe much as long as *they're* annoying the herd."

"They'll be gone soon enough." Ogilvey leaned back and made himself comfortable. "Meanwhile, we can observe things other than behavior. Those colossal nose horns, for instance."

"I've been meaning to ask you about those," Kit said, "ever since Chase's pickup got punctured by one."

"Ask away," the professor said.

"Since when do pachyrhinosaurs have long nose horns? Where are the flat nose bumps you always see in books and movies?"

"That answer is simple, Kit. There were multiple different species of pachyrhinosaurus. Some did indeed did have stupendously long nose horns, as we see here."

"But that goes against everything I've learned about pachyrhinosaurus."

"Learned? From whom?"

"From books. And from Disney's *Dinosaur* movie—"

"Ahh!" Ogilvey said.

"From *Dinotopia*—"

"Ho!"

"And *Walking With Dinosaurs*."

"Heeh!" Ogilvey laughed. "Now Kit, you must admit that

those are not exactly *scientific* sources of information."

"Of course. They're popular books and movies."

"Indeed. And all of them subscribe to what always was just one of several views of the creature."

"But I've read scientific papers that claimed the bump was covered with a hard shell of horn for use as a blunt battering ram."

"Heeh!" Ogilvey screeched. "A mere speculation, written before we had the chance to see the actual creature in the flesh and, er, horn. Perhaps you should have read more thoroughly in the scientific literature. If you had, then you would have come across other papers that made the case that the large lump of bone on the creature's nose was there to solidly anchor a stupendous nose horn—much better for fending off a T rex attack."

"I thought the battering ram looked pretty effective."

Perhaps, but consider this—in order to bump a huge carnivore with a blunt nose, a pachyrhinosaur would need to run in close under the predator's body. Now, I hope I need not remind you that getting in close to a rex would put the pachy's back and flanks in easy reach of the carnivore's deadly jaws. It seems a poor defensive strategy. But look at these creatures. In some cases their nose horns extend a good ten feet ahead of the protective frills covering their necks. With such long horns, they can engage a rex at a distance, rather than rushing in close and exposing their flanks. No, Kit, nose-bumping pachyrhinosaurs were the exception, not the rule. Otherwise, the rexes would have made short work of them and their stubby armament."

"But people who grew up loving nose-bumping pachies will be disappointed! Including me!"

Ogilvey thought for a moment. "Aha!" he said at last. "I've got the answer. We needn't dispose of the nose-bumping pachyrhinosaur completely."

"What do you mean? We can see the long horns in front of us right now."

Ogilvey raised a pedantic finger. "The fossil record clearly shows at least three separate species of pachyrhinosaur and the one in front of us is a fourth. If we must continue to allow the cherished notion of a nose-bumping pachy, then why not assign that status to the others and let this species be the exception? The others are all extinct anyway, so no one will ever know for sure."

"That's a good idea," Kit said. "So people can keep their model pachyrhinosaurs with nose bumps, and watch Disney's *Dinosaur*, and *Dinotopia*, and *Walking With Dinosaurs*, without getting confused."

"Precisely," Ogilvey agreed. "And yet we can still present to the world our new scientific discovery—that the longest nose horn to ever grace any animal in the entire history of the world, sat atop that nose bump!"

The professor had been casually observing the pachyrhinosaur herd outside the canopy glass as they talked. Suddenly his owlish, gray-bearded face took on a look of amazement. "Oh, my!" he said just audibly.

"What is it?" Kit looked around as if searching for danger.

Ogilvey knit his brows and thought deeply for a moment. "Um-hum. Yes. Most certainly. Indeed!" he said, apparently having an internal debate and then resolving it.

"What?" Kit demanded.

"I have it!" he said, smiling his slightly buck-toothed grin with his magnified eyes twinkling behind his thick glasses. "I have solved the riddle of why these pachyrhinosaurs have a bump of bone, rather than a full, bony horn core on their noses. Hmmph. Um-hum," he continued his internal debate.

"Well!" Kit cried. "Don't keep me in suspense. What's the secret?"

In answer, Ogilvey gestured toward one of the pachyrhino-saurs. "Take a good look at the nose horn on that nearest big male."

"Yeah? What about it? It's big. I know that only too well. One of those poked clean through the cab of Chase's pickup and knocked him out cold."

"Er, yes, indeed. It is quite a formidable weapon. But you have not perceived what I am most concerned with."

"What?" She looked again. "It's incredibly long. Almost eight feet, I'd say."

"And?"

"It's got a very sharp point."

"Correct. Almost as if it has been honed on rocks and trees. And?"

"And— Oh. I see. It's practically encased in snow and ice!"

"Exactly!" Ogilvey cried. "That is my point!"

Kit thought a moment. "Your point is that it can get ice on it?"

"Yes, indeed! Now here is a little information you may not have learned in your biology classes so far. Bone is a living tissue. Horn is not. If bone is subjected to freezing conditions it will not only freeze but it will die. Horn, on the other hand, is no more than a mass of keratin protein. It cannot die of cold because it is not alive in the first place! Hence, even if coated in ice by a winter storm, the boneless horn of a pachyrhinosaurus will not be harmed at all. On the other hand, consider the centrosaurs, pachyrhinosaur's ancestors from warmer times and places. They had tall bony cores in their nose horns. Therefore, if we were looking at a centrosaur right now instead of a pachyrhinosaur, we would be looking at an animal whose nose-horn was being damaged irreversibly as we speak. The bone inside would rot where it had frozen, perhaps becoming a dangerous bone infection. Or the horn might fall off completely, leaving the centrosaur defenseless against predators!"

"You never cease to amaze me, Dr. O."

"Then you like my theory?"

"I love it!"

"That horn," Ogilvey mused, looking at the pachy again, "is a hardened, solid mass external to the animal's body. It can freeze and thaw any number of times, because it is not a living part of the creature any more than your hair is, Kit. And hair, as you know, may be exposed to freezing temperatures and even gather ice with no consequence at all. Hence, the identical situation applies to the pachyrhinosaur's long, boneless nose horn—it may ice up without consequence to its owner. It's a brilliant solution to the problem of having a long horn in a sometimes fiercely cold environment. It's very much the same solution that our wooly rhinoceros utilized during the Ice Ages, and for the same reason. But pachyrhinosaurs came up with the solution sixty-five million years earlier!"

"Now, wait a minute," Kit said. "There have never been any fossils found of pachyrhinosaurs showing even a hint of a nose horn."

"A point well taken," Ogilvey admitted. "However, consider this—the keratinous claws of carnivorous dinosaurs are almost never preserved, even though the bony core of the claw is preserved. Furthermore, the Natural History Museum in London houses a fine mummified specimen of a wooly rhinoceros that was found in a bog in the Ukraine. It is so well preserved that even its skin and some internal organs are intact. However, the animal's keratinous nose horn had become detached after death. It is entirely missing from the specimen, which by the way, had also lost most of its keratinous hair."

"I get the picture," Kit said. "But maybe it was a hornless species of rhinoceros."

"An astute suggestion, Kit, but unfortunately incorrect. Cave dwellers of the time painted images of the rhinoceros with a very long nose horn and heavy fur. In addition, quite a few detached horns have been found lying on the arctic tundra. So the detachment of a keratinous horn after death is well established for rhinoceroses. Why couldn't it also be true for pachyrhinosaurs? In fact, given the London rhinoceros specimen, we have a precedent for *expecting* a dead pachyrhinosaur to lose its horn, not keep it."

"I yield to your great wisdom," Kit said a little sarcastically.

"As you should, Kit," Ogilvey said, ignoring her jibe. "Now if only my arch nemesis Professor George Summerlin would follow your example."

"Oh-oh," Kit said. "Is Summerlin involved in this one, too?"

"Indeed, he is. And on the wrong side of the argument, as usual. He is a chief proponent of the theory that the thick nose bones constituted a battering ram. But as we see, the thick bump was simply a solid attachment point for a world-record-breaking, rhinoceros-style horn."

"Maybe some of the other species of pachyrhinosaurs really did have battering rams."

"Of course, that could be possible for the other species that flourished and then became extinct before this creature— *Pachyrhinosaurus lakustai, canadensis,* and *perotorum.* Although I personally doubt it."

"Which species is this?"

"An altogether new one, I believe. Based on its incredible horn, I intend to propose the name, *Pachyrhinosaurus longicornus,* the longhorned pachyrhinosaur. You and I must prepare a paper proposing the name to the International Commission on Zoological Nomenclature. But never mind that. I am in the midst of another revelation regarding pachyrhinosaurs."

"And what is that?" Kit asked incredulously.

"It occurs to me there is another advantage to a keratinous, rather than a bony nose horn. A horn is lighter, if made of protein rather than bone. Therefore, it can be swung side-to-side quickly to impale even the most agile attacker."

"The horn that mangled Chase's truck was lightning fast."

"Exactly. A bony horn could never have moved so quickly. Its mass would have made it difficult to maneuver. "

"I think you're onto something, Doc. A light-weight sword like a duelist's rapier."

"Yes indeed, Kit! I can hardly wait to see George Summerlin's humiliated expression at the next meeting of the Paleontological Society when we present our findings."

"That's fine for you, Doc, getting your revenge on Summerlin. I'll be more interested in my colleagues smiles of delight."

"As well you should be, Kit. But I have put up with Summerlin's sniping for years, and his unceasing folly. Can you name another creature, modern or ancient, that has a battering ram on its nose?"

"Well, um—"

"Don't strain your brain, Kit. There are none. Battering ram forehead, yes. Witness the boneheaded pachycephalosaurs, or our heavy-horned musk oxen and bighorn sheep. But the battering ram in those cases is atop the cranium, not on the nose. The cranium is at the end of the spinal column, which delivers the power thrust from the legs. Summerlin's nose-ramming pachyrhinosaur is physically preposterous. An impacting snout would have an extra segment between the impact point and the spinal column—and a flexible hinge that would dissipate the energy coming from the body. The force of the blow would be *lessened* by the hinging of the head on the neck upon impact. That is why all known battering ram creatures use the crown of the head, not the nose."

"I get your point," Kit said. "All creatures that strike with the nose use a horn. They stab, gouge, or toss their opponents. They don't smash into them."

"Exactly!" Ogilvey smiled triumphantly. "*Quod erat demonstrandum.*" He patted his plump sides in satisfaction.

"Enough talk, Doc!" Kit suddenly exclaimed. "Look what's happening now!"

CHAPTER 23

Thera McArty had taken her place again behind Bobby Everett. He gunned the engine of the snowmobile, driving down off the overlook and out among the congregated animals. As the snowmobile's noise scattered bison and pachies, Thera raised her camera to snap shots of the animals in motion.

"That witch," Kit hissed. "Something bad is going to happen."

"Something bad *is* happening," Ogilvey concurred. "Look down by the river." He pointed to the frozen surface of an oxbow of the Lamar River, where the fifty-foot wide expanse of the channel was solidly frozen into blocky sections of blue-white ice covered in drifted snow. Six of the youngest pachies had run down the sloping bank to escape the noise and smoke of the snowmobile. Now they trotted out onto the river's frozen surface.

"It looks like the ice can take their weight," Kit said hopefully.

"It's not the young ones I'm worried about," Ogilvey said. "Here comes Mamma!"

They watched, open-mouthed, as a big female pachy came down the slope to the river. She bawled out a summoning cry to get her wayward young back on solid ground. They started in her direction, but the snowmobile's engine roared again and they turned back toward the middle of the channel.

Braying despairingly, the mother took one careful step onto

the ice—and then another, and another. Kit and Ogilvey held their breaths as she joined her calves in the middle of the ice floe. She turned back toward the shore, unconcerned about the noise of the snowmobile. Her brood took heart and followed her until—with a sickening crunch that could be heard within the sealed quahka—the ice cracked.

"Oh, no!" Kit cried as one of the mother's hind legs plunged down and jagged sheets of ice rose around it. The babies sprinted for shore and the mother gamely tried to follow them. But the ice cracked again, and then again, and finally she dropped heavily into the frigid river, sending out waves of gray water onto the ice on either side of her. As her babies scrambled back onto the bank, the brave mother sank into the deepest part of the channel until only her head was above water. She thrashed at the surrounding ice with her horn and forelegs, sending frigid spray tens of feet into the air, but she made little progress toward the shore.

"Oh, my gosh," Kit gasped. "She'll drown."

"Or die of hypothermia," Ogilvey added.

"What's the difference?" Kit growled. "Those fools have killed her as surely as if they used a gun. Look at Thera! She's still taking pictures!"

Ogilvey reached over Kit's shoulder and took a radio handset from the quahka's dashboard. He pressed a button on it and called, "Chase Armstrong! Chase, do you read?"

After a moment, Chase's voice came back casually. "Sitting here in a comfortable quahka with my feet up, watching my wolves squabble with some coyotes over a frozen iguanodont carcass. Pretty interesting stuff."

"Oh, really?" Ogilvey remarked, momentarily forgetting his purpose. "Do they prefer meat on the bone or are they after entrails?"

Kit snatched the mike from the doctor's hand. "Listen Chase," she shouted. "You've got to get over here right away!"

"Oh?" he responded a little coolly. "Have you had a change of heart about our—problem?"

"It's not about that. A mother pachy has just fallen into the

Lamar River. She'll die if we don't do something."

"Sounds bad," he said, taking a serious tone. "You think we should try to fish her out?"

"Well," Kit said heatedly, "what else would you propose?"

"I didn't propose anything. I've learned that making proposals to you can be a painful experience. You got a plan?"

"We'll think of something. Just get here, quick!"

"All right. I'm on my way."

The female pachy had made some progress toward the bank. But she had foundered at the broken edge of a thick ice sheet that barred her progress up the slippery underwater slope of the river channel. Her fur was matted with cold water and her eyes were wide with terror. Her babies stood on the bank bleating in fear as she struggled against the ice barrier.

Ogilvey shook his head. "I don't know, Kit. If we drive down there to help, she might smash the quahka. We could be killed ourselves."

Kit thought for a moment. "If I had a rope, I could get it around her horn. We could try to pull her out."

"If any cowgirl could lasso her," Ogilvey said, "that would be you."

"But my ropes are all in our barn sixty miles away."

Ogilvey put up an index finger. "I believe the Kra keep some sort of cable or fiber in the tool compartment."

Kit put on her heavy shearling coat and her cowboy hat, popped the quahka's canopy open, and jumped down into the knee-deep snow. Ignoring the chill on her blue-jeaned legs and cowboy-booted feet, she moved quickly around the quahka, opened a hatch on the rear of the fuselage, and pulled out a thin, coiled rope. "It doesn't look thick enough to drag her out without snapping," she called up to Dr. O.

"Don't be so sure," Ogilvey responded. "If I recall Gar's description, it's made from pure carbon nanofibers. Their tensile strength is greater than high-carbon steel. And besides, it's your only option, isn't it?"

Kit quickly fashioned a lasso from the rope and moved to

the river's edge. The pachy mother was still thrashing desperately, but she had slowed somewhat, as if hypothermia were already setting in. She paused, panting, and her breath puffed icy billows that drifted away on the stiff cold breeze like geyser steam.

Kit spun the lariat up over her head, cowgirl-style, and made her throw. The circling rope spun with scarcely a wobble, carrying out over the blue ice and gray water, propelled by Kit's expert toss. As planned, it fell over the cow's nose horn and draped down across her face. As it did so, Kit yanked the rope to draw the noose tight. The rope slipped into the cow's puffing mouth and tightened on the space between the beak and the rear chewing teeth. "That'll do it!" Kit exclaimed. Her rope had gotten the best possible grip around the animal's muzzle.

Now came the question of what to do with the lifeline she had secured to the animal. Unaware that Kit was trying to help, the pachy bellowed and shook her head in an effort to throw off the noose. But the noose held.

"Bring the rope here," Ogilvey called from behind her. "There's a roller inside the laser arm."

Kit scrambled to the right arm of the quahka with her end of the rope as Dr. O switched to the driver's seat and pressed a button. A small cover opened on the arm and, inside, Kit saw a metal roller with a notch at one end. She looped the rope around the notch and called, "Okay!"

Dr. O engaged a motor and the roller began to wind the rope around itself. As the rope tightened, it began drawing the pachy toward shore. Frightened by this new force, she panicked and resisted with all her might, thrashing and shaking her head.

"She's not helping the situation any," Kit cried.

Suddenly, one of the pachy's fierce tugs caused the quahka to slip on the snowy slope and lurch downhill. "Oh, dear!" Ogilvey cried, momentarily losing his composure. He flipped a lever that let some of the rope out and provided slack. Then with uncharacteristic deftness, he stood the quahka on its two metallic legs and backed it toward the trees. Using a joystick to reach out with the left arm's pincer, he gripped a lodgepole pine trunk. Then he resumed winding with the right arm, pulling the rope tight again.

"Heeh!" he cried gleefully as the rope tightened on the pachy's snout. "That should suffice! Ingenious, if I do say so myself. Don't you agree, Kit?"

Instead of an answer, he heard Kit's terrified scream. Simultaneously, he heard a new and more monstrous bellow.

The biggest of the bull pachies had approached unnoticed while Kit and Ogilvey were preoccupied with the cow. Now the colossal animal pawed the snow in preparation for a charge. For her part, the cow seemed to have realized that the lasso was helping rather than harming her. She strained at the edge of the ice just below the quahka, but the ice continued to bar her way. The riverbank was so steep and covered in such thick ice that each time she almost got out, she slid back into the frigid water.

The bull, however, did not understand Ogilvey's good intentions. It bellowed again and threatened the quahka by digging at the snow with its fore- and hind-paws. It lowered its head and tossed its prodigious horn from side to side as nimbly as Kit and Ogilvey had discussed. Its bristle-tufted tail stood high behind it, poised in balance for a charge.

"Oh, dear," Ogilvey cried. "I would zap him with the electric bolt but the gun arm is… er… preoccupied." With the rope stretched tight to the cow's snout, the arm's electric gun barrel could not be aimed at the bull. "Whatever shall I do?"

"I don't know," Kit cried, moving behind some boulders near the nose of the quahka and feeling very exposed to the bull's anger. "But you had better think of something, fast!"

The bull bellowed once more and then charged—not at Ogilvey, but at Kit!

"Not this again!" she screamed as she ducked down behind the boulders.

The bull tried to circle the boulders to get at her but was

impeded by the quahka on one side and the precipitous river slope on the other.

"Perhaps this will help?" Ogilvey pressed a button that sounded a loud blast from the quahka's loudspeaker—the electronically generated thunder of a parasaurolophus's warning call. As it echoed in the woods and nearby hills, the monster retreated a few steps and Kit took the opportunity to rush through the snow to the far side of the quahka. There, she stumbled in a deep snowdrift and went down as Dr. O called again into the radio mike, "Chase my boy, if you're coming, get here quickly! We are about to become pachyrhinosaurus fodder!"

"I'm moving as fast as I can," Chase replied. "It's a blizzard up this way."

The male pawed the ground again and bellowed louder.

The female finally got sufficient footing on the muddy shore to lurch out of the river with the aid of the rope. She struggled out of the water and trotted several steps onto the solid shore, and then paused to shake herself much the way a dog does, throwing a shower of drops on all sides and clearing her fur of the bulk of the cold water. Then she stood still on the bank, trembling and appearing lethargic and shaky on her feet. Her bison-sized babies quickly gathered around her, bleating with joy at their reunion.

"She's too wobbly to move far," Ogilvey called. "And that rope may entangle her."

"I'm on it," Kit replied, rising from the snowdrift. "The rope is tight around her snout. Let it go!"

Ogilvey reversed the spool direction and the rope slacked and then fell free of the arm entirely. He swung the arm to face the bull, preparing to unleash the electric bolt if it was needed.

Kit grabbed the loose end of the rope and gave it a deft flick with her wrist. A ripple propagated along the rope to the cow and the knot on the side of her beak loosened. Another flick and another ripple caused the noose to go slack. Feeling it drooping, the female swiped her horn in the snow and the rope came loose, lying like a thin brown snake over the white ground. She turned and walked away with her babies gathered around her as if trying to warm her with their smaller but drier bodies.

Kit looked up at Dr. O and smiled. She raised her hands to the sides. "I guess that's that!"

"Not quite my dear. Look out!"

Kit heard the thudding of the male's feet charging through the snow. She didn't even look in his direction, knowing the sight of his charge might freeze her in panic. Instead, she ran quickly to get behind the quahka, as Ogilvey turned it to deal with the charge. Once behind the quahka, she heard the crackle of the electric bolt discharging from the weapon arm.

Dr. O cried out, "It's not working too well!"

Kit couldn't see much from her position behind the quahka, but she could tell from Dr. O's desperate cries and the bellowing of the enraged beast, that the bolt was insufficient to drive it back. Suddenly the quahka lifted entirely off the ground. It had been hooked under its belly by that awful horn! "Who-o-a!" Dr. O howled as the machine tipped backward onto its stubby tail and then fell over on its side, spilling him out of the open canopy into a snowdrift beside Kit!

"*Now* what do we do?" Kit asked as she helped the paleontologist to his feet.

"Pray?" Ogilvey responded, brushing away a rather comical dusting of snow that had covered his red flannel shirt and brown shearling vest, which fit his portly body rather too tightly. "We've made some trouble for ourselves, haven't we?"

The male began circling around the quahka on the riverbank side, where the cow and the rope had barred his way before.

Kit sprinted away from the quahka and ran to a nearby boulder that stuck up with a snowcap on top that made it nearly as tall as Kit. Ogilvey attempted to follow her to her somewhat inadequate cover, but slipped halfway and went down on one knee in the open.

"Save yourself Kit," he cried as the bull pachy lumbered toward him, lowering its horn.

"No!" Kit cried in response. And then she shouted at the pachy, "Hey yah!" She raised her arms and waved, but could not catch the big animal's eye. She came out from behind her cover and, desperate to intervene, took up the only weapon available to her—digging into a snowdrift, she made a snowball. Packing it hard, she reared back and let go a hard toss. The snowball impacted the animal's snout and burst apart in a spray of white. The bull flinched and blinked his dark brown eye, but he kept his attention riveted on Ogilvey, who was floundering in the snow and making little progress.

Kit made another snowball, tossed it, and shouted "Hey! Over here!" just as it hit the big beast on the cheek. This made the bull turn from Ogilvey and wheel in Kit's direction, lowering its ten-foot horn to point at her.

"Uh-oh," she said under her breath. "What do I do now?" The huge beast moved forward slowly until the point of its horn was just a few feet from her chest. Knowing the pachy could run her down quickly if she left the scant refuge of her boulder to run across an open space, Kit set her feet wide and poised her arms to the sides for balance. Seeing that her best chances were among the trees of the forest, she tried to fake out the beast before running that way. She took a quick, feinting step to the left and then just as quickly jumped back to the right. She had planned to start her sprint when the animal followed her feint to the left, but the bull thwarted her plan by demonstrating exactly the phenomenon Dr. O had predicted. The pachy reacted to each move she made, flicking the point of its long but lightly built horn instantly to match her, move-for-move. Kit froze in place, dismayed at how easily the great animal could maneuver to keep that horrendous horn pointed at her heart. She swallowed hard, feeling a sense of imminent doom. "Doc," she croaked in a tremulous voice. "I guess you're right about these horns being easy to maneuver. You'd better get away while you can. I think I'm a gonner."

"Where the devil is Chase Armstrong!" Ogilvey growled. "Has he forgotten us?"

At that moment, the roar of the snowmobile engine announced that at least Bobby Everett hadn't forgotten them. His red-cheeked face was drawn into a fearful, wide-eyed and round-mouthed expression of terror, but nevertheless he gunned his engine and raced straight toward the colossal animal. He shouted, "Run, Kit!" and steered his roaring machine around the flank of the pachyrhinosaur and up the side of the boulder, which was banked with snow. The snowmobile flew into the air while Thera screamed, clutching Bobby awkwardly but holding her camera tightly in one hand. They slammed down hard in front of the beast's nose and raced away as it swung its long-horned nose and charged after them. Kit ran to the safety of the trees as the beast pursued the snowmobile.

Thera continued snapping photos. And she wasn't the only person on the snowmobile keeping a close eye on the thundering beast. Bobby turned his head to measure the distance between him and the animal, but that was a mistake. A thicket of snow-laden sagebrush lay dead ahead of him. Thera spotted the threat first. "Watch out!" she shouted.

"I am watching out!" Bobby shouted back.

"Not this way," she hollered. "That way!" He looked forward again just as the snowmobile plowed into the sagebrush thicket and came to an abrupt halt. Both Bobby and Thera were tossed into the snow-covered bushes. Bobby was up in an instant, wrenching at the overturned snowmobile's handlebars to set it upright, but it was too heavily entangled in branches.

When the bull caught up, it lowered its horn and gouged at the snowmobile, lifting it out of the sagebrush and sending it cart-wheeling into the air. As it crashed down on a mound of sagebrush, apparently ruined, the beast turned to put Bobby and Thera at bay with its incredibly maneuverable horn. Astonishingly, Thera was still snapping photos.

"Well," Kit said uncertainly, "I guess we'd better try to help them."

"What can we do?" Ogilvey resisted. "Throw more snowballs? Our quahka is topsy-turvy!"

Suddenly a new sound tore the frigid air. It was the foghorn honk of the parasaurolophus alarm on Chase Armstrong's quahka.

When Chase arrived at the scene of the fight, he slowed his quahka from a dead run to a fast walk while he sized up the situation. To his left, a snowmobile lay overturned in a thicket with a man and a woman cowering while a pachyrhinosaur bull bellowed and aimed its horn at them. To his right, a fighter-walker lay on its side with Dr. O and Kit in not-much-better circumstances.

The enraged pachyrhinosaurus bellowed and pawed the ground, seeming uncertain which human to attack first. Its long dinosaurian tail, heavily covered in black, bristling hair, was held high behind it. Chase knew through experience with bison that this tail posture signaled an impending charge. He needed a rescue plan—quickly.

At the overturned quahka, Dr. Ogilvey grabbed the radio mike from inside the cockpit. "Chase!" he warned. "Don't forget our experience with that Coahuilaceratops in Mexico! This creature is also immune to the electric bolt. The horns and frill shield it somehow. I don't think you'll have much luck if you try it."

"Only one way to find out!" Chase radioed back. He approached the pachy, and when it turned to face him, he blasted it full in the face with his bolt. This enraged the creature but it was unwilling to retreat. Instead, it bent low and stood firm as the blast played over its horn and frill.

"It's no use, my boy!" Ogilvey cried. "You'll have to use lethal force. Fire your laser cannon."

"Can't do that, Doc," Chase responded flatly. "My job's protecting wildlife, not killing it, remember? Now, let me think."

Meanwhile, the bull had a mind of his own. Confronted by opponents on three sides and the river on the fourth, he chose the least of his antagonists. Dropping his horn low, he charged the snowmobilers, singling out Bobby Everett, who waded desperately into the thicket as the pachy barreled toward him.

Chase saw the opportunity for one last trick. The bull bared its left flank as it crossed in front of him, and Chase aimed his electric bolt at the space beneath the big beast's frill. The bolt struck true, just behind the ear hole. At first the animal roared and resisted, but Chase had indeed found a tender spot, and it ultimately broke off its charge. Wheeling and leaving Bobby tangled helplessly in the sagebrush, the bull trotted away shaking his head, following the cow and calves as they retreated onto the flats. Chase pursued the retreating bull for a short way, nipping at its tail tip with his electric bolt. Once all the pachies were far enough afield to represent no further threat to humans, he about-faced his quahka and returned to the riverside.

Bobby Everett was struggling to wrench his snowmobile out of the sagebrush.

Chase opened his canopy. "Here, let me help with that," he offered, swinging the quahka's left arm into action. Using the finest of touches on the joystick control, he slid the pincer end under the snowmobile and gently flipped it upright on an open patch of snowy ground. "Good luck getting it running again," he said to Bobby.

"It doesn't look too banged up," Bobby replied, checking the machine over.

Thera approached and snapped a picture of Chase in his pilot's seat. "Nice rescue, Tall, Dark, and Handsome," she said. "I got it all at twenty-four megapixel resolution." She snapped more shots as Chase smiled at her and touched the short bill of his fleece-lined green Park Service winter cap. Then he turned his machine and walked it over to where Kit and Ogilvey stood looking at their own downfallen transport.

"Is it damaged badly?" he asked them.

"Not too," Kit replied.

"A dent or two on the belly of the fuselage," Ogilvey said. "But no punctures or signs of injury to the arms or legs."

"Good," Chase said. "Let me help you get it right-side up."

"I can do it," Kit replied. "I've learned as much from Gar as you have about how to drive these things."

THOMAS P. HOPP

CHAPTER 24

Even in its tipped-over configuration, the versatile machine was not fully disabled. Kit settled as best she could into the sideways cockpit. She hooked the toes of her cowboy boots into the foot-pedal straps. Then, tugging deftly at the left and right joysticks, she got the arms to push and twist until the quahka was nose-down. Then she used the foot pedals to maneuver the three-toed feet under the forward part of the fuselage and stand it up. "Ta-dah!" she exclaimed when it was upright.

Chase nodded and gave her that wide, handsome grin she had seen too rarely lately. Ogilvey climbed up the hand- and foot-holds on one of the quahka's legs, huffing and puffing in the frosty air, and then settled his round body into the seat behind Kit. "I wish I had worn a full snowsuit," he complained. "Turn on the heat."

Bobby Everett's snowmobile roared to life. He drove it a short way to see that it was fully functional and then pulled up near the quahkas, letting the engine idle. He looked up sheepishly and asked, "Are you all right, Kit?"

"I was fine," she said testily, dusting some snow off an arm of her coat, "until you guys came along and messed everything up. You scared that mamma pachy into the river and you nearly got her and me both killed!"

"But you'd have died famously," Thera interjected. She had come to join them and now gestured at her prodigious camera. "I would have gotten it all on record. I've still got another fifty shots worth of memory left in this baby. I can imagine the headline now: Cowgirl Gives Her Life To Save Dinosaur."

Kit glowered. "Every time you come around, somebody gets hurt—or worse!"

Thera shrugged off the remark. She turned and smiled up at Chase in his quahka. "Every time *you* come around," she cooed, "I get rescued, and you—"

She climbed up onto Chase's machine, leaned into the cockpit, wrapped her arms around his neck, and tugged his face to hers. She gave him a lingering kiss that he resisted, but not too strongly. "—get kissed." she concluded.

Kit scowled harshly. She put her hands on her hips. "Is that how it is, Blondie? You think you have your pick of the men around here?"

Thera grinned at Kit, still hanging onto Chase. She shrugged. "Basically, yes."

Without a word, Kit jumped down from the quahka and went to Bobby, who stood beside his snowmobile looking confused. She reached up, threw her arms around his neck, and said, loudly, "Chase Armstrong's not the only man around here who's brave enough to get a kiss." She pulled Bobby's round face down to hers and laid a big wet kiss on his lips. And her kiss lingered longer than Thera's had on Chase. Then she linked an arm in Bobby's and turned to face Thera and Chase. "Two can play at that game."

"F-Four," Bobby corrected. A blush had turned his pink cheeks solidly red.

Thera threw an arm around Chase's wide shoulders, smiling smugly at Kit. She pressed her cheek sensually against Chase's green-jacketed shoulder.

Chase gently undid her arm from around him. "I've gotta go," he said, looking uncomfortable. "Gotta finish writing up my wolf observations." He turned to Ogilvey. "The Bison Creek pack has got quite a battle going on with some coyotes over who owns that iguanodont carcass, Professor. I want to go see how things turn out. Their survival through the winter may depend on it. So long, everybody."

"I'll come with you," Thera suggested.

"No, you won't," Chase replied.

Thera reluctantly climbed down and Chase lowered the quahka's canopy glass. He turned the machine and, without another glance at anyone, drove away across the snowy plain. Soon he came to a full seventy mile-an-hour sprint over the snowdrifts, heading back to his observation site.

Watching Chase go, Kit sighed. A big puff of condensed breath drifted off on the breeze.

"Oh, dear me," Dr. Ogilvey remarked. "Love triangles and quadrangles. It's just a bit confusing to an old codger like me, I'm afraid."

"Never mind," Kit said despondently.

Ogilvey addressed Thera. "Miss photographer, I am thoroughly surprised you had the guts to do what you did."

"What?" she responded with a humorous smirk. "Kiss a man? Oh that's the easiest thing—"

"No," the professor interrupted. "I didn't mean that. I meant how you kept snapping photos even when you were in mortal danger."

Thera grinned wider. "I just thought about winning a Pulitzer Prize."

"Posthumously, I hope," Kit muttered.

They eyed each other coolly for a while. Then Bobby Everett got on his snowmobile and revved the engine several times. He called, "Are you ready to go, Thera?"

Thera continued looking icily at Kit and vice versa. "Keep a lid on it, hot stuff!" she snapped at Bobby without looking at him. Then she looked meaningfully at Kit and muttered, "The weather *does* seem to have gotten a little chilly around here." She turned and walked toward the snowmobile, calling to Bobby, "All right, Beefcakes, I'm coming!"

She stowed her camera in a hatch and got onboard, wrapping her arms around Bobby much more thoroughly than was necessary. When she ran her gloved hands sensually over his chest, he grinned sheepishly in Kit's direction, still glowing beet red. Then he gunned the engine and took off across the snowdrifts, heading back the way he had come.

As the snowmobile sounds faded, peace returned to the hot spring area. Kit lowered the canopy and soon the quahka's heaters had the interior comfortable enough for her to take off her coat.

"That's better," Ogilvey said. "But I take back what I said about wildlife observation being as cushy as an office job."

"Not when you consider the kind of wildlife we're observing," Kit agreed. Her attitude was improving with the return of warmth and calm.

Ogilvey peered through the snow-streaked canopy glass at the herd, which was slowly moving away on the flats. "Where did that mother pachy go? I'm worried she'll be too chilled to survive the coming night."

Kit chuckled. "Over there," she said, pointing in the other direction. "And look what she's doing!"

The hypothermic mother pachy had waded out into the warm waters of the hot spring and sat down on her haunches. Her six babies were timidly testing the steaming shallows nearby. Beyond her, the geyser bubbled and frothed in the center of the pool, sending out clouds of steam that swirled around the hunkered-down pachy mamma like the warm air of a sauna bath. The big beast raised its nose high, closed its eyes, and let out a long, steamy sigh.

"I must say she looks delighted," Ogilvey remarked, "if a pachyrhinosaur can express such feelings."

Suddenly Kit had an idea. "Well, well," she said, fishing in a coat pocket and taking out her cell phone. "Looks like Miss National Photographic missed a good shot." She raised the canopy partially, framed the pachy family warming in its steam bath, and clicked off several pictures. "We'll see who gets the Pulitzer Prize now," she said as she lowered the glass again.

"You shouldn't start competing with that photogenic female," Dr. O responded. "You'll be far too busy with other matters, Kit. Consider how well your paleontology training is going. Despite some, er, difficulties today, we've learned much more about pachyrhinosaurs than anyone else could hope to know. We'll write up our findings and perhaps you can include that photo in a treatise on the habits of Yellowstone's newest winter inhabitants. And don't forget you've already got plenty of work cut out for you in your senior thesis project. Why, your tyrannosaurus skeleton is complete right down to the cricoid bone! Think of it. You'll have two major scientific papers in the world's preeminent scientific journals even before you get your bachelor's degree. Quite prodigious accomplishments for a college student. What more could you wish for?"

Kit pushed down the accelerator pedal and steered the quahka out onto the snowy prairie. As she drove past the pachyrhinosaur herd and began the long trek home, she murmured, "What more could I wish for?" Two words came to mind that she didn't speak out loud. *Chase Armstrong.*

As they moved across the mountains, heading north toward the ranch, Kit was quiet.

Dr. Ogilvey was uncharacteristically silent for some time. Then he said, "Perhaps we should recommend a name other than *Pachyrhinosaurus* for those amazing beasts."

"What have you got in mind?" Kit asked half-heartedly, still wrapped in thoughts about Chase Armstrong.

"Perhaps something that draws attention to their rather striking resemblance to the wooly rhinoceros."

"How about '*Rhinosaurus,*' then?" Kit tossed out disinterestedly.

"Why, yes!" Ogilvey exclaimed, sitting upright. "That's it, exactly! *Rhinosaurus!* The international nomenclature commission could hardly argue with a name that reflects the fact that the animal is so much like a rhinoceros. What could be a more appropriate name, and one that implies by its very sound, the close similarity of their forms? That way, we could avoid confusion with the snub-nosed pachyrhinosaurs portrayed in books and films. *Walking With Dinosaurs*, indeed. They should have seen *these* creatures before they made their movie!"

"Oh well," Kit said, warming to the conversation, "*Walking with Dinosaurs* wasn't so bad. At least it showed them in snow."

"Yes, my dear. That is one thing they got right, isn't it?"

CHAPTER 25

Professor Ogilvey hosted a small get-together of friends at his new home adjacent to his museum on the plains of Arran Kra. The occasion was a housewarming of sorts for the newly completed mansion built by the Kra with painstaking precision in College Gothic style, reminiscent of Branford College at Yale University, where the professor had studied for his PhD degree in paleontology. Attending were Gar, Gana, and little Jonak, as well as Kit and Chase. A luncheon of roast-iguanodont-and-cucumber sandwiches was served, although the three Pteronychi preferred iguanodont steak tartar with pickled pig's feet on the side. Gar had developed quite a taste for the latter, consuming them bones-and-all. The group convened around a large, elegantly set table in a much-more-than-ample dining room. Little Jonak, who was by now nearly half adult stature, amazed all with his fine grasp of the English language and the advanced state of his education in both Kra and human learning—all this despite his tender age of barely five months.

After lunch, they adjourned to a spacious parlor, well furnished with couches and chairs for humans, as well as the backless, hassock-like seats and benches preferred by the long-tailed Kra. On one wall of the parlor, and nearly covering it entirely, was a wide-screen television. It made a tone and Ogilvey responded by calling out, "Screen on!"

The wall lit with an image of two soldiers sitting in the front seats of a military vehicle.

"General Suarez! Major Abercromby!" Ogilvey called over

THOMAS P. HOPP

the two-way video stream. "To what do we owe the honor of this call?"

"Good afternoon, ladies, gentlemen, and dinosaurs," Suarez said, smiling. "Just reporting in with the latest news from the great Northwestern migration."

"Excellent!" Ogilvey cried. "What news?"

"News is," Crom said, "the big beasties and their babies are home, safe and sound in the Hoh River Valley rainforest."

"Congratulations," Ogilvey said. "I trust you had no further incidents along the way?"

"None worth reporting," Suarez said. "Although things got a little touchy when they turned north just past Olympia and circled the peninsula counterclockwise to get here."

"Oh my," Ogilvey said. "I'll bet you were surprised."

"Affirmative," Crom said. "And so were the people along the way."

"We'll have to hear all the details," Ogilvey said. "And, your timing is excellent. I have some guests who will be very interested in every detail."

"And we'll be glad to oblige," Suarez said. "First, have a look at this." He had been speaking into a video camera, which he now swung around to give an entirely different view, a panorama of rainforest with huge green trees overhanging sword-fern-covered glens. Among the many tall tree trunks were some other tall vertical objects that were in motion—the necks and heads of sauropod dinosaurs, several dozen of them, large and small.

"Wow!" Kit exclaimed when the camera focused on the herd, which was interspersed among the giant trees of the rainforest, the heads of the largest animals rivaling the height of tall conifers and bigleaf maple trees.

"Wow is right," Crom said. "*Jurassic World* has got nothing on this place!"

"Look at the babies!" Ogilvey cried. "When last we saw them they were hatchlings barely a yard long. Now, in just months, they are ten times that length!"

As they watched, an adult that had been cropping off Spanish moss that hung from the bottoms of the highest branches of a tall Sitka spruce tree, leaned its head down and vomited a mass of green, slimy material directly into the open and waiting mouth of one of its ten-yard-long offspring.

Kit said, "Still a lot of barfing going on, I see."

"Affirmative on that," Suarez replied. "And the young ones never spill a drop."

"I'm just glad I'm not there to smell it," Kit added.

Crom replied, "We're parked upwind."

"Regardless of the indelicacy of their feeding habits," Ogilvey said, "I am interested to see them eating lichen hanging off the trees."

"There's tons of that stuff around here," Suarez noted.

"I wonder why there is no modern large mammal there that eats lichen off trees?" Ogilvey puzzled.

Chase said, "Maybe the mammoths and mastodons that lived there ate it, before they were wiped out by Stone-Age hunters. The remains of spear tips in mastodon bone have been found right there on the Olympic Peninsula."

"Astute, Chase," Ogilvey replied.

"So, I'm thinking the alamosaurs might restore the balance of nature a little by trimming the Spanish moss."

"And, speaking of alamosaurs," Ogilvey said, "Gar informs me the Northwestern variety are a distinct genus and species from the alamosaurs down in Texas. When I communicate with the international nomenclature committee, I think I shall propose a new name for them as well as for rhinosaurus."

"What name you going to choose?" Suarez asked.

"Something appropriate to their location, perhaps. Thinking along the lines of *Alamosaurus* being appropriate for a Texan dinosaur... let's see. They are grazing in the Hoh River Valley. Perhaps we can combine the name of the river with 'saurus.' What would we get? Er. *Hohosaurus*. What do you think, Kit?"

"Hohosaurus?" You've got to be kidding, unless you plan to get eight of them to pull Santa's sleigh at Christmastime."

The professor looked at Kit for a moment, uncomprehenddingly. And then his expression changed to one of humor. "Oh, yes, of course," he said. 'Ho-Ho-Ho,' like Santa says. You are absolutely right, my dear. *Hohosaurus* is not such a good name after all. No one would take it seriously. Perhaps the name of another nearby river valley—" He took up a notepad computer and tapped it to bring up a map of the Olympic Peninsula in a corner of the big wall screen.

Kit shook her head, looking over the map. "I don't think *Queetsosaurus* has quite the right ring to it, either."

"Nor *Snahapishosaurus,*" Ogilvey concurred.

"Or *Humptulipsosaurus,*" Chase said, getting a laugh from everyone. "So, what's it going to be?"

"Wait!" Kit cried, pointing to a mountain peak marked in the center of the map. "I've got it! *Olymposaurus!*"

"Yes!" Ogilvey said. "Yes indeed. *Olymposaurus!* What a fine choice. Named for the mountain, and for the national park in which they spend the majority of their time!"

"Brilliant," Chase said.

"As usual," Kit concurred immodestly.

"Olymposaurus it will be then," Ogilvey concluded.

Watching the big beasts graze serenely, Kit sighed happily. "So all is right in the new world we all inhabit."

"Not quite," Chase said.

"Oh?" she responded. "What's still wrong?"

"Saurgon."

Gar growled, deep in his chest.

Gana hissed just audibly.

"Hmmm, yes," Ogilvey murmured. "A study in treachery, that one. Have you heard anything of his whereabouts, General Suarez?"

"Nada," Suarez replied.

"Then I must agree, Chase," Ogilvey said. "You have identified the greatest source of uncertainty for all our futures."

"I wonder where he could be?" Kit asked.

Saurgon sat in a finely appointed nautical cabin, in a vessel deep beneath the surface of a tropical sea. Blue-green daylight rippled through the ocean waters and into a large, round porthole, through which the Kra commander had a sweeping view of the coral-studded ocean bottom where his underwater war machine had set its anchors.

"Hoonahs," he murmured as saliva dripped from his fangs. "I have not tasted your blood for the last time."

***

"The Kra sure work fast," Frank Johnston said to Diedre Porter.

"They sure do," Diedre agreed.

They were standing in one of the corbelled secondary-cannon towers atop the step pyramid at Illik Moon Base in Phaeon Crater. From the tower windows they had a sweeping view of the main turret dome, whose repair was now entering its final stages. Its crumpled structure had been restored, and once again a prodigiously huge gun-barrel-like object protruded from it.

Diedre let out a satisfied sigh. "Just think, Frank. They're doing all this just for you and me!"

Frank looked at the long barrel in awed silence for a moment. And then he murmured, "The most powerful telescope ever built, and we're part of its operating team. I still can't believe it."

"Believe it Frank. According to Tekkoo, it will be capable of seeing the faces of individual people and Kra on Planet Earth—and seeing individual planets revolving around other stars. I can hardly wait to get started!"

"Me too." He put a big, beefy arm around her slim shoulders and hugged her. "We've gotta be the luckiest space scientists of all time."

It was almost as if spring had returned to the high country of Yellowstone Park. Snow-covered and windswept only two weeks before, the landscape was again warm, dry, and clear of snow, with the exception of the tallest mountain peaks. Winter had abated for the time being, but would return with gusto soon enough. But this day was a fine day for a picnic in the high country. Chase Armstrong had parked his walking machine on a grassy, sloping hillside overlooking the broad Lamar River Valley. Below, herds of dinosaurs grazed, interspersed with bison, elk, and moose. Chase and Kit had spread a blanket on the grass and enjoyed a picnic lunch while watching a new, small wolf pack explore the valley. Two adults and five nearly-grown pups, they were the beginnings of a pack Chase had been studying when he first met Kit, on a day that seemed almost an eternity ago, given the events that had transpired since then.

"Look at 'em go!" Chase exclaimed, following them through binoculars as they streamed, single file, through the sagebrush thickets on the far side of the valley. "Healthy, beautiful—and looking for something to eat."

Kit wasn't watching the wolves. She was watching Chase. "Okay," she said. "I surrender."

"Surrender to what?"

"Your irresistible charm. By that I mean I'll marry you."

He lowered the binoculars with look of shocked surprise coming over him. "You're serious?"

"I'm serious, Chase Armstrong. You can have your wife, your house, and your kids, just like you want."

"I... Well... Oh... That's great! But...?"

"But there's just one catch."

His expression fell. "I knew there was something. What is it?"

"I'm just not quite ready right now. Not for a couple of years, anyway. What do you say to that?"

He thought a moment. "I'd say... Well, what *can* I say when you put it that way?"

"How about, okay?"

"Okay."

"Oh. And one more thing," she said. "What about that Thera McArty witch? Do I have to worry about her?"

"You never did have to worry about her. She's not the first woman to come after me that way. And I can't swear she'll ever stop being the way she is. But I can promise you this—I'll never let her get to me. Is that good enough?"

"You promise?"

"I promise."

"Then you've got yourself a deal." She held out her hand like a rancher ready to shake on an unwritten contract.

He took her hand and shook it. "Deal!" he said.

They both laughed at the sight of themselves making such a serious decision in this way. Then she threw her arms around his neck and embraced his broad shoulders. He wrapped his arms around her waist and they kissed, long and tenderly.

"I love you, Kit Daniels," he whispered in her ear.

"I love you, Chase Armstrong," she whispered back.

He kissed her again and her heart pounded until she felt dizzy and her body grew limp. Then, perhaps taking a cue from the wolves they had been watching, she uttered a small animal growl deep in her throat and pulled him close. He continued kissing her until she felt almost delirious, wishing the kiss could last a lifetime. She knew this was dangerous thinking for a girl who intended to guard her independence. But for the time being it was bliss to be wrapped in Chase's loving embrace.

Somehow, she knew, everything would work out just fine.

Not too many miles distant from them, in regal chambers within Arran Kra, Gar and Gana strutted the Kra love dance. They fanned glorious, iridescent, greenish-black wing feathers at each other as they moved.

Elsewhere, much farther away, on the front walk of an officer's mansion on Joint Base Lewis McChord in Washington State, stood General Victor Suarez, just arrived home from what had been the front but was now a treaty line. He embraced his wife, Maria, who cried with joy and kissed his face repeatedly. At their feet, the two small boys, Evan and Manny, tried to climb their father's legs like tree trunks.

###

ABOUT THE AUTHOR

Thomas P. Hopp was born in Seattle, Washington, where he lived his earliest years in a housing project. Despite a tough start in life, good grades at West Seattle High School and the University of Washington as well as a perfect score on the Graduate Record Examination gained him entry to the Biochemistry Ph.D. program at Cornell University Medical College. He studied genetic engineering at Rockefeller University and went on to help found the multi-billion-dollar biotechnology company, Immunex Corporation. He patented the gene for the immune system hormone, interleukin one, and advised the team that created Immunex's blockbuster arthritis drug, Enbrel. He also created the first commercially successful nanotechnology device, a molecular handle called the Flag epitope tag. He worked with paleontologist Jack Horner, excavating bones of the nest-building duckbilled dinosaur *Maiasaura*. He published the brooding-to-flight hypothesis, in which wing feathers of birds developed first for nesting and then for flying: http://thomas-hopp.com/pdf/DinoBrooding.pdf. He plays guitar and bass, and has performed onstage with blues legend John Lee Hooker and rock supergroups The Kingsmen and The Drifters. He has lived in San Diego and on Manhattan Island. Nowadays he lives near Seattle. Visit his official web site at: http://thomas-hopp.com/blog.

ACKNOWLEDGMENTS

Cover and interior art for this book was created by the author using Poser software and dinosaur 3D models developed by Dino Raul Lunia, including Bistahieversor, Coahuilaceratops, Pteranodon, and Argentinosaurus.

OTHER BOOKS AND STORIES BY THOMAS P. HOPP

The Dinosaur Wars Trilogy

Earthfall
Counterattack
Blood on the Moon

Peyton McKean Mysteries

The Smallpox Incident
The Neah Virus

and coming soon:
The Sabertooth Amulet

Short Stories

The Treasure of Purgatory Crater
A Dangerous Breed
The Re-Election Plot
The Ghost Trees
Blood Tide

Visit the Author's Official Web Site

www.thomas-hopp.com/blog